'Please . . .' Sh

He took no ⟨...⟩ ⟨...⟩er bodice from h⟨...⟩ ⟨...⟩er down across th⟨...⟩ ⟨...⟩ed itself to hers. H⟨...⟩ ⟨...⟩e lacing at the b⟨...⟩ ⟨...⟩g became more o⟨...⟩ ⟨...⟩e erratic beating ⟨...⟩

A flush of persp⟨...⟩ation had broken out on her skin, causing her face to glow in the lamplight, and she cried out, 'No, Red, please, not yet . . . Not like this. No gentleman would force himself upon a lady against her will!'

His arms gripped hers, prising her body away as he glared into her upturned face. 'That, my dear Aimée, as I told you before, I have never claimed to be!' He gave a bitter laugh. 'In fact, there's hardly a soul in the whole of this doggone County would credit a Redmayne with that title! No, my dear, I may be many things, but I ain't no gentleman! And coming here like this, if I may say so, makes you no lady!'

F8

Eileen Townsend was born in Scotland in 1945, and brought up in England. She has since returned to Scotland and lives with her husband Colin, a University lecturer, and two sons Alan and Stephen, in a rambling converted rectory in the beautiful Perthshire glen of Strathardle. She is an MA Honours graduate in history and politics, and has travelled extensively, living abroad for several years, in North Africa and Germany, before settling down to the rural life.

She wrote her first novel two years ago and has since had eight published. *Lorena* is her first historical and she looks forward to writing many more.

LORENA

Eileen Townsend

MILLS & BOON LIMITED
ETON HOUSE 18–24 PARADISE ROAD
RICHMOND SURREY TW9 1SR

*First published in Great Britain 1987
by Mills & Boon Limited*

© Eileen Townsend 1987

*Australian copyright 1987
Philippine copyright 1987
This edition 1987*

ISBN 0 263 75950 4

*Set in 10 on 10½ pt Linotron Times
04–1287–82,200*

*Photoset by Rowland Phototypesetting Limited
Bury St Edmunds, Suffolk
Made and printed in Great Britain by
Cox & Wyman Limited, Reading*

PROLOGUE

HIGH ON A plateau in the foothills of the Blue Ridge Mountains one hot late July day in the year of Our Lord 1860, a man sat tall in the saddle, his black-booted legs gripping the glistening flanks of the black stallion as he pulled the animal up sharply to gaze on the scene below. His dark-lashed, sleepy-lidded eyes narrowed as they took in the colourful panorama of fluttering flags and gaily attired guests on the smooth, green lawns some few hundred feet beneath him. North Georgian society had seen nothing like it since General Robert E. Lee himself had led the Thanksgiving Ball almost two years previously. That, too, had taken place at Four Winds. But even that splendid affair was nothing like this.

His bronzed hand caressed the windblown mane of the sweating beast, and his eyes continued to scan the scene spread out before him beneath the backdrop of rolling red hills with their huge outcroppings of underlying granite, the towering pines, and the acres of rich red earth that was the Four Winds plantation.

Wildwood, his own estate, was just as big, just as profitable, but the Redmaynes had never possessed, or sought to possess, the glamour and mystique of the MacDonalds.

He was not even sure why he had come—why he had accepted Charles Stuart MacDonald's invitation to meet his new bride-to-be. It was not as if he even liked the man! And he detested barbecues—especially in the late summer when the mosquitos rose in their millions from the stagnant river-beds to plague guests and slaves alike.

Why, then, had he come? After all, it was not as if an English bride was uncommon in the high society of the Deep South . . . But this one was half French—

and few had ever come from such a dubious background as the beautiful Miss Aimée Charlotte Sophia Fitzwilliam!

CHAPTER ONE

'HUSH YOUR MOUTH, Maybelle McCrae! If Charles Stuart MacDonald chose a jackass for a bride, it would become a lady—and the most envied in all Craven County— and you'd do well to remember that!' Mrs Euphemia Carnegie smoothed an imaginary wrinkle from the voluminous folds of her black bombazine skirts and glanced nervously over her right shoulder. She had already heard far too many disparaging remarks since arriving at Four Winds that afternoon, and still felt obliged to rally to the raven-haired stranger's defence. As Charles MacDonald's godmother, it was the very least she could do!

The young woman in question stood on the steps of the mansion alongside her husband-to-be at the head of the long queue of guests, as the cream of North Georgian society lined up patiently to be presented to her—Miss Aimée Charlotte Sophia Fitzwilliam, the future Mrs Charles Stuart MacDonald, master of Four Winds, one of the finest plantations in the whole of the *ante-bellum* South. The sea-green eyes that had captured the young American's heart in London barely three months before flashed a smile from beneath their frieze of thick dark lashes at each guest in turn. Her cool composure was unflagging, despite the relentless rays of the early afternoon sun still high in the cloudless azure sky.

There was no denying that they made a handsome couple. Since he had come of age ten years previously, Chas MacDonald had broken more female hearts than almost any other male in the whole of Craven County. With his lean, firm-muscled, six-foot frame, his shock of pale blond hair and wide-set grey-blue eyes, it would have been difficult for any red-blooded Southern girl to avoid falling head over heels in love with him. And when he inherited the Four Winds plantation barely a year back, his appeal had soared even higher, but the shock-waves that reverberated round the countryside that summer when he chose a complete foreigner for a wife—and an actress at that—could be felt right up to the Mason-Dixon line and beyond.

Not that Miss Aimée Fitzwilliam wasn't beautiful —she was that all right; quite stunning, in fact, with her waist-length blue-black hair, now demurely caught up in a chignon and net. Her neck, rising from the swathed muslin sheath of her basque, was creamy-skinned and slender, and the pale pink rose behind her right ear matched to perfection the fifteen yards of shell-pink muslin that made up her dress. Up to now, Becky Madison was known to have the neatest waist for miles around, but as the guests eyed the seventeen-inch hand-span of the bride-to-be, even that distinction seemed to have gone to the beautiful stranger.

'High time you got yourself hitched, you ol' varmint! You landed a wily ol' devil, and no mistake, when you landed this 'un, young lady!' Old Jake Buchanan's blue eyes glinted mischievously as he turned from Chas to shake Aimée's lace-mittened hand. The stem of his walnut-bowled pipe stabbed in Chas's direction. 'Been on the loose too long, I reckon! He needs the love of a good woman like yourself to calm him down. He's broke a few hearts in his time, I can tell you!'

Aimée's black lashes were lowered demurely and the green eyes flashed a glance at the young man by her side. 'I can believe that, sir. But wild young stallions need a tight rein if they're to be tamed properly, and I pride myself on being an expert horsewoman!'

The old man threw back his grey-bearded head and snorted in glee. 'D'you hear that, eh, Chas? Landsakes, you've got a good 'un here! A gal with a bit of spunk! You'll be a mighty fine addition to these parts, my dear—a mighty fine addition!'

Chas MacDonald's eyes narrowed as they watched the old man head for the beer tent, still chortling quietly to himself. His lips brushed the petals of the pink rose as he bent to speak, and his voice was ice-cold in the young woman's ear. 'This is Craven County, Georgia, you're in now, ma'm, where men are men, not dandified fops such as you left back home in London. I'll thank you to remember that!'

Aimée's colour rose as she glanced up at her fiancé. 'I'm sorry, Chas. Forgive me—it was only a jest!'

'Mrs Amelia Mear, my dear, and this is my daughter Sarah-Jane.' The mauve-taffeta-swathed matron now before them prevented further conversation, and a bead of perspiration formed on Aimée's brow as she extended her hand once more to be politely shaken. They had been receiving guests for over an hour, and the temperature, now in the high eighties, was already taking its toll. The pink-frilled parasol did little to alleviate the broiling rays of the sun, and beneath the basque of her dress, the whalebone of her stays dug cruelly into her perspiring flesh.

'An actress, so I hear, Miss Fitzwilliam . . . How very interesting!' This time the speaker was a tiny bird-like woman in black and aubergine taffeta, whose husband, Willard Sykes, had twice run for Governor. 'Why, Ah remember my dear mother saying how, as a child, she saw the great Sarah Siddons herself on stage in London! Can't say as Ah remember what the play was, though . . .' The narrow lips pursed in thought. 'No —it's gone . . .'

Aimée's green eyes gleamed. 'I knew her niece, Fanny Kemble,' she said, with new-found enthusiasm. 'She was a wonderful actress—until she gave it up to marry a Southerner, too. Pierce Butler, I believe his name was.'

A silence descended as she felt her husband-to-be's fingers grip her elbow until she winced with pain. As the woman nodded briefly and moved quickly on, murmuring her goodbyes, Chas's voice hissed in her ear, 'Unfortunately, honey, the good Mistress Sykes was a Butler before her marriage!'

'So?' Aimée's eyebrows rose in two elegant curves as she turned to meet his eyes.

'So—that particular marriage you referred to proved quite a scandal in these here parts. She was an actress, you see. Fanny Kemble was an actress!'

Aimée's dark head swirled round to stare straight ahead, eyes flashing, as the colour flared in her cheeks. The implication was obvious, but she was glad to hear it from his own lips. 'Say it, Chas, say it!' she said, her voice rising. 'For actress, what do we substitute? What do we substitute, Chas—whore?'

There was an audible gasp from those guests within earshot, and an even louder exclamation from Chas MacDonald himself as he stared white-faced at his fiancée. His lower jaw fell open and he stepped back as if physically struck. She had gone too far, much too far! No lady could possibly utter such an obscenity and retain her place in Southern society.

Dismayed at her own outburst and its effects on those around her, with a sob Aimée gathered up her skirts and dashed through the assembled guests, her hooped skirts swaying alarmingly as her feet sped on up the gravelled drive. She did not stop until the sound of music and voices became inaudible and the drive turned eastwards round the back of the Four Winds mansion. A small slave child, a boy about four years old, watched her through large, brown, saucer eyes, his stick-insect legs painfully thin beneath the shapeless calico smock as his new mistress-to-be increased her pace, her head bent, sightless now with the blinding tears that streamed down her flushed cheeks.

The drive became rougher as it neared the slave quarters and she gave a sharp yell of pain as the toes of her right foot, encased in its soft satin slipper, hit an unexpectedly large piece of rubble. She toppled forward on the rough ground, the hoops of her skirt tipping up behind her at a ridiculous angle as her face scraped on the dusty gravel.

Hooves pulled up in a cloud of red dust within a few feet of her prostrate figure, the black stallion snorting through flared nostrils and tossing its head as its rider drew in the shining leather reins. The young woman looked up from the ground, her face dirty and tear-streaked, the thick black hair escaping in wayward tendrils from its encasing net. Towering above her, the sweating animal pawed the ground while the black-booted legs swung down from the saddle to land barely three feet from her startled eyes. A pair of well-muscled legs in elegant fawn pants bent at the knee, the black leather riding-boots squeaking slightly as the stranger squatted beside her. A tanned hand was extended, and Aimée took it gratefully as she scrambled up from the dirt.

He stood a good foot taller than her own five feet four inches, and her gaze was barely level with the burgundy cravat tucked into the fine lawn shirt. Too embarrassed to look up, her eyes travelled down over the watered-silk waistcoat as a deep voice drawled, 'The barbecue can't be that bad, miss—or can it?'

Still spiked with tears, her dark-lashed eyes fluttered to meet his brilliant blue gaze. He was without doubt a most attractive man—in a rather odd, foreign way, she thought. Odd because he appeared both rough and smooth at the same time. Rough, with the deeply bronzed skin and the shock of wildly curling dark hair, the mutton-chop whiskers that decorated the lean lines of his face were just that bit too long, the look in the sleepy-lidded eyes just a shade too intimate to be honourable, the slight twist to the smile on the well-drawn lips just that bit too cynical to be genuine. But the outfit . . . The outfit was smooth, all right. Almost too dandified, she thought, with its well-cut burgundy velvet jacket, the embroidered silk waistcoat and immaculate pants.

'I haven't had the pleasure, I believe?' the deep voice

intoned, reminding her of the smooth black molasses that flowed freely over the hot waffles served up every morning by Angel, the small mulatto table-maid. 'Allow me to introduce myself. My name is Redmayne—Daniel O'Connell Redmayne, but you can call me Red. Everyone else does!'

Aimée allowed her hand to be shaken in the giant paw of the man before her. 'How do you do, Mr Redmayne. I—I'm Aimée Fitzwilliam—Charles's fiancée.'

The astonishment on his face was only too obvious. 'Well I'll be darned—if you'll excuse the language! Old Charlie-boy's bride-to-be!' He took a step back, keeping hold of her hand, as his eyes surveyed her from top to toe. His low whistle only served to embarrass her further, aware as she was of her dishevelled state. 'Well, I'll say this for him. He may be a son of a—a man not exactly after my own heart, but ol' Chas can sure pick 'em!'

Aimée's colour heightened beneath the tear-streaked dirt as she raised a tentative hand to her wayward locks, pulling her right one free of the stranger's grasp as she struggled to tuck the escaped wisps back into the chignon at the nape of her neck. How exactly was she supposed to react to such a double-edged compliment? 'You know my fiancé, then, sir?' she enquired demurely. 'You're a—an acquaintance of Chas's?'

A deep boom of laughter burst from within the massive chest as he stood, hands on hips, regarding her with some amusement. 'Let's just say that's a mighty pretty . . . mighty diplomatic way of putting it!'

She glanced down at her dress, unable to face the brilliant blue gaze. The pink muslin skirts were now caked in dust and there was a slight tear just above the bottom flounce of her hem. Even the palms of her white lace mittens were now holed and filthy, and she regarded them with despair, giving a deep shuddering sigh.

He took a step forward, grasping her by the elbow. 'Are you sure you're all right? You're not going to swoon on me or anything?'

She shook her head. 'No—No, I'll be all right . . . really.'

He took hold of her hands and turned them over, palms upward. Blood was beginning to ooze through the cotton mesh. With a low whistle, and a frown, he reached into his coat pocket and extracted a white cotton handkerchief. 'I'm afraid I've only got the one,' he said, wrapping the clean cloth round the worst hand, 'but perhaps it'll do until you get back to the big house. One thing's for sure, though—you're in no fit state to walk back!'

Aimée could merely nod miserably. The past hour in the broiling sun and the sudden rapid exit from the festivities had left her hot, sticky and not a little faint.

'I'll take you back,' he said. It was not a question, but a mere statement of fact. 'You can ride in front of me. It'll be quite safe!'

A barely suppressed giggle sounded from behind them, and Aimée whirled round to see three pairs of dark eyes regarding her from round, bitter-chocolate-coloured faces. The girls, obviously well past puberty, were still dressed in the same rough shirt-like garment of the younger slave children.

'Ignore them!' Red said sharply. 'You'll be the talk of the cotton fields in a moment. Just don't let it upset you.'

Before she could reply, his tanned capable hands had encircled her waist, lifting her off her feet and depositing her on the front of the leather saddle. With a single leap he was up behind her, his black-booted legs straddling the shiny flanks of the horse as he bent to grasp the reins firmly. Aimée could feel her face flame, and she gripped her parasol defensively to her breasts as, pressing forward to gain better control of the horse, he completely enclosed her in a heart-stopping embrace.

His breath was warm on her face, and his lips, now positioned just above her right temple, asked softly, 'Comfortable?'

She nodded, quite unable to speak, as a multitude of

scents overran her senses: the sweet, musky odour of the horse, mingled with the tang of the well-oiled tack, but most unsettling of all was the scent that emanated from the man himself—a warm masculine aroma of old bourbon, heavily disguised by fresh mint and chewing tobacco, and the very faintest hint of perspiration, as her head pressed hard against the beautiful waistcoat.

To her relief, the black stallion did not canter but broke into a slow trot, its master urging, 'Steady! Steady there . . .' as they set off down the wide, curving drive.

From her elevated position, Aimée took in the colour-ful vista on the front lawns of Four Winds. Young men in fawn and grey trousers and fine, ruffled, lawn shirts vied for the attention of girls in crinolines as bright as butter-flies who tried to evade the eagle-eyed glances of the bombazined matrons.

A haze hung lazily in the tops of the tall trees, and even at this distance the mingled aromas of burning hickory logs and spit-roasted mutton and pork wafted invitingly on the gentle breeze. Next to the spits stood huge iron washpots brought into service to cook the delicious stews and barbecue sauces that were tended by teams of white-coated house-servants, their black faces shining in the combined heat of sun, spits and cooking-pots. They would have their own feast of yams, hoecakes and chitterlings later, but now their task was to ensure that none of the milling crowd of ladies and gentlemen lacked for a thing. MacDonald hospitality must never be found wanting. Even if the object of the festivities—the bride-to-be herself—was absent, the party would go on.

The stallion slowed to a halt, and Aimée scanned the crowd anxiously. The long, winding serpent of guests waiting to be introduced had dissolved into the throng on her abrupt disappearance, and at first she could see no sign of Chas. On closer examination, however, there was no mistaking the tall figure on the steps of the mansion itself. The big house, as it was known to all, stood in all its perfect white symmetry, totally dominating the scene being played out on the rolling lawns. Its tall Grecian columns and wide verandas lent it a dignity not at present apparent in the pacing figure on the wide wooden steps beyond the front door. To her horror, immediately her eyes alighted on the face of Charles Stuart MacDonald, the black-booted legs behind her dug into the horse's flanks, and it shot forward.

The crowd at the foot of the mansion steps was particularly dense, but making no concessions to the exquisite crinolines or the elegant attire of the men, the black stallion ploughed on, scattering the guests with a cacophony of squeals and oaths from them that brought the colour to the cheeks of the young woman atop the horse. All eyes turned towards the pair—the dirt-streaked, dishevelled, mistress-to-be of Four Winds and the tall, dark, inscrutably smiling face of Daniel O'Connel Redmayne. But the eyes that stared the longest and the hardest belonged to the owner of the mansion itself.

Aimée stared at her fiancé, the colour draining from her flushed face as the steel of his gaze cut deep into her heart.

'Chas . . .'

He stepped forward and stood quite still, hands on hips, his long legs almost two feet apart. 'Get down, madam!' he hissed between fiercely gritted teeth. 'Get down from that horse this instant!'

Before Aimée could move an inch, the tall figure behind her swung down from the saddle. His large hands encompassed her tiny waist, and with a fluid, easy movement he lifted her from the sweating animal's back. She was aware that every eye was on them as, with a flourish that left her gasping, he lifted her right hand, complete with its makeshift bandage, to his lips. 'It has been the greatest pleasure and honour, ma'am,' he said slowly, the soft, liquid vowels of North Georgia even more noticeable as his voice caressed her ears.

Without releasing her hand, he led her slowly up the steps, in front of the amazed gazes of the on-

lookers, until at last he stood before the master of Four
Winds.

'Sir . . . Your bride-to-be!'

CHAPTER TWO

AIMÉE GLANCED AT her aching wrist; where his fingers
had dug into the soft white flesh, livid weals were already
appearing. With the fingers of her right hand she mas-
saged the painful skin. Chas had thrown her on to the
buttoned-velvet sofa by the window after hauling her up
the steps of the house and through the main hall into the
front drawing-room. His silver-buckled shoes paced
noisily on the polished oak floor. He did not look at her,
nor she at him, but she was well aware of the fury in his
eyes.

When at last he spoke, his voice was little more than a
hiss. 'Goddamn you, ma'm—and I don't apologise for
the profanity! What in God's name do you think you are
doing? Have you any idea what this little shindig has cost
me? Almost a thousand dollars! There are nearly two
thousand people out there, don't you know? Almost two
thousand folks invited to Four Winds to meet its new
mistress. You, Aimée Fitzwilliam, goddamn you—
you . . .'

'I—I know, Chas, I know . . .' Her voice was barely
above a whisper, and her fingers tugged nervously at the
bandage on her hand.

He swung round to face her, his eyes now a cold steel-
grey. 'If you know, then why . . . In God's name—
why?'

She shrugged her shoulders helplessly. 'I shouldn't
have used that word,' she said slowly. 'I know that,
Chas. I was upset, that's all. Can't you understand? That
woman . . . Even you . . .' Her voice trailed off in a
strangled sob. 'An actress is an honourable profession,
Chas, not one to be ashamed of!'

'Have I ever said otherwise?' he demanded, glaring
down at her.

'It-was insinuated,' she said softly.

He spread his hands in a gesture of futility. 'Old ideas die hard—especially over here. You're not in London now, Aimée. This is North Georgia, not even Atlanta or Savannah, where folks might be more . . . er . . . worldly about these things; here, they are conservative. Why, they don't even think it fitting for a gal to do any sort of work, never mind act on the stage!'

Aimée took a deep breath and stared out of the window. 'I did hear tell that Fanny's—the Butlers' —marriage broke up,' she said at last. 'Tell me the truth, Chas—I have to know. Was it because of her background? Did they hold it against her for being an actress?'

In the long silence, she looked up at him, a deep frown creasing the clear skin of her brow while she waited for his reply.

'To tell the truth, Aimée, I don't rightly know,' he said slowly, 'and that's the truth. Some folks claim as that's the reason—others give something else . . .'

'Something else?' Her brows rose enquiringly, and her green eyes widened.

He walked to the window, and gazed out over the lawn still thronged with guests. 'I did hear say it was the slave issue,' he said, his voice dropping so much that she had to strain to hear. 'She kept interfering, always complaining . . . wanting better quarters—better this —better that. Caused no end of unrest, that woman did!' His voice had risen again and anger flared in his eyes as he turned towards her. 'It don't do to go giving them ideas above their station. You know that, don't you? The slaves are the master's affair, and no one else's. When a woman tries to interfere it brings nothing but trouble—for everyone, the slaves included! I trust I'll have no cause to worry with you in that regard?'

His eyes cut straight through her, and she could only shake her head dumbly. The question had never entered her head. In fact, the knowledge that Chas was the owner of over five hundred slaves had come as a complete shock after her arrival the previous week. It was something that he had never mentioned during the period of their courtship in London. She knew he was a landowner, of course—and rich. He would have to be that to be able to enjoy the best hotels that were home to him during his three-month tour of Europe. But actually to own other human beings—and so many of them —was something else entirely. Now, however, was certainly not the time for argument. 'I—I have no intention of interfering in how you run your affairs,' she said softly, nervously smoothing the pink muslin of her skirts as she glanced up at him through lowered lashes still glistening with tears.

'Good!' he said, forcing a smile that was not reflected in his eyes. 'So let's put this unfortunate episode behind us. I shall go outside and rejoin our guests while you repair upstairs to change your gown. You may join us again in—shall we say—no more than fifteen minutes?'

Aimée got up from the sofa, willing to obey any command that might in some way make up for what she now regarded as her unpardonable behaviour. 'Of course, I'll go immediately!'

He strode ahead of her, but stopped at the door and turned, his fingers on the handle, to address her once more. 'And, by the way, my dear, a further word of warning. I would prefer it if you did not associate—either now or in the future—with that man!'

'That man?'

'Daniel O'Connell Redmayne!' The name was spat out. 'He is trouble, nothing but trouble . . . We don't want any more of that, do we?'

The door closed with a quiet click straight into her face. She stared at it, as a deep fatigue overwhelmed her. It had never been like this in her dreams back home in Lambeth, or in the flights of fancy she had experienced every day as she stood on the rolling deck of the ship, imagining she was already at Four Winds—already Mrs Charles Stuart MacDonald.

Was this really the same beau who had wined and dined her, every single night, in Mayfair? The same man who had fallen head over heels in love with her after seeing her play the part of Kate in *The Taming of the Shrew* at the Lyceum?

She could do no wrong then. Everything she said or did brought the most extravagant of compliments to his lips. And when he discovered her illustrious forebears, she thought he would simply swoon with excitement—if that had not been too unseemly a reaction for a man!

'Well, I'll be . . .! Royalty, indeed! You'll be telling me next that your granddaddy was king!' She could see him now, slapping his plaid-clad knee and throwing back his head, laughing heartily at what he regarded as her little joke.

'Great-granddaddy, actually,' she had said truthfully, ruffling his blond, baby-soft hair as they sat, side by side, in the private dining-room at the Hotel Charlotte. 'My great-grandfather was King William IV—and that's the truth! Why do you think I carry the name Fitzwilliam, pray?'

His eyes had clouded momentarily. 'Fitzwilliam? I can't rightly say. Whatever do you mean?'

She had sat back against the plush wine upholstery of the booth and savoured the moment. 'To have the prefix Fitz,' she explained carefuly, 'is to indicate that you are descended from a noble family—often the Royal Family itself—but always on the wrong side of the blanket!'

'You mean your granddaddy was a bastard? A right royal bastard?'

She had laughed to see the incredulity on his face. 'Correct, sir! The son of William IV and Marguerite Duval—one of the most beautiful actresses of her day. Grandpapa was conceived before William ascended the throne, of course. Great-granddaddy, as you put it, actually married a German princess—Amelia Adelaide of Saxe-Meiningen—eminently more suitable than the daughter of a French revolutionary exile!'

She could hear his laughter still, as it had rung out in that tiny room. 'Well, if that isn't the darndest thing I've ever heard! The great-granddaughter of the King of England—that'll be quite something to tell my buddies back home!'

She had laughed with him, carried along with his boyish enthusiasm. There was something refreshing, she thought, almost child-like, in American beaux. A girl could get more than a little bored with the weak-chinned charms of so many of the English aristocracy!

Flowers had arrived every single day at her lodging-house—great bouquets of red and white roses. 'Red for love, white for honour,' he had said when she had thrown her arms about him and thanked him with a shower of kisses. 'Wear them on your wedding day. Red and white roses in your bridal bouquet—wear them for me, Aimée. Wear my promise to love and honour you for ever, for all the world to see!'

She would keep that promise. Not for all the world, but certainly Craven County to witness.

She turned and walked to the window. It seemed as though the whole of Craven County were out there now, all those that mattered socially, that is. Her eyes narrowed as she stared out over the lawns, then turned towards the broad steps to the left of the window where the tall figure of her fiancé swaggered down to join the milling crowd.

'Love and honour,' she murmured, as he moved into the middle distance, to be surrounded by a giggling group of Southern belles. He had certainly loved her in London—loved her with a fervour and panache that had quite taken her breath away; perhaps it was silly to imagine things would be completely the same immediately she arrived at Four Winds. There were still all of two weeks to go before the actual marriage itself —time enough for the flames of passion to rekindle in his

eyes. But honour . . . After today, honour was quite
another matter!

Just look at them, she thought with not a little bitterness, worthy matrons all, with their well-upholstered
figures. It was strange, really, but the thought that she
might not be fully accepted into Georgian society had
never really entered her head. Why, an actress of her
standing was welcome in some of the best drawing-
rooms in England—if not in most of Europe. But
England and Europe were not Craven County. That fact
was becoming more and more obvious with every minute
spent in this beautiful, but very foreign, land. With a
defiant tilt of her chin she swung round and swept from
the room, across the great hall and on up the wide,
sweeping staircase.

She had barely closed the door to her room when two
light taps made her turn, and a slim, coffee-coloured
figure entered.

'Tizzy!' With a sigh, Aimée sank on the satin-covered
stool by the dressing-table, turning her back on the
maid. 'You'd better help me out of this gown—they're
waiting for me outside.'

Long, slim fingers undid the back-fastenings of her
basque as Aimée watched silently in the dressing-table
mirror, for she found it quite unnerving to be served
night and day by this slim, silent figure with the enormous saucer eyes and the strangely Caucasian look to
her long straight nose and finely-drawn lips. Her hair she
could not see, for it was wrapped in the traditional white
turban.

'Which one will it be, miz?' The maid slipped the
undone bodice from her mistress's shoulders to fall in
pink crumpled folds on top of the hooped muslin
skirts.

Aimée stood up to facilitate the complete removal of
her dress, and kicking off her soiled satin slippers,
padded over the cotton rug to the wardrobe. 'I think
the white organdie should do nicely,' she murmured,
flicking through the rack of gowns. 'Don't you agree?'

The maid's face remained totally impassive as she nodded her assent.

Twenty minutes later the transformation was complete, and Aimée stepped back to admire the result in the full-length swing-mirror on its rosewood stand by the window. Not a hair was out of place nor a speck of dirt visible on the pale, creamy skin of her face, and the hands that fussed nervously with the broad, pink satin sash were cleanly bandaged beneath new white net mittens. She had intended keeping the white, rosebud-spangled organdie for her honeymoon, but this afternoon was no time to stint on her appearance after what had just gone before.

Extracting the matching parasol from the stand, she gave an impulsive twirl and turned to the figure watching silently from the side of the bed. 'What do you think, Tizzy?' she asked breathlessly. 'Will he approve? Will the master think I look pretty enough for him?'

The maid continued to watch her with an unblinking stare that she found both unnerving and not a little insolent. 'I asked a question,' Aimée said irritably. 'Are you deaf—or just singularly lacking in manners?'

'It's a very nice frock, miz.'

Aimée snorted and picked up her skirts. The emphasis on the gown, and not on her person, did not go unnoticed. She had tried to be pleasant—heaven knows, she had tried, she thought—and would waste no more time on the insolent hussy. She might even have a word with Chas, and get her exchanged, perhaps, for a more amenable personal maid. But that was for later. Now she must fly, otherwise he would be further enraged by her behaviour. For what remained of the day, she must try to make amends for the disastrous beginning to the festivities.

She had made many important entrances in her young life, but none had caused her heart to palpitate quite so alarmingly as when she began her descent of the wide wooden steps of the mansion. Her eyes stared fixedly ahead and a dignified smile was frozen on her lips as she walked slowly towards the small knot of guests. Chas was nowhere to be seen in the immediate vicinity so she paused momentarily, and a female voice at her elbow caused her to turn.

'Miss Fitzwilliam?' The speaker was a young woman of about her own age, or perhaps a trifle younger, her pale skin a striking contrast to the vivid titian-red of her hair. 'I'm Rebecca Madison—Becky to my friends.'

A pale, slightly damp hand was extended, and Aimée shook it warmly. 'I'm very pleased to make your acquaintance, Becky,' she replied.

'I saw your exit—and your re-entrance. It was quite a show!'

Aimée blushed to the roots of her hair. 'I can assure you that no show was intended!' she said heatedly. 'Quite the contrary, in fact . . .'

'Oh, don't go gettin' all fussed up!' Becky interrupted. 'I'm spunky myself at times. Too spunky for my own good, Pa says!'

In common with so many redheads, her eyebrows and eyelashes were so fair as to be almost invisible, giving her the lashless look of a startled rabbit, but she was pretty nevertheless, and Aimée found herself relaxing and warming to her new acquaintance. 'I'm afraid I've got a good deal to learn about Southern ways,' she said softly, giving a twirl of her parasol behind her shoulder as the two continued across the velvet lawn.

'I'd ignore them, personally,' Becky said sympathically, ' 'Specially Widow Sykes—that ol' peahen! Why, she's got me in more trouble with my daddy than almost anyone I know!'

Aimée suppressed a smile and glanced round nervously; her new companion's voice was a trifle too loud for comfort, but the music of the band and the laughter and chatter of the other guests more than drowned any private remarks.

'He's a mighty fine-looking man, don't you think?

He's quite a skylarker with the ladies, that's for sure, and not always of the right sort! All my girl-friends just swoon clean away when he's around, but I guess they're a bit too strait-laced for the likes of him!'

Aimée turned her head, puzzled. 'He?' she said. 'You mean . . .'

'I mean Red!' Becky said firmly. 'Daniel Redmayne! A gal could get herself into all sorts of trouble over a beau like that!'

Aimée coloured slighty and nodded in agreement. 'To be honest, I was too flustered at the time to notice his looks. But, come to think of it, he was rather nice!'

'Rather nice!' Becky hooted. 'Why, how very English, I do declare! If he's not just the most handsome man in the whole of Georgia, then my name's not Rebecca Emily Madison! It's too bad about his reputation,' she said with a sigh. 'They'd rather kill me back home than have me keep company with the likes of him!'

Aimée's brows furrowed and she gave a doubting laugh. 'Really? Surely no one can be as bad as that? What did he do—murder his grandmother?'

'Worse—much worse!' Becky replied, shaking her head. 'He's Irish!'

They sat down on one of the rustic benches beneath the tall plane trees at the edge of the lake, and as their lavishly flounced skirts were manoeuvred into position, Aimée looked curiously at her new friend. 'I don't quite understand.'

Becky's pretty rosebud mouth pursed slightly, then broke into a wry smile. 'You'll learn soon enough. Living in Georgian society, dear Aimée, is like living in a very opulent, but very stuffy, room. If anyone tries to open the door and let in some fresh air—or a fresh face—there are howls of objection from those within. At least among the older generation, that is. In a way, the MacDonalds here at Four Winds and the Redmaynes at Wildwood typify exactly what I mean . . .'

Aimée sat forward, listening intently, as Becky said, 'You see, Aimée, Southern society, in areas such as this, was founded by Scottish settlers fleeing their country after the Jacobite rebellions of the last century. Even the famous Flora MacDonald herself fled to Virginia after the defeat of Bonnie Prince Charlie at Culloden! Did it never occur to you why your fiancé Chas was baptised Charles Stuart MacDonald?'

Aimée shook her head. Chas had hinted that she was not the only one with a famous ancestor, but he had never got round to enlarging on the subject.

Becky paused to swat ineffectually with her parasol at a cloud of mosquitoes that had risen from the lake, then continued, 'Well, anyway, the Scotch have formed the bedrock of our society ever since . . . Oh, quite a few English families, and one or two French, have been admitted, but Craven County is still very much as it was in the last century—and too many people want it to remain that way! After the Irish famine a dozen or so years ago quite a few Irish settled around these parts and tried to—well, to break into society, but they would have none of it. The trouble is,' her voice dropped, as though she were divulging the most intimate secret, 'Red's daddy succeeded—or partly! He bought Wild-wood—the estate right next door to the MacDonalds themselves—and, oh boy, that did not go down too well, I can tell you!'

'But that's terrible!' Aimée protested. 'That's just blind prejudice! It seems to me there are too many people here who think they're superior to others!'

Becky gave her blue silk parasol a twirl and toyed with the tassel. 'Sure are—I wouldn't argue with you on that. But that's just how things are, I guess. Just thank the good Lord you were born white, that's all!'

'We're certainly in the minority,' Aimée mused. 'Why, I'd seen only one negro in my entire life before I came here. But, of course, he was a free man, not a slave.'

'How do you find the household ones?' Becky

asked. 'I always say a good personal maid is worth her weight in gold. Has Chas picked out a good one for you?'

Aimée grimaced. 'I'll reserve judgment on that for the moment, if you don't mind! Her name's Tizzy, and she's . . .'

'Tizzy, did you say?' Becky interrupted, her jaw dropping.

'Yes. Do you know her?'

Becky's pale face went paler still, the freckles standing out like splashes of amber paint across the bridge of her pert nose. 'Let's just say that I know of her,' she said slowly.

'And?'

Her companion half-turned on the wooden bench, so that her face was no longer visible. 'It's of no import!' she said quickly. 'Please, let's talk of other things. In fact, I must go now. You must forgive me. It's been so nice to make your acquaintance. Please always regard me as your true friend!' She stood up, turning round to offer her hand.

Aimée took it reluctantly, standing up to face her as she grasped her slim fingers. 'Please, Becky, what did you mean? What do you know of Tizzy? If you won't tell me, then I must ask Chas!'

'No!' Becky gasped. 'Don't do that, Aimée, I beg you! For your own sake, don't do that!'

With that, she was gone, the tiny slippered feet hurrying over the green grass, the blue taffeta hooped skirts swaying gracefully as her slight figure disappeared into the crowd in front of the biggest of the refreshment marquees.

A vague sense of unease pervaded Aimée, and her eyes scanned the milling figures who surrounded her. Becky's peculiar reaction to the mention of the maid's name was distinctly odd. But that was something to ponder on later, perhaps. Not now—for she must rejoin the guests and attempt to make up for her long absence. She had still seen no sign of Chas and knew he must be

absolutely furious with her by now. I must find him, she
thought, anxiously gathering her skirts, when a soft
masculine drawl made her head turn sharply.

'Miss Fitzwilliam! All alone, I see! May I join
you?'

'Mr Redmayne!' Her lips blurted out the name, and
her cheeks coloured at the unexpected appearance of
the man by her side. He had come up from behind, a
slow grin spreading over his bronzed features as he
looked down at her from his immense height.

'I would appreciate it if you did not associate—either
now or in the future—with that man . . .' Chas's voice
rang in her head as her eyes met the brilliant blue ones
smiling down at her.

'I'm sorry, Mr Redmayne,' she flustered, looking
about her in embarrassment. 'I—I really must find my
fiancé!'

The dark eyebrows above the sleepy-lidded gaze
rose quizzically, and his lips curved in amusement.
'Then allow me to escort you!' he said in a voice that
brooked no argument, proffering his velvet-sleeved
arm.

Aimée blenched visibly. How on earth could she
refuse without giving the utmost offence? 'Thank you,
sir,' she said faintly, as she slipped her lace-mittened
hand on to his forearm. 'That's very kind . . .'

It seemed as if every head turned as they moved
forward into the crowd, and she could feel the panic
rising within her as both men and women melted from
their path to allow them a free passage across the lawn.
The heads of the matrons inclined together, their tight
lips whispering unheard comments, as their daughters'
eyes followed only the tall figure on whose arm she now
walked.

'You see how the men are looking at you?' the smooth
molasses voice just above her right ear said softly. 'I
guess I'm the envy of every man here today!' As she
glanced up and met the deep blue of his eyes, he laughed
and corrected himself. 'Every man but one, that is! I

guess ol' Charlie-boy will be none too happy, don't you agree, Aimée?'

She did. And he was right.

CHAPTER THREE

THE DINNER-TABLE gleamed, all twenty feet of its mahogany surface glowing a rich reddish-brown under the flickering lights of the crystal chandelier. As usual since Aimée's arrival, it was set with only three places: Chas at the head, herself to his right and Great-aunt Effie directly opposite.

Euphemia Morrison was Chas's great-aunt on his mother's side; a formidable lady of uncertain years, but certainly well into her seventh decade. She had come out from Scotland as a girl of thirteen with her father, the Reverend John Ross Morrison, her mother and her elder sister Kate—Chas's maternal grandmother. Great-aunt Effie was the only one of Chas's family left at Four Winds, and she ran the house like clockwork. Her one failing, if you could call it that, was that she was almost stone deaf. As usual, she had been the first to take her place at the table, followed by her great-nephew, and the two waited silently for the English girl to join them.

Aimée entered the room with a pounding heart, closing the door gently. The old lady did not turn her head, but the grey-blue eyes of the young man to her right narrowed to two steel slits as he stared at the pale, drawn face of the young woman he was about to marry.

He had not uttered one word to her since the moment when he had received her, for the second time that afternoon, from the arm of Daniel Redmayne. For another two hours they had gone through the motions demanded, mingling with the guests and making the necessary introductions, but as the carriages for the ladies began to reassemble towards six o'clock and the men collected their horses from the stables, the tension increased. And, at six o'clock exactly, he had left her side. In total abjection she had watched his tall figure marching across the lawns towards the big house, then ascending the steps, two at a time, to disappear through the great pine door. To see him now, two hours later, seated at the dining-table, was in itself something of a shock, for she had thoroughly convinced herself that she would not see him again for the rest of the evening.

She took her place silently, murmuring her thanks to the wizened white-coated negro who held out the high-backed mahogany chair, enabling her to slip her taffeta skirts comfortably beneath the damask cloth. She managed a strained smile of greeting to Aunt Effie, seated directly opposite, and was rewarded with a slight upward twist of the lipless mouth. Aunt Effie seldom spoke, and Aimée had not yet ascertained whether this was a by-product of her profound deafness. It was a fact of life that she bitterly regretted, however, as the reverberating silence in the large dining-room made her stomach quake, and it was all she could do to stop herself from turning and running.

The food at Four Winds was excellent, ordered and presided over by Aunt Effie and cooked to perfection by Sarah, the buxom, ebony-skinned cook, with a small army of assistants. The title and position of 'house-slave' was much prized within the slave community, for although the hours were long, the increased status and better food and clothing it afforded meant much to those lucky enough to attain the 'high rank'. Next to Sarah, the most senior of the house-slaves was Ebenezer, the long-serving butler who supervised the serving of the meals and whose grey wire-wool head was now bent over the large silver platter of breast of fried chicken accompanied by a yellow yam, cut open and steaming, with melted butter dripping from it in long golden rivulets.

Normally the very thought of such food would have made Aimée's mouth water—but not tonight. Tonight she could only watch in dismay as the third plate was heaped with succulent fare and deposited in front of her.

The personal hurt in the old man's eyes when, twenty minutes later, he removed her barely touched plate, filled her with remorse.

'Just the tiniest drop, please, Ebenezer,' she said softly when he produced a large cut-glass bowl of melon and blackcurrant fool. 'I don't really feel quite up to eating tonight.'

Chas refilled his glass from the large bottle of Château Anjou Blanc on the trolley by his elbow, and Aimée could feel his eyes on her, cold and penetrating, as she bent her dark head over the purple-coloured sweet. She wished with all her heart that there had been no one else in the room, for then she could have had it out with him—plead for forgiveness, understanding—whatever it was she needed to do to regain his approval. As it was, in the presence of Aunt Effie, old Ebenezer and two lesser men-servants, she could only keep her peace and pray for the meal to end quickly.

Aunt Effie excused herself before the coffee, and although Aimée accepted half a cup, Chas declined, preferring to finish the bottle of white wine. It took very few sips to finish her coffee, and as the last bitter dregs met her tongue, she replaced the tiny gold-rimmed cup in the saucer and looked across at the man who was soon to be her husband. 'Chas?' She spoke the name so softly that she thought at first he had not heard.

At length his icy, blue-grey eyes turned towards her with an indifference that sent an involuntary shudder through her body. 'Yes?'

Her eyes blurred as she looked down, plucking nervously at the narrow band of rucking on the aubergine taffeta. 'Do you love me, Chas?' she whispered, her voice breaking as she said his name. 'Do you still love me?'

The wine-glass remained at his lips for a moment, and then he replaced it on the cloth, his fingers still gripping the slender stem. He said slowly, 'I'm marrying you, ain't I?'

Her face draining of colour, she stared across at him as

her fingers gripped the edge of the table. 'That's not
what I asked,' she said quietly. 'That's not what I asked,
Chas. Please, I . . .'

She stopped in mid-sentence, when he stood up,
pushing back his chair with one hand, the other still
holding the empty wine-glass, glaring down at her. 'I
have promised you my name,' he said in a voice that
matched the look of steel in his eyes. 'You will be
mistress of Four Winds. Do not ask for more.'

There seemed to be a cold hand gripping her heart as
his hand curled more tightly on the delicate stem of the
glass. With a sharp crack it snapped in two, its foot
dropping to the table, where it shattered into a dozen
crystal pieces.

For a long time, after he had left the room and his
footsteps had died away in the distance, she sat still.
Huge tears formed as she gazed unblinkingly at the
broken glass, acutely aware of the presence of the old
butler and the other servants. It seemed that the whole
world had stopped when Chas left; it had become
frozen, like her heart, and she had no idea how to change
it. She knew no one would make a move until she did,
so, blinded by the tears that were now streaming down
her face, she rose from the table and walked from the
room.

It seemed that everywhere she went, every move she
made, was monitored by the silent presence of the
servants, their black eyes aware now, as ever, of the
slight figure who rushed past them and on up the sweeping staircase. Even in her own room she was not alone,
for within minutes she was aware of the presence of
Tizzy at the foot of the bed.

'What do you want?' she demanded, raising her
swollen face from the satin-covered quilt. Was she to be
allowed no privacy in this place?

For a moment she was sure she could detect the
faintest hint of triumph on the beautiful coffee-coloured
face. 'I's come to undress you, miz.'

Aimée sat up, wiping her wet face impatiently with the

back of her hand and pushing the wayward locks of black hair back behind her ears. Her green eyes still glistened as she watched Tizzy walk to the dressing-table, and opening the top drawer, extract a clean lawn nightdress.

Coming over to the bed, the nightdress folded carefully over her arm, she looked down, from her full five feet ten inches, at the figure of her mistress on the crumpled quilt.

'Don't look at me like that!' Aimée snapped, wheeling round. 'I have a headache, that's all! Haven't you seen anyone with a headache before?'

The white-turbaned head nodded, and the dark eyes glanced towards the small drawer of the medicine-cabinet.

'Don't bother!' Aimée commanded. 'I'll see to it myself. There is still a little laudanum left in the bottle, I believe. Just—Just go now, please.' With a deep sigh, she flopped back on the quilt as the maid laid the nightdress carefully over the carved camphorwood chest at the foot of the bed and took her leave.

All she wanted was peace—time to herself to reflect on the day and what had gone so disastrously wrong with her life since her arrival in this strange foreign land. She got up and opened the glass doors to the right of her dressing-table, and went out on to the ornate wooden balcony that overlooked the soft, rolling acres of the Four Winds plantation.

The sun was now below the horizon, and as she watched, the red glow at the rim of the world faded to a dusky pink. The whole sky was turning slowly from azure to the delicate blue-green of a robin's egg, and the unearthly silence held a magic like nothing she had ever experienced in cold, grey London. As the twilight descended, a shadowy dimness crept over the countryside, changing the blood-red furrows of the fields beyond the gardens back to plain brown earth. The tall, spreading plane trees that edged the small lake at the foot of the lawns loomed ink-black in silhouette, while round the big house itself the house-swallows soared and swooped in their evening ritual, before taking up residence in the eaves for the night ahead. A fresh breeze whipped at her loose strands of hair, and crossing her arms in front of her breasts, she shivered slightly and turned back to the sanctuary of the bedroom.

Within minutes she was regretting her cursory dismissal of the maid, for it proved almost impossible to undo the intricate back-fastenings of her basque, and the very thought of the contortions that would be required to undo her stays made her quail. There was nothing else for it. She would simply have to go downstairs and borrow one of the housemaids.

The flurry her entrance caused in the kitchen made her feel instantly guilty, and she resolved to make her visit as brief as possible. 'I've done a rather silly thing, I'm afraid, Sarah,' she said, addressing the cook, who was hastily drying her chubby fingers on a linen tea-towel. 'I've dismissed Tizzy for the night, and completely forgot I'll need help with this,' she said, indicating the back of her bodice. 'May I borrow one of the others, please? I'll keep her only a few minutes.'

'Oh, yes'm!' Sarah said, relieved that the request was so easily granted. With a nod of her turbaned head, she gestured to a small, pretty child of about thirteen. 'Go with Miz Aimée, Sadie!' she commanded.

The child's eyes grew wider and the generous lips broke into a nervous smile as with a small curtsy she followed her new mistress from the room.

The relief when the stays were removed was enormous, and Aimée turned to beam her thanks. 'You did wonderfully well, Sadie. Would you prefer to be a personal maid some day—rather than a housemaid?'

'Oh, yes'm!' Sadie replied, her enthusiasm overcoming her shyness. 'Dat be real good!'

'Then so you shall!' Aimée said impulsively. 'So you shall! I see no good reason why the job should be done by the same person all the time.

'But, miz—Tizzy . . . Oh no, ma'm . . . She be real sore!'

'Fiddlesticks!' her mistress replied. 'I shall tell her in the morning. You will make a perfect little maid, and shall certainly have your chance!'

When the child had gone, Aimée stared into the small swing-mirror on top of the dressing-table and carefully removed the hairpins from her luxuriant locks. They tumbled down her shoulders in thick dark coils, emphasising the pale skin of her face. The day had taken its toll, but perhaps it might not end too badly. Once in her dressing-robe, she could slip along the corridor and have a quiet word with Chas—to apologise to him for what he had perceived as her misbehaviour. He was angry tonight, there was no doubt about that. But anger was a fleeting thing. She would talk to him quietly—explain how things were still strange for her here at Four Winds. She had made mistakes, but she would learn from them and see that they never happened again. And she could tell him of her plan to train Sadie as her personal maid. Surely anything that made life happier for her could raise no objections from him? He did want her to be happy here, didn't he? After all, that could only add to the sum of their joint happiness!

Without further ado she shed the remains of her undergarments and slipped the fine lawn nightdress over her head. With trembling fingers she did up the tiny mother-of-pearl buttons, adjusting the broderie anglaise frill round the bodice and neck before slipping her arms into an emerald-green dressing-robe.

It was quite improper, of course, to visit anyone, let alone a man, in such attire—but they were to be married within two weeks! Her heartbeats quickened at the thought. They had had so few opportunities to be alone —really alone—since her arrival on this side of the Atlantic. Perhaps the misunderstandings of the day were not so disastrous—perhaps they might even recapture some of the old magic they had known in London before the day ended! The small carriage-clock on the mantelpiece showed that it was almost ten o'clock. With nothing keeping him downstairs, and no plans that she knew of to go out, the chances were that he was already in his room.

With a last anxious glance in her mirror, she slipped her feet into a pair of embroidered green velvet mules and crept out of the room. The landing was quite dark, as the lamps had not yet been lit, and a shiver ran through her slight figure as she slid silently along the passage. Chas's room was at the very far end—a large sunny room that straddled the front upper-left part of the house, giving a spectacular view over miles of the estate. Aimée had been in it just once, and then only as far as a foot inside the panelled oak door. Her immediate impression had been one of beautiful polished wood —whole walls of it that surrounded the magnificent four-poster bed in the centre of the floor. A thin film of perspiration broke on her brow at the thought as the door came into sight.

Aimée stood before it, wiping her palms on her robe, before raising her hand to knock, when a sound from inside the room made her halt, her hand in mid-air. He was definitely there—but had already gone to bed, for she could hear the unmistakable creak of bedsprings. Her head bent forward, her straining ears heard the creaking become louder and more rhythmic. Then, with a gasp, she leapt back, as though stung, at the peal of laughter that came from the other side. By the greatest stretch of imagination, that could not be Chas! It was a woman in there—and they were not discussing the price of cotton!

Her first inclination was to throw open the door and confront them—Chas and whatever trollop was in there with him. But something made her draw back, freezing her hand inches above the brass handle of the door. What would it accomplish? Perhaps this was simply how things were out here. Perhaps it was normal for Southern men to have mistresses—after all, Frenchmen did, didn't they? With a sigh, she leant back against the door-jamb as another peal of laughter reached her ears, this time the deep, resonant laugh of a man, followed by a muffled female giggle. Was she one of those strumpets —those wantons—that Becky Madison had referred to that afternoon? Surely, if they could attract a man like Daniel Redmayne . . .

Her mind was in turmoil as she headed back along the landing to her own room, closing the door. Through the window opposite, she could see the pale silver orb of the full moon rising like some spectre in the darkening sky. As though drawn by a peculiar force, she opened the doors and stepped out into the balmy night air of the balcony. As the breeze caressed her face, Aimée realised to her surprise that her cheeks were dry. She was shedding no tears, although the pain inflicted by what she had just encountered was acute. She glanced back into the room, at the ornate four-poster bed, with its heavily embroidered drapes and soft, duck-feather pillows. Could she really retire there tonight, knowing that just along the passage the man whom she was about to marry was lying in an identical bed with another woman?

She could not—and would not. She had to get out of here. This house, for all its outward show of dignity and beauty, was rotten at the core! Air was needed—fresh, clean air to clear her head and help her to put the events of the last twenty-four hours into some kind of perspective.

The fact that she was still in her night attire meant nothing as she ran down the main staircase, her tread in the velvet mules almost silent on the polished wood. Luckily there was no one in the hall to see her leave, and she slipped out through the front door like an ethereal being—a fleeting, phantom-like figure barely visible in the dark shadow of the front porch, which ran almost the full length of the house.

Automatically her feet led her round the back towards the stables, which were almost directly adjacent to the slave quarters, separated only by the huge cobblestoned courtyard. Although it was not yet totally dark, the lanterns inside the main block had been lit, because one of the mares was in foal, and she pushed through the swing-doors with a rapidly beating heart.

The pungent smell of polished leather and saddle-oil assailed her nostrils as she passed through the tack-room and on into the first block of stalls, where Tartar, the chestnut gelding allotted to her, was kept. The sweet, highly scented odour of fresh hay filled her senses, and one of the horses whinnied at the soft whisper of her footsteps on the stone-flagged floor. 'It's only me, boy,' she called softly. 'Easy, now, easy . . .'

The animal raised its head, whinnying louder, its soft brown nostrils flaring in the ghostly lamplight as she entered the stall. The noise brought one of the stable-boys scurrying in from the depths of the main stable beyond.

'It's all right—it's Miss Fitzwilliam,' she said reassuringly to the wide-eyed youth who stood in front of her, clutching a pitchfork to the front of his rough cotton shirt. 'Could you saddle him up for me, please?'

The lad's eyes, now jet-black in the lamplight, grew wider as they took in the unexpected state of *déshabillé* of the lady before him. Young men like him had been flogged, if not hanged, for less than setting eyes on a white woman so attired. A flush of sweat broke on his forehead as, murmuring, 'Yus'm,' he led the animal past her towards the tack-room.

His reaction was not lost on Aimée, who immediately regretted the impulsiveness of her actions. The last thing she wanted was to bring trouble on the heads of others. The thought of returning to the big house and what it contained was, however, quite beyond her. All she really wanted to do was to ride—and ride—until her hurt and confusion disappeared into the background, like the Four Winds mansion itself.

Once in the saddle, her spirits immediately lifted at the feel of the living power of the animal beneath her. She had never ridden side-saddle in so soft a garment as the velour robe, and urging the gelding forward, she felt both exhilarated and extremely vulnerable as they headed off in the direction of the mountains beyond. She had ridden this path in daylight, but never at night, and the landscape was disconcertingly unfamiliar. The odour of the pines came to her before she reached them, their heady scent wafting pungently on the fresh breeze that swept across the foothills of the Blue Ridge Mountains. The air was alive with the sounds of the night, and she gasped aloud in fright as she ducked her head low over the horse's flying mane to avoid the giant fruit-bats that wheeled and soared before swooping low to within inches of her streaming black hair. Once or twice a jack-rabbit leapt out from underfoot, causing the horse to shy, flinging its head into the air, as she fought desperately to keep control. If it threw her and bolted, she knew she would never find her way home unaided.

When the path led deeper into the woods, she felt the exhilarating freedom of the ride change to apprehension as familiar landmarks became blurred, or disappeared altogether in the inky blackness. She thought she knew this way reasonably well in daylight, but now . . .

The shot rang out without warning. The bullet whistled past her bent head so close that she could feel it within inches of her face. Her scream coincided with the horse's reaction to the shock. Within a split second it had reared and bolted, disappearing into the depths of the forest, while she flew through the air to land like a broken doll by the side of the track.

At first she was conscious of nothing but the deep, velvety blackness that enfolded her—then the pain, as she struggled to stop herself from sinking into oblivion. She groaned out loud as she attempted to raise herself from the bed of dry rye grass at the edge of the path, then the moan became a scream as the massive figure of a man appeared behind the barrel of a gun that was still pointed menacingly at her.

He walked towards her, halting about ten paces away and stared down at her crumpled figure. Her eyes fixed on the dark knee-booted legs and travelled their terrified way upward, as a deep masculine voice gasped, 'Landsakes—it's a woman!'

The man bent one of his black-booted legs to kneel

beside her, and she lifted her petrified face to look up into the eyes of Daniel Redmayne.

'Dear Mother of God, it's you! What in heaven's name . . .?'

Aimée shook her head as tears of relief swept down her colour-drained cheeks. 'Mr Redmayne! I—I was so frightened . . . so terribly afraid . . .'

'And so you should have been!' he said in astonishment. 'I could've killed you! I shoot first and ask questions afterwards when there are strangers on my land. So does everyone. It's a lesson you learn very quickly round these here parts.'

'Your—Your land?' she repeated faintly. 'I'm on *your* land?'

'You have been for the last half-mile,' he said, taking off his jacket and draping it over her. 'Didn't you know?'

She shook her head. 'I thought this was still Mac-Donald country. I'm—I'm so sorry.'

There was a moment's silence as he wrapped his garment more closely round her slight shoulders, then he murmured, 'You're in night-clothes! What happened, Aimée?'

His use of her first name sent another tremor through her shivering frame, and she shook her head hopelessly. 'Please don't ask,' she said softly. 'I just had to get away, that's all . . .'

'You had words with Chas?' he insisted. 'He hurt you?' His voice was harsher now.

'No. No, nothing like that. I discovered something tonight I would rather not have known, that's all . . .' Her voice trailed away as the memory of that laughter —that awful laughter—from behind the closed bedroom door invaded her mind.

There was a silence again, and then his voice was soft, almost gentle. 'I think I may know.'

She stared at him in the darkness, Becky Madison's words echoing in her head, 'He's quite a skylarker with the ladies, that's for sure—and not always of the right sort!' Her body stiffened under his hands. 'I should think you might, sir!' she said coldly. 'For I believe you are not unacquainted yourself with such behaviour!' She winced with pain as his fingers increased their grip.

'No!' he said harshly. 'No, not that—never that! I have been guilty of many things, but never that! I do not own even one slave.'

Each pair of eyes sought the other in the faint beam of moonlight that broke through the tall pines looming above them. 'Are we talking of the same thing—the same sin?' she asked softly. 'Tell me what you know . . . Help me to understand . . .'

'No, Aimée,' he said quietly. 'No, it's not for me to tell you. It's not my fingers that will place a ring on your finger some days from now. It's not me you should ask. You cannot run away from the truth for ever. You must go back now and ask him yourself. Just remember one thing, though. When—or if—you do, think on this. This is not London, Aimée—this is the South—this is Georgia. They do things differently here.'

She felt her eyes fill as they gazed into his. 'Don't they fall in love the same way here, Red? Is that so very different, too? Don't they fall in love in the South? Don't they feel the same emotions here? Don't they suffer when wounded? Don't they ever fall in love—really in love?'

Very gently, as though afraid she might break into a thousand pieces under his hands, he lifted her back to her feet and stood looking down at her. 'I cannot speak for my fellow countrymen, my dear. I can only say that some of us do . . . Some of us still do . . .'

His face swam before her, and as the tears rolled silently down her cold cheeks, she felt his fingers tighten once more, pressing through the soft velour of her robe, as his head bent towards her. A tiny gasp rose in her throat as his mouth found hers, pressing her cold lips apart, infusing her whole being with such an intimate, all-pervading warmth that she could do nothing but surrender to the sweet sensation of the moment. Propriety, however, reasserted itself, and her momentarily pliant body became rigid. She should not be enjoying this! This was not the man she was about to marry . . . What on earth was she thinking of?

Summoning all her strength she wrenched herself free, stepping back, raising her hand to strike him across the cheek. 'Sir, you disgrace yourself—and you shame me!'

He caught her wrist in mid-air, and his eyes—now midnight-blue in the moonlight—found hers. 'There is no shame, Aimée, in what is freely given—and accepted. Your words may say one thing, but your lips have told me another . . .'

'No, it's not so! I pray you not to taunt me! I am bethroted to another . . . I am going to marry Charles MacDonald!' Why was he looking at her like this, causing this confusion within her, making her heart beat so alarmingly beneath the thin fabric of her nightgown?

He let go of her wrist, to cup her face in his hands and lift it towards his. His breath was warm on her skin as he said softly, 'If you still love him, really love him, then I apologise for what passed between us. But if not, I have no regrets. *Non, je ne regrette rien, ma belle* Aimée . . .'

'I didn't know you spoke French,' she whispered, her body trembling like a frightened bird in his grasp.

He smiled—a slow, intimate, enigmatic smile that sent a tremor through her entire being, as he said quietly, 'But then, my dear Aimée, there is a lot about me that you do not know.'

CHAPTER FOUR

THE BRITTLE CHIMES of the small ormolu clock on the bedroom mantelpiece struck six as Aimée opened her eyes. Already the sun was streaming through the open drapes of the tall windows, bathing the whole room in a golden glow.

She slipped out of bed and threw open the doors to the balcony, and a soft, balmy warmth, heady with the smells of summer, poured into the room. Under the wooden floor of the balcony, mocking-birds and jays engaged in their age-old battle for possession of the old magnolia tree beneath her feet, the mockers as sweet voiced and plaintive as ever, the jays as insistently shrill in their perpetual argument with their adversary. She had stood here enjoying their battle every morning since her arrival at Four Winds, content to lean on the broad sill, drinking in all the scents and sounds. Life had been nothing like this in England, for it was almost impossible to persuade flowers to grow in the pocket-handkerchief gardens, and the only birds she could remember were the starlings and the half tame grey pigeons that infested the foggy London pavements and rooftops. Yes, life was certainly different here in the South, but this morning she had little time to spare for its delights. Today was different. Today she had something more important to do.

Turning from the sun-soaked magic of the balcony, she picked up her robe from the chair by the side of the bed, and after a rudimentary examination for any tell-tale signs of her ride the previous night, slipped it on over her nightgown, knotting the sash belt tightly. Tizzy would not appear with the hot water for her morning toilet for half an hour yet. That would give her just enough time to slip back along the landing and do what

had to be done. She must have it out with Chas before he
left on his daily round of the estate. If she waited until
she saw him later in the day, her courage would fail
her.

Thank goodness no one had noticed her exit or return
last night, she thought, as she pulled the bristles of the
silver-backed hairbrush through her tangled locks. She
had made sure that she had been dropped from the black
stallion's back well out of sight of the big house, or
anyone near it. In her haste to get back to the sanctuary
of her room, she had even forgotten to thank her rescuer
or to bid him goodbye. But her short and dramatic
relationship with Daniel Redmayne had never been
exactly predictable. She only hoped he would keep his
promise and attempt to capture her wayward horse
before its absence from the stable was noticed by Chas
himself.

Her heart was pounding as she closed her own door
quietly behind her and set off down the passage. What
exactly she was going to say to Chas she had not completely thought out—but surely, if their love meant
anything, it meant honesty between them—if fidelity
was too much to hope for?

To her dismay, his door was slightly ajar, and taking
her courage in both hands, she gave two light taps and
stepped back to wait. There was no sound from inside,
and she tapped again, this time louder. When there was
still no reply, she pushed the door gently, peering into
the sun-filled bedchamber.

'Chas?' Tentatively she stepped into the room, and
with a sinking heart, found that it was already empty. He
had gone, disappeared out into the red rolling hills of the
plantation before she was even awake.

With a groan of frustration she sat down on the edge of
the rumpled bed. It creaked loudly, and she leapt up
again, her mind flying back to that same awful sound and
its associations of the night before. Wide-eyed, she
threw back the patchwork quilt to stare in anguish at the
bottom sheet and pillows. 'Why, Chas, why?' she

whispered into the emptiness, as hot tears filled her eyes.

They glistened a bright sea-green as they travelled to a small miniature watercolour of herself in a silver frame on the bedside table. He had had it painted in London, before sailing back to North America. 'I shall sit it by my bed, my love,' he had promised. 'You shall smile on me and guard me through the long hours of the night . . .' How many scenes similar to that of last night had she been unwittingly smiling on since those words had been uttered? With a sob, she turned and ran from the room, slamming the door behind her.

At the door of her own room, Aimée was met by the tall, silent figure of Tizzy, and she stared at her with a mixture of embarrassment and anger. How dared she look at her like that, with that superior, mocking light in those dark, liquid eyes!

Grabbing the pitcher of hot water from the maid's hands, she pushed in past her. 'I'll take that!' she snapped, blinking back the tears still stinging her eyes. 'And please send Sadie up to assist with my toilet. You're dismissed, as from this minute!'

The young woman's eyebrows lifted. 'Beggin' yo' pardon, miz—massa done give me dis job. Him the only one . . .'

'Don't you dare to be pert, girl!' Aimée flamed. 'I'm your mistress now—and don't you ever forget it! Now just do as you are told and find Sadie—please!' The last word was given undue emphasis, and Aimée's teeth bit hard into the flesh of her lower lip as she watched Tizzy disappear back downstairs. What on earth had made her flare up like that? What was it about this particular young woman that made the ire rise within her every time those saucer eyes looked at her?

She was still pondering the question at midday as she sat at the drawing-room window, her *petit point* on her lap, while she awaited Chas's reappearance for luncheon. Her thoughts were cut short at twelve-five precisely, when his tall figure loped into sight, ascending the steps to the front door at the double.

'Why, Aimée, my dear, you look real pretty this morning!'

His appearance at the door of the drawing-room took her by complete surprise, and she stood up in confusion as he crossed the polished floor to sweep her briskly off her feet, whirling her round twice before setting her down in front of him with a beaming smile.

'Tell me now, what have you been getting up to today? Don't say you have been plying that needle and thread all morning!'

She smiled up at him as they walked arm in arm towards the dining-room. It was almost like old times, she thought, with his long-lashed grey-blue eyes smiling down into her own.

A large pile of buckwheat cakes dripping with syrup was on a plate in the middle of the table next to a platter of cold meat and a dish of pickles. Chas poured two glasses of wine from the open bottle on the trolley, and handed one to her. 'Aunt Effie's still down in the slave quarters,' he said. 'One of the older women is in accouchement. Seems there may be some difficulty with the birth, and Auntie prefers to be there herself at times like that.'

Aimée's brow furrowed. 'I should be with her . . . I really had no idea.'

'Don't let that worry your pretty li'l head. You'll have time enough to worry about servant problems when we're married!'

He smiled across at her reassuringly, but the furrow remained firmly between her brows as she remembered the altercation with Tizzy that morning. 'Chas—about the servants . . . Well, about Tizzy, the maid you allotted to me. I—I dismissed her this morning.'

'You did what?' His voice was harsh, and she looked at him in alarm.

'I don't know what it is, but we do not get along. She—She intimidates me somehow, with her super-cilious look. It's as though she's laughing at me, as though she knows something I don't know, or feels in some way superior . . . I just don't like her, I expect!'

He was listening intently, leaning forward in his chair as she spoke. When she had finished, he was silent for a moment, then said quietly, 'I'm sorry, Aimée. I gave Tizzy the job of looking after you—and she stays.'

'No!' she exclaimed, much louder than she intended. 'No! I don't want her. I want Sadie. Why can I not have whom I want?'

His eyes narrowed. 'Because I am the master in this house, madam. And you would be wise to remember it.' Then suddenly he laughed.

The loud peal made a cold hand clutch at her heart, at the terrible thought that had just crossed her mind. A dreadful thought that unnerved her totally. No—surely not! Not Tizzy . . . Not that slave and Chas—her future husband!

She could eat nothing in the half-hour that followed, except with the utmost difficulty, and it was with some relief that she pushed the half-eaten buckwheat cake from her as Chas got to his feet.

'By the way, my dear, there's a musical evening at the Madisons' tonight. I may have forgotten to mention it to you before. Wear one of your prettiest frocks, won't you?'

She nodded dumbly as he kissed her lightly on the cheek and took his leave, striding across the room with the same easy grace that had attracted her so much all those months ago, back home in London. As his footsteps receded into the distance, she gazed after him, at the half-open door; then, with a small strained smile at the waiting servants, she stood up, wiping the corners of her mouth on the linen napkin and replacing it by the side of the syrup-sticky plate, and left the table.

She knew what she had to do and she would do it now, before doubts set in and her resolve melted. She would go down to the slave quarters and see for herself, or hear from another's lips, what she could not ask the man she was about to marry.

Never had she ventured into that part of the grounds allotted to the slaves, but had merely walked past them, avoiding the eyes of the children still too small to work in the cotton fields. Only the old, the sick and the very young were allowed to remain in the huts during the day; even the nursing mothers had their children brought to them three times a day for feeding, so that their work would not be interrupted. Her excuse could be that she was looking for Aunt Effie; she could even offer assistance at the birth. She had never attended any birth before, let alone a slave's delivery, and she felt uneasy at the thought of what awaited her three-quarters of a mile away at the compound.

What struck her first was the silence. Even the children huddled together round the open doorways of the shacks remained mute as she passed, their black-grape eyes wide with a mixture of interest and anxiety as she picked her way among the scrawny chickens and over the pot-holes in the sun-baked soil. She had no idea the place was so big, for it was hidden by trees from the windows of the big house, and her brows knitted as she looked at the identical rows of cabins that seemed to stretch in unbroken lines into infinity. From the drive one got no impression of just how many dwellings were down here, and she glanced about her helplessly in a vain attempt to locate the one which might contain Aunt Effie.

Suddenly a small child appeared on the wooden step of the nearest cabin, but as Aimée walked forward, he disappeared back inside with an alarmed cry, 'Massa's missus! *Ndoomba! Weeza!*'

She stood still, unnerved by the reaction the sight of her had provoked, and at length an old man appeared, his dark face more lined than any she had ever encountered.

'*Yinga?*' he said, his seamed face breaking into a toothless smile.

Aimée's heart sank. From his age and his greeting he was obviously one of the few original Africans left, and he might not speak English. But she persevered. 'I'm Miss Fitzwilliam—the master's lady . . . Can you tell me where I might find Miss Morrison?'

'*Ukola?*' the old man replied, still smiling. '*Quer quenda?*'

It was obviously no good. Then Aimée had an idea. 'Tizzy!' she said. 'Where is Tizzy's family?' She knew the maid had lived here until her own arrival at Four Winds. He must recognise the name.

'Ah!' the old man nodded. 'Tizzy!' He said something to the child that Aimée did not understand, but indicated for her to follow him.

With a smile of thanks, she followed the small boy down the narrow path between the houses until, a few minutes later, they emerged outside a much larger cabin at the end of the row. The child pointed to the closed door of the shack directly opposite. 'Tizzy!' he declared in a piping voice, before disappearing whence he came.

Aimée looked apprehensively at the closed door, then checked herself. How ridiculous to be nervous about meeting a servant, she thought, striding forward, the grey taffeta flounce of her skirts trailing in the brick-red dust. There was no answer to her knock; then, as she was on the point of knocking a second time, the door opened.

On the step stood the most beautiful child she had ever seen—a girl of about seven, whose golden skin and long straightish brown hair at first led her to wonder what on earth she was doing here—a white child playing in the slave quarters.

'Tizzy?' she asked softly. 'Is Tizzy here?'

The child shook her head, and the thumb of her right hand remained firmly embedded between the finely-drawn lips. She answered quietly, 'No'm . . . Tizzy —my ma—no here.'

As Aimée continued to stare at the child, wondering what on earth to do or say next, a toddler stumbled into the daylight from the depths of the shack. He clung to his sister's short calico smock as he stared at the strange white woman before them.

'Good God!' It was a blasphemy, but it was the only possible response to the shock of light brown hair on the coffee-coloured head of the infant. The eyes were brown, not grey-blue, but even the bridge of the nose was unmistakable. It was there—the slight crookedness that could only denote MacDonald ancestry.

For one terrible moment Aimée felt she was on the verge of swooning as a hot, then a cold, flush washed over her body. Breathe deeply, she commanded herself, as her legs, unable to bear the weight of her body any longer, staggered over to the wooden steps of the cabin. It was no bar-room trollop in the four-poster at Four Winds last night but she, the woman he had installed in his own home as the personal maid of his bride-to-be—it was Tizzy, their mother!

Aimée leaned back against the wooden handrail, closing her eyes against the sight that she found so unbearable. So oblivious of all but her own inner pain was she that she she failed to hear the barefooted tread of the tall figure pass her, or see the look in the dark eyes as they took in her slumped and dejected form on the steps. When Aimée came to, Tizzy was standing before her as her dazed eyes travelled slowly over the blue and white striped blouse that encased the full, heavy breasts. In her arms was a small bundle—a child no more than six months old with cream-coloured skin and light brown, tightly-frizzed hair. As Aimée continued to stare, Tizzy turned the infant towards her, and she gazed into the round dark grey eyes.

With the greatest difficulty she stood up, clinging tightly to the handrail, and passed her other hand over her glistening brow. 'I—I really haven't got used to this climate yet,' she said awkwardly. 'This heat makes me quite swoon!'

Tizzy smiled enigmatically. 'You be lookin' for some-one, miz?'

Aimée stared dumbly at her. This tall, beautiful creature—this slave—who had no more rights than a piece
of property, a table or chair that could be bought or sold
at whim, this human being, who was owned body and
soul by the man she was about to marry, was her rival. It
was simply too much to take in. Surely she should do
something, say something, to intimate that she was no
longer blind, that she was well aware of what had
been going on—what was still going on—under the
roof of the very house of which she would soon be the
mistress?

'You be lookin' for someone, miz?'

The question was repeated, louder this time, breaking
into the turmoil of her thoughts. 'Yes, I am,' Aimée said
faintly, looking around her with a distracted air. 'I'm
looking for Miss Morrison. I understand she's down
here.'

'Miz Morrison done gone fifteen minutes now, ma'm.'

Aimée gave a long shuddering sigh of relief. 'You
mean that she's back in the big house? Oh dear, I'm just
too late. What a pity . . .'

The two older children were now clinging to their
mother's skirts as they gazed up at the white-skinned
stranger, and the baby stretched out a chubby arm in her
direction. Fighting to keep her tone light, gathering up
her skirts, Aimée said, 'It's a beautiful baby. What do
you call it?'

There was a long silence, then the baby's mother
looked her straight in the eye, and there was no disguising the hint of triumph in her voice as she said, 'She'm
called Zola, ma'm. It be African for "love".'

The two women stared at each other, eyes locked,
over the child's head. No further word was spoken.
There was no need.

With a deliberately raised chin, Aimée swept up her
skirts and turned, walking quickly down the rickety steps
of the shack and on up the dusty dirt track. By the time
she reached the drive round the back of the mansion she
was running, skirts uplifted and swaying alarmingly, as

she made for the main door of the house. But, incredibly, she was not crying. Her eyes were quite dry, but a curious numbness had taken hold of her mind—a numbness that was matched only by the icy hand of fear that clutched her heart.

The afternoon passed in the same numbed daze, and still the tears did not come. Aimée sat on the window-seat in her room, staring with unseeing eyes out over the rolling countryside that was the Four Winds plantation. The scent of magnolia blossom permeated the room from the open doors to the balcony, and the sun, still high in the azure sky, cast a golden glow over the exquisite fabrics and furnishings. She could be happy here, as Chas's wife, she knew that. But could she do what so many other Southern wives were forced to do and turn a blind eye to what went on behind their backs—or even, as last night testified, under their very roofs?

She had heard before she came out that this kind of thing went on between master and slaves. It was one of the perquisites of being a slave-owner, wasn't it? Or so she had once been informed by a Southern gentleman some years before. In fact, it seemed that many men pleasured a selection of different slave women every night—a fact of life that was only too obvious from the numbers of mulatto children to be found on every plantation south of the Mason-Dixon line. But, in a way, if such dreadful violations had to continue, such fleeting unions must be infinitely preferable, for the master's wife, to this. This was no casual sexual gratification: this was an affair that had lasted at least seven or eight years—perhaps longer—and had produced children.

She twisted the tiny lace-trimmed handkerchief into a tight ball as the faces of the three children—his children —down there in the slave quarters haunted her mind. How did one cope, watching them grow up—his own flesh and blood, but still slaves, still held in bondage, to be bought or sold, despite the MacDonald blood that ran in their veins? Completely unable to find an answer, she gave a deep sigh as her eyes clouded. But they remained dry.

They were still dry that evening when she informed the cook that she would not be present for dinner.

'Please inform Aunt Effie and the master that I won't be dining tonight, Sarah. But I shall be joining Mr MacDonald for the soirée at the Madisons'. You will let him know?'

'Oh, yus'm!' Sarah assured her. 'Ah sho' will!'

Aimée relaxed visibly with that accomplished, and satisfied what hunger pangs might arise later by helping herself to a tray of fresh peaches, a cooked chicken-leg and a glass of milk, which she took back to her room. She also ordered a hip-bath of hot water to be brought up at five o'clock precisely, well aware that her penchant for regular bathing caused much head-shaking and mutterings of 'weakening of the constitution' among the Mac-Donald's friends and relations. But she cared little for the opinion of others in that regard, as she wallowed luxuriantly in the zinc tub. Tonight she would outshine every other woman at the gathering. Tonight she would look her best, she resolved, so that even Charles Mac-Donald himself would wonder what on earth she ever saw in him!

She took gown after gown from the wardrobe and then discarded them as she stood in the middle of the bedroom floor clad only in her best lace-trimmed pantalets, linen corset cover and three billowing lace and linen petticoats. First the sky-blue organdie with the long navy sash was tried and rejected, then the pink barred muslin with the wide insets of lace on the bodice, then the black bombazine frothing with flounces, each one edged with silver-grey ribbon, until at last she held up the apple-green watered silk, each flounce edged with the finest Brussels lace trimmed with dark-green velvet ribbon. This had always been a favourite, for it darkened her sea-green eyes to a deep emerald, especially in lamplight. She had to be laced her tightest for this one, of course, for its seventeen-inch waist meant a lot of puffing and pulling on the part of her maid—but the effect would be well worth it!

To her astonishment it was not Tizzy who appeared to minister to her dressing requirements, but Sadie. She refrained from enquiring the reason for this, preferring to believe that it was perhaps a goodwill gesture on Chas's part, in the hope of getting the evening off to a good start. And, if that was the case, she would attempt to respond in kind. Her innermost thoughts on what she had learned this afternoon would remain a secret kept locked within her heart—something to ponder on in the sanctuary of her own room later on. Nothing could be accomplished by creating a scene before the evening had even begun, and, anyway, knowing how much it meant to him, she desperately wanted to redeem herself in the eyes of his friends and neighbours. Or did she? A slight frown, accompanied by the hint of a wry smile, flickered across her delicate features. If she was entirely honest with herself, there was still a tiny part of her that got a secret pleasure out of shocking the elegantly-attired matrons of Southern society. 'Get thee behind me, Satan!' she murmured, to the astonishment of the attendant Sadie as she gave a last twirl in front of the mirror at seven-thirty precisely.

Her thick dark locks, released from their daytime net, now fell in abundance of 'Follow me, lads' ringlets over her shoulders. The crown of her head was left smooth, the hair pulled back from her high forehead and the sides turned into the sleek roll that typified the 'Coiffure Ristori', the hairstyle popular with smart young ladies in London. Her full breasts, pushed above the ruffled top of her basque, swelled into the creamy whiteness of her bare shoulders, and she passed her finger tentatively across her smooth skin. Was it done, in Craven County, Georgia, to wear an off-the-shoulder gown to a musical soirée? She really had no idea, and she cared less! Tonight all eyes would be on her—and her alone— and dared Charles Stuart MacDonald look at a coarse cotton-clad maid after this?

He was waiting at the foot of the main staircase when she appeared, his dark brown velvet frock-coat sleekly cut and braid-bound to match the single-breasted waist-coat beneath; his legs in the fawn shepherd's plaid trousers and brown buckled shoes were firmly planted apart, as he watched her descend the curving stair step by step.

'Beautiful,' he murmured, extending a velvet-clad arm, while his eyes moved approvingly over the gown.

She smiled her thanks, but found herself unable to meet his gaze as her fingers rested lightly on his forearm and they walked sedately towards the front door.

Even in the carriage during the short journey to Magnolia Mount, the Madison estate, she kept her eyes firmly on the passing landscape. She was well aware of saying all the right things in reply to his light-hearted small-talk, but found herself curiously detached. Whether he noticed or not, she could not be sure, but neither did she particularly care. Even the desire to impress him with her beauty, in comparison to others, had gone. She had little time to dwell on the matter, however, for their carriage soon joined the others making the journey up the winding drive of the Madisons' white-columned home. Within minutes they were among the other guests who stood on the wide stone steps, exchanging pleasantries before continuing on up into the well-lit hall.

Through the wide windows Aimée caught sight of lace-capped matrons already seated sedately in their dark bombazines, as they fanned themselves and talked of the only subject on everyone's lips at the moment, Secession and the threat of confrontation with those 'damned Yankees' in the North. Within half an hour every chair in the massive drawing-room was occupied and an excited buzz of conversation filled the air while the assembled company awaited the first act of the evening—a group of girl singers from Savannah.

Aimée could just make out the back of the titian head of Becky, sitting next to the buxom figure of her mother,

Martha Madison, in the front row. The glimpse of a friend brought a comforting glow as she sat up in her chair, her hands neatly folded in her lap, waiting for the events of the evening to begin.

A hush descended as Martha Madison stood up on the small wooden podium, and lifting her lace-mittened hands, confronted the assembled guests. 'Ladies and gentlemen—good friends and neighbours all—it gives me the greatest pleasure to welcome you here to Magnolia Mount this evening. Ah know Ah can promise y'all a most enjoyable experience. May Ah crave silence now for four very pretty young ladies—the Savannah Soubrettes!'

All eyes turned towards the wide open doors to the left of the company, as Martha Madison descended the steps to take her seat again next to her husband and family. A ripple of applause began at the sound of approaching footsteps, and Aimée's eyes swivelled to the left along with the others. Her mouth broke into a smile of welcome for the expected young ladies from Savannah, only to drop open in astonishment. Between the wide doorposts stood the resplendent figure of Daniel O'Conell Redmayne, a broad smile etched across his handsome bronzed features.

As the waiting audience watched, his brilliant blue gaze fell on Aimée, and with a gesture much too expansive to be deemed proper, he swept her the most wonderful bow she had ever seen.

'Miss Fitzwilliam—how lovely to see you!' he drawled in his deep voice, while all eyes turned in unison to stare at the object of his homage.

'How lovely to see you, Mr Redmayne!' she replied with a barely suppressed smile. Her eyes locked with his, and held for just long enough to be regarded as quite shocking.

CHAPTER FIVE

'HARLOT!' THE WORD was shot across the elegant drawing-room, and Chas MacDonald's mouth twisted contemptuously.

The object of his wrath shrank visibly and steeled herself in preparation for what was to come. He had not uttered a single word to her throughout the remainder of the entire evening at the Madisons'. Even in the carriage home he had sat, clench-jawed, staring out into the dark velvet night, during the journey back to Four Winds.

'Not in front of the servants' was not usually a rule meticulously obeyed by the tall fair-haired Georgian, but tonight he had waited until the heavy door of the drawing-room had been well and truly closed before venting his ire on the pale-faced young woman before him. 'Landsakes, Aimée, are you plumb stupid—or just plain wicked? How many times do I have to tell you to keep away from that no-good Redmayne? Consorting with that varmint is akin to washing in pitch. You're defiled, madam—defiled! And, what is worse, you've made a jackass out of me!'

His right fist smashed into the palm of his left hand as he turned to glare at her, impaling her with a stare that turned her blood to ice-water. 'I—I'm sorry—so sorry . . . I simply conversed most civilly with Mr Redmayne . . .'

'Simply conversed! Simply conversed!' he mimicked savagely. 'Made eyes at him for the whole darn' evening, that's what you did! And in front of the whole County, at that!'

No—he had it all wrong! Her lips opened to protest, but her mouth was dry, her throat constricted with nerves. She put out her hand in an attempt at mutual reassurance, but he slapped it away with such ferocity that she was sent staggering backwards.

'Don't play the innocent with me! Not tonight—not ever! You've disgraced me once again in front of my own friends and neighbours—my own kith and kin—madam. And I don't take kindly to that!'

Suddenly all the hypocrisy and deception became just too much. How dared he? How dared he, of all people, claim that *she* had disgraced *him*? Her fists clenched in the dainty lace mittens as she took a step back and fought to control her crazily beating heart. 'Don't talk to me about disgrace, Charles MacDonald! Don't you ever claim that I've disgraced you! Don't think I don't know your dirty little secret. Don't think I don't know what goes on under this very roof—in that very bed upstairs —behind your closed door!'

He sucked in his breath harshly as his pale brows furrowed. 'What d'ya mean by that, pray? Explain yourself, woman!' His voice was little above a hiss as he stared at her in a mixture of shock and mounting anger.

'You know very well what I mean! You're not a fool, Chas. But neither am I the silly innocent you would have me be. I've seen them, Chas! I've seen your little coffee-coloured bastards down in the slave quarters. Dear God, forgive me, for I know. I've seen them with my own eyes!'

'No!' The word was barked out as he swung on his heel and strode to the window, staring out at the star-spangled sky. His shoulders in the brown velvet frock-coat were tensed, his knuckles showing white through the skin, his hands gripping the back of a carved rose-wood chair.

'Yes! Yes!' She scarcely recognised her own voice screaming her insistence at him. 'It's Tizzy, isn't it, Chas? Admit it! You have the gall to call me a harlot —you, who would defile a slave under the same roof as your own bride-to-be! Admit it, if you have any honour left in you. Admit your sin before you presume to cast judgment on mine—if such it be!'

He was silent for a long time, his tall figure still turned from her in the frame of the window. She could feel a knot in the muscles of her stomach. Perhaps she had gone too far. Perhaps, like the hapless Fanny Kemble, she had committed the unpardonable sin in this so-called God-fearing land, where wives and sweethearts were to assume that the dozens of doe-eyed, mulatto children round them had simply dropped from heaven. Perhaps the truth was not always the best policy.

When finally he spoke, his voice was low, with a hard cutting edge that was meant to lacerate—and did. 'For far less than what you have just said, madam, I have had others horsewhipped. Ay—and worse!'

He swung round and began to walk towards her, his face deathly pale except for two bright spots of colour along the high cheekbones. His eyes burned with a glow so fierce that Aimée shrank immediately.

Hoop-skirted evening gowns, with their slight train at the back, were not designed for retreating, and her slipped feet tangled hopelessly in the apple-green flounces that skirted the floor behind. With a cry, she toppled back on to the polished floor and almost disappeared in the centre of the silken hooped cage.

He towered above her, glaring down with eyes the colour of polished steel. 'Get up, damn you!'

His right hand shot out and caught her wrist, pulling her roughly to her feet. The force of his fingers pressed the tiny jade inserts of her gold link bracelet into her skin, making her cry out in pain. Hot tears sprang to her eyes as they stared at one another across the few inches of space. 'Let . . . me . . . go!'

The words came out jerkily. It was more a command than a plea, but he chose to ignore it, his grip tightening on her wrist as he twisted it, forcing her to look at him. 'You know better than that, my dear! You know better than to issue orders to me . . . Very soon there will be a golden band on this lily-white hand—a band that will symbolise your promise to obey me for ever!'

Both pairs of eyes stared down at the pale fingers

protruding from the white lace mitten that covered her palm. Then slowly, very slowly, their gazes moved upwards to lock in silent combat.

'Go to bed, Aimée! Just get out of my sight, will you?'

The slam of the door resounded in her head as she stood quite still in the middle of the room, her face buried in her hands. A tiny drop of blood oozed from the inside of her wrist, cut by the jade, and trickled down to stain her mitten. She could hear his feet, in the shiny buckled shoes, storming through the hall and on out of the front door. Stifling the tears that relentlessly flooded her vision, she gathered up her skirts and ran to the window. His tall figure, like a ghost in the pale yellow glow of the lamplight, descended the steps at the front of the house and strode angrily down the drive in the direction of the slave quarters. Aimée stared out until her eyes glazed into a sightless blur. He was going to her—to Tizzy. The knowledge brought a sick feeling to the pit of her stomach.

But even more dreadful than the humiliation that was being perpetrated on her was the fact—the awful fact —that this situation was liable to continue as long as she lived under the MacDonald roof. She was trapped here at Four Winds. She knew it, and Chas knew it. And there was not a single thing she could do about it.

Or was there? Her brow furrowed, and her fingers twisted nervously on the green velvet tails of the ribbon bow at her waist, as the bronzed, smiling features of Daniel Redmayne swam before her. 'Red!' The name came to her lips, and her pulse began to race. There was somewhere she could go . . . to Wildwood! She would throw herself on the mercy of that enigmatic Irishman who seemed to arouse such fury in the man she had promised to marry.

Her heart pounded as the thought crystallised in her mind. The very idea of spending one more hour in this house was intolerable. How could she possibly climb those stairs to her room knowing that her husband-to-be, the man to whom she had pledged her life, was with another woman—and a slave into the bargain? No, —she might have very little in this life that she could call her own—but she still had her pride.

Gathering up the green watered silk of her skirts, she hurried from the room and headed for the staircase, only to be met at the foot by Ebenezer. Something told her he had been there for a while, and could probably bear silent witness to every word that had passed between herself and his master a few minutes before.

'You want yo' maid, Miz Aimée? Ah git Tizzy?'

The name was painful to her ears as she stared at the old man, acutely aware of her tear-stained face. 'No thank you, Ebenezer. I have a feeling that Tizzy will be detained elsewhere. Please see that I'm not disturbed tonight, unless I specifically ring for assistance.'

Her slippered feet ran up the broad, curving stairs, and she was aware of the old man's watchful eyes on her as she disappeared along the top landing. How much did he know of what was going on? How much did any of them know? Probably more than she did herself, she thought bleakly, as she threw open the door to her room and slumped on to the chair by the fireplace.

There was no question of packing a valise. She would have to arrange for that to be done tomorrow—or the day after—once the heat had gone out of the situation and Chas had accepted the fact that she had left him. He need not know where she had gone. No one need know. She would simply take the basic necessities, just enough to fit into a saddlebag, and borrow one of the horses from the stable. If she followed that forest track, she would soon be on Redmayne land. She had already discovered that to her cost on her earlier encounter with the master of Wildwood!

Resolute in her determination to leave, she got up and opened the top drawer of the bow-fronted tulipwood chest that contained her most personal possessions. One by one the essentials for her flight were extracted: a bar of her favourite gardenia-scented French soap that she had brought specially from England, a clean face flannel, the round cherub-decorated tin box that contained the rice powder so essential for disguising a flushed complexion on special evenings, the black net reticule containing her most precious pieces of jewellery.

She paused, frowning, then opened the small bag and extracted several items. The gems flashed defiantly at her in the yellow glow of the lamp as she laid them on top of the chest. Every single one was a present from him—Charles Stuart MacDonald—the man she was to have married. The pearl-studded black velvet choker, the silver filigree rose with the emerald-encrusted leaves, the garnet and opal bracelet he had produced on the occasion of their first meal together. And, of course, the one she was wearing. She glanced down at the jade and gold links encircling her wrist. A small scar of dried blood had formed where the gem had cut into the flesh, and a bitter smile contorted her delicate features as she opened the catch and laid it with the others. Let him give them to her—to that haughty negress. She would owe him nothing—not ever again!

Within five minutes she had gathered together all she regarded as essential and had wrapped the small bundle tightly in a paisley shawl. This she inserted into the specially-made inside pocket of the black woolcloth cloak she had worn for her journey across the Atlantic. As she fastened it round her slim shoulders, a flush of gooseflesh stippled her skin. 'Please don't let him see me,' she prayed aloud, bending to extinguish the lamp. 'Please don't let me be caught.' For Chas to discover her intentions before she got to the sanctuary of Redmayne land would surely be a disaster.

She calculated that it would take about half an hour, at a steady canter, to reach the outskirts of Wildwood. In fact it took almost double that time, for although there was a bright moon, its light failed to penetrate the tall pines that edged the twisting path between the two estates. Twice she lost her way completely and had to backtrack for at least a mile to find the right road again. The sounds of the nightbirds filled her ears, and in the distance a coyote—or some such animal—howled into the sky, making her flesh creep and her fingers tighten their grip on the reins.

In London, she had always thought of trees as tall, silent sentinels one encountered in parks, but here in the depths of the forest they were living, breathing creatures whispering at her through the darkness, reaching out to tangle their long sinewy fingers in her hair and brushing against the soft cloth of her cloak as she urged her horse on into the night. Just when she felt she would never get out of the dark, whispering prison alive, the trees suddenly parted. She pulled up on the leather reins, calling to the mare to halt.

The Wildwood mansion soared out of the darkness straight ahead, huge and imposing, and if the back view was to be trusted, even grander than that of the Mac-Donalds. The path led round the side of the house, past the stables and various outbuildings. A few lanterns at infrequent intervals added their ghostly glow to the scene, but there was no sign of human life. Then a dog barked—and another, until the whole night was alive with the baying of a hundred hounds—or so it seemed, as she bit her lip and coaxed her mount forward along the dusty road.

The house looked even bigger from the front, and she dismounted by the main steps and tethered the animal to the ornamental balustrade to the left of one of the six stone pillars that supported the upper balconies. It was three storeys high, with verandas that ran the full length of all three floors, each one bordered by carved balustrades, the details of which it was impossible to make out in the dim light. The whole place appeared to be in darkness, apart from one solitary light burning in the room directly above the front door. Tentatively she climbed the front steps, her hand gripping the wrought-iron rail as though her very life depended on it. Her eyes were fixed directly ahead on the huge white-painted door, while her mind conjured visions of what might lie behind it.

It took her precisely five minutes to find out. After several hard, long tugs on the bronze knob of the bell, the door was finally thrown open by none other than Daniel Redmáyne himself.

'Well, I'll be . . .!' The genuine astonishment in his voice and face remained, and he took a step back and stared at the now shivering figure. 'What in heaven's name brings you out here at this time of night?'

He was dressed in what appeared to be dark blue silk pyjamas beneath a quilted burgundy smoking jacket, and his hair was slightly dishevelled, as if her presistent ringing of the bell had got him out of bed.

His obvious surprise and the momentary furrowing of his brow disconcerted her. She had somehow imagined a delighted smile of welcome. 'I—I am sorry to disturb you . . . There was nowhere else—nowhere I could go. I—I won't put you to any trouble . . .' Her voice had a strange, high-pitched quality that sounded foreign to her ears as she looked at him imploringly. Suddenly the whole idea of running away to spite Chas seemed ridiculously childish, and almost impossible to explain without going into the awful details that she could never disclose to another human soul. It was almost impossible to keep her teeth from chattering, despite the heat of the night.

He shook his head, then ran a hand through the tangle of curly dark hair over his brow. 'Well, I can't say as I understand what's going on, but it sure ain't doing any good you staying out here on the front porch.' Stepping back to allow her to enter, he picked up the lamp he had placed on a small table inside the door. 'Mrs O'Mara's gone to bed, but I'm sure I can rustle something up in the way of refreshment. You look like you could sure do with something a little stronger than coffee right now!'

She smiled wanly and followed him into the hall and through the echoing gloom towards a small, cosily furnished room at the back of the house. 'It's my den,' he said with a faintly roguish smile. 'I don't usually have lady visitors in here, but I'll make an exception with you.'

'Come into my parlour, said the spider to the fly?'

'If you like!' He laughed softly—a musical chuckle that resonated from deep down in the broad chest. 'I will own up to feeling distinctly predatory where you are concerned, Miss Aimée Fitzwilliam . . . But then I guess you already know that?'

She glanced down at the floor in confusion. 'I have no gift of second sight, sir, or ability to see into the minds of others—particularly of gentlemen such as yourself!'

He paused, his hand on the door knob. 'Now there is a mightily loaded description, if you like . . . A gentleman such as myself. And, pray, what type may that be?'

She backed off, slightly nonplussed by the question. Even in the soft glow of the lamplight his eyes had a twinkle that spoke volumes, but she was determined not to be intimidated. 'It would appear you have quite a reputation in this County, sir . . . Not least among the ladies!'

'Then can I assume you have come here tonight expecting me to live up to it?'

Despite her resolve to remain composed, the colour flared in her cheeks. Her body stiffened as she fixed him with a cold, hard stare. 'I have come here tonight to the home of a gentleman, a proper Southern gentleman, and I expect nothing more and nothing less from you, sir, than the behaviour of such a person!'

His left eyebrow lifted quizzically, and the lazy grin that quirked the well-drawn lips totally negated her attempt to lift the conversation on to a level of greater propriety. 'I would have thought that your beloved intended, the gentlemanly Charlie-boy, would have put you right on that account before now, my dear. Ol' Daniel Redmayne never has—and never will be— granted the status of "a real Southern gentleman", as you term it, in these here parts . . . And, to tell the honest truth, I don't give a damn. They're a bunch of darned hypocrites, the lot of 'em!'

He fixed her with an even broader smile before throwing open the door to the study and executing a perfect bow as he gestured for her to enter. 'Beggin' your pardon for referring to your fiancé in such a way, but there ain't no more fitting word I can think of at present —not that would be appropriate for your delicate ears, that is!' He went over and lit an ornamental brass lamp that hung in the centre of the room, then set the lamp he was carrying down on the writing-desk. 'But we'll not spoil the evening by polluting it with any more talk of ol' Chas. You must be exhausted by that ride, and I'd be neglecting my duty if I didn't do something to put that to rights. What'll it be—coffee and a piece of pie, or something a mite stronger?'

Aimée gave an embarrassed attempt at a smile. 'I think, under the circumstances, something a little stronger wouldn't go amiss.'

He beamed, and gestured to her to take a seat on an overstuffed sofa, turning to a silver tray on a small table beside him. 'Cognac suit you?'

'Lovely—thank you.' She undid the braid loop at the neck of her cloak and slipped it from her shoulders, laying it neatly over the back of the sofa, before sitting down. Her eyes darted around the room as he poured from a decanter into two balloon-shaped goblets, and handed her one. Just being in here alone with him, in what was most obviously his own special room, brought a nervous tingle to her skin. The whole place reeked with aspects of his character that she could only have guessed at before. Beautiful oil paintings of ships in full sail hung on the walls, and exquisite examples of similar craft in bottles were arrayed along the marble top of the fireplace. In a tall, polished pine bookcase on the far wall stood rows of matching leather-bound volumes, with more books, obviously well thumbed, stacked on every available surface. The inscrutable master of Wildwood was obviously an avid reader . . . Yes, despite his declarations to the contrary, Mr Daniel Redmayne had all the material attributes of a gentleman of the very best breeding.

The pungent smell of tobacco still hung in the air, indicating that he had spent the evening here, with one of the many pipes from the rack on the wall by the fire as his companion. She must have disturbed him just after he had retired for the night.

While her eyes roamed round the room, fascinated by the sheer maleness of it, he remained standing, his right elbow leaning on the marble mantelshelf as he regarded her thoughtfully, a faint smile playing around the corners of his lips. 'Here's to your first visit to Wildwood, Miss Fitzwilliam. And, whatever the reason for it, let us pray to God it will not be your last!' He raised his glass in salute, before taking his first sip.

Silently she raised her own in return and took a gulp of the cognac. It left a burning trail down her throat, but brought a warm glow, and she took another mouthful almost immediately—to her consternation almost emptying the glass.

'That's what I like to see!' Daniel Redmayne's eyes gleamed as he picked up the bottle and leaned over to refill her glass. 'Now just what makes a little lady like you feel the need for a drop of the hard stuff?'

There was that twinkle in his eyes that was still all too easily discernible, even in the dim shadows of the lamplight, but she blushed nevertheless. 'There's no point in lying to you, Mr Redmayne,' she said softly. 'I've left Chas.'

A low whistle escaped his lips, and his blue eyes narrowed as he took another swig of the cognac. 'And?'

'And I've come to you.'

'Mother of God, girl, have you gone mad?'

His exclamation made her catch her breath sharply and sit up straight on the sofa. 'No, sir, I assure you, I'm not mad—but I must have been ever to have left London and come here to this awful place!'

There was the suggestion of a sob in her voice that caused his dark brows to furrow as he finished his drink and placed the empty glass on the mantelpiece. 'What's happened, Aimée?' he said wearily, as though her admission had come as no real surprise to him. 'You'd better tell me.'

'No, I can't. It's personal—very personal.' How could she tell him? How could she tell anyone what she had witnessed this very afternoon?

'It wouldn't have anything to do with children, would it? Or should I say "piccaninnies"?'

She stared at him. Even he knew! Dear God, everyone must know! She nodded miserably, unable to bring herself to speak.

'Whose did you see?'

'What—Whatever do you mean?'

'Charlie-boy's offspring—were they Leila's or Tizzy's?'

That now familiar sick feeling welled again in her stomach. 'I—I don't understand . . .'

'Oh, Aimée, Aimée . . . Do I have to spell it out? Whose little MacDonald bastards did you come across—Leila's or Tizzy's?'

When there was no response from the stunned young woman on the sofa, he sighed deeply and reached into the pocket of his jacket for his favourite pipe. 'I reckon they were probably Tizzy's,' he said, lighting a spill from the nearest lamp and puffing the coarsely-shred tobacco into life. 'If I remember rightly, Leila's been out of favour since she jumped the broomstick with that big buck from the Madison place some years back. Real sore ol' Charlie-boy was about that, and no mistake! Never asked his permission, it seems. If she wasn't already the mother of two MacDonald piccaninnies, she would have been flogged to within an inch of her life for that piece of disobedience. As it was, I believe her lord and master —ol' Charlie—got old man Madison to sell the buck up-state, then he got himself a new lady-love to teach his two-timing little slave gal a lesson she'd never forget!'

Aimée felt the blood drain from her face as she stared at the man before her. For one wild moment she hoped he might be jesting with her, but his face had never been more serious. She shook her head once, then again, and again, as if the action of denial could somehow negate the truth of what she had just heard. 'How—How do I know you're speaking the truth?' she whispered hoarsely, for want of something better to say.

'You don't.' He stuck the meerschaum in the corner of his mouth and puffed quietly for a few seconds. 'But I'll tell you this, Aimée Fitzwilliam. I have no reason to lie to you. To Charles MacDonald, yes. I'd lie through my teeth to that double-dealin' varmint, but to you, no —never. You're different from the others—the feather-brained little dolly-moppets he's taken a fancy to in the past. You've got a brain in that pretty head of yours. I sensed that the first time we met.'

Her mouth fell open. 'Why, Mr Redmayne, you're making fun of me! The first time we met, if I remember rightly, I appeared to throw myself at your feet—or at least your horse's! In fact, it would seem I've made something of a habit of that . . .'

A slow smile spread across the bronzed features of his face. 'You've not heard me complaining.'

'I expect you're quite used to that type of thing—from what I've heard. You're quite the Casanova with the young ladies around Craven County, I believe!'

'You'll have to enquire as to my right to that title from the young ladies in question—and I dare say few would disagree with you!' His eyes glinted wickedly in the lamplight as he added, 'Unless the object of your exercise in coming here tonight is to find out for yourself!'

'Why, you . . .!' She jumped up from the sofa, her hand shooting out in the direction of his cheek, but he was too quick for her, grabbing her wrist and almost swinging her off her feet, as his eyes blazed down into hers.

'Don't try it, Miss Fitzwilliam. Don't ever try it! No man has ever tried that with me and remained standing afterwards—and if I won't take it from a fella, then I certainly ain't gonna take it from a little bitty gal like you! Now sit down there and behave yourself, and tell me what this is all about before my patience runs out and I send you back to where you come from!'

He all but threw her back on to the plump cushions of the sofa, irritation etched across his tanned features. With an impatient gesture, he tapped the meerschaum bowl of the pipe into the fireplace, then turned to fix her with an admonishing glare of the startlingly blue eyes.

Embarrassment stung her cheeks as she perched once more on the edge of the sofa, dropping her eyes to her hands clasped in her lap, suddenly very aware of the bulge of her possessions inside her cloak. 'You—You'll not send me away, please, Red? Say I can stay here at Wildwood—at least for the time being?'

He was silent for a long time, the furrow on his high forehead growing deeper as he gazed down at her. 'You put me in one helluva position, honey child.'

'Why, Red, why?' She was using his Christian name again, and it sounded right on her tongue, as her eyes pleaded with his. 'I wouldn't be any trouble, truly I wouldn't. And it wouldn't be for long—just time enough to make proper plans for the future.'

He sighed deeply as he shook his head. 'I don't doubt that for a second—not for a single second. But life's not quite as simple as that, my dear Aimée. There is such a thing as honour—your honour. You could never return to Four Winds, having spent the night here under my roof.'

'You don't want me to stay . . . Is that it? You want me to go? You would send me back to that man, rather than give me shelter?' She had not bargained for this and leapt from the sofa, her fingers clutching the sleeve of his jacket.

'No, Aimée, I never said that. I most certainly never said that . . .' His voice was husky as he set his pipe down in a glass ashtray on the mantelpiece and gazed down at her.

His face swam before her, and she gave a small gasp as his hands reached out to cup her pale cheeks. Two large tears hovered for a moment on her lower lashes, than trickled slowly towards her mouth. He gently wiped them away, his fingers lingering on her trembling lips.

The nearness of him was almost overwhelming. There was a dark, brooding power about him that she had never sensed in Chas. It seemed to envelop her—to engulf her in a potent aura that vibrated with both danger and security. He was sending her away, but every breath in her body would beg him to allow her to stay.

'So soft . . . So very soft . . .' His fingers continued to caress the tender flesh of her lips, and she felt him move perceptibly closer.

Her senses were filled with the smell, touch and taste of him, and a strange ache welled within her that she had never experienced before—not with Chas, not with anybody. 'Please don't send me away, Red, not to-night . . .' As her hands moved up over the smooth satin of his lapels and she whispered the words into the silent room, she knew she was not pleading to stay in order to avoid returning to Charles MacDonald. She was begging to be allowed to stay with Daniel Redmayne. It was something she had asked of no other man.

But even as she spoke the words, the expression in his eyes was subtly changing. 'You don't know what you're saying, honey. If I let you stay here, you could never hold your head up in Southern society again.' His words poured over her like a sudden shower of cold water as he released her hold on his lapels.

'But what if I don't want to? What if I said I'd rather do anything than go back to him—to Four Winds?'

'Anything, Aimée? You'd do . . . anything?' His eyes burned into hers. There was no mistaking the implication of his query.

Her mind whirled. She had never thought this thing through properly; she always had leapt before she looked, even as a child. But what was the alternative —to go back to Chas? She couldn't bear that. . . . 'I—I don't want to go back. I'm sure of that. If I choose to stay with you and not him, that's my business, isn't it? I thought about my choice before I left tonight. I made it, and I chose you.' The words poured out of her, and she was lying. Her emotions had, as usual, ruled her head, and very little thought had been involved, but he must not know that.

'What do you mean—you chose me?' he declared in exasperation. 'Mother of God, can't you see? You can't stay here, Aimée. It—It's just not possible!'

'Not possible? Why not?' Her voice was almost childlike in its petulance, and she searched his eyes in the lamplight. What was he telling her?

He reached out his hand and touched her cheek, saying quietly, 'Aimée, my dear innocent little English girl, for you to stay under my roof . . . Well, it would be possible only as my wife, and no matter how desirable I may or may not find you, I can never marry you. I can never marry anyone—not now, perhaps not ever. I'd make the world's worst husband—I can promise you that! The world's worst.'

She stared at him in confusion. 'I—I never mentioned marriage! I only said I couldn't go back there . . . I can't marry him.' Why was he making it so difficult for her?

Scepticism filled his eyes, for he clearly did not believe her. He continued softly, 'I don't doubt I could make you happy for a night, but a night is not a lifetime, my dear. A lifetime is for ever. And I am not ready to promise you—to promise anyone—for ever. For ever is a long time, Aimée. For ever is a very long time . . .'

She shook her head, her long hair tumbling wildly round her bare shoulders. He didn't understand. She was not asking for a lifetime, but only for a little while —enough to get things sorted out in her mind. She must make him understand—and, besides, what was so appalling about the idea of marrying her? Was it really so horrendous? As the thought took shape, she found herself begin to bristle in indignation that he should have considered the idea, then dismissed it so summarily. 'I would not really be a bad catch—even for such as you!'

she protested. 'Certainly plenty of others, long before Chas MacDonald, have thought so!'

He shook his head slowly, as though despairing of ever making her comprehend, but when he finally spoke, his thoughts were elsewhere. They had flown back over the years to a Georgia she did not know—and could never imagine even in her wildest dreams. 'My father worked long and hard for all this, Aimée— burying a wife and three children in the process. He came from Ireland, a land riddled with famine and unimaginable poverty, to America, a land of plenty and unimaginable riches—for those willing to work. And he worked. My God, how he worked! Blood, sweat and tears were shed to make this place what it is now. It's still not finished. But I am the only one left to complete the task—and, by God, I shall do it! And when it is complete—and only then—shall I consider taking a wife. It would not be fair on any woman otherwise . . . And, apart from that, there's a war coming. I can smell it in the air. Secession from the North is not only on everyone's lips—it's in every Southern heart. It'll be upon us by Christmas, whether we wish it or not.' He turned to face her, a look of infinite weariness on his face. 'This is no time to think of marriage, if that's what's on your mind, or even of just moving in with me, my dear. I'd be making you a bride only to make you a widow by the time it's over. Maybe the likes of Chas don't mind the idea of that, but it's not for me.'

'Don't say those things! Nothing is going to happen to you . . . Nothing!' Why was he talking of war and death now—telling these things to frighten her? She crossed the floor to take his arm, her nails digging into the smooth skin that stretched across the taut muscles beneath his jacket. Her cheek was against the soft mat of hair on his chest as she whispered savagely, 'I won't go, Red. I won't!' She could feel him tense, and sensing that she was beginning to break down the barrier he was so resolutely building between them, her eyes found his. 'Do you really want me to go, Red? Really want to throw me out into the night?' Her lips parted as her hand moved slowly up across his chest to rest intimately on the back of his neck, her fingers teasing the fringe of dark curls beneath his collar.

His kiss was as sudden as it was brutal, leaving her gasping for breath, and his hands gripped her shoulders. The latent power she could sense in every muscle sent a surge of panic mixed with exhilaration through her. 'Is this what you really want, Aimée?' His lips moved hungrily down the slim curve of her throat, his fingers slipping the lace-trimmed edge of her gown from the pale skin of her shoulder. His fingers found the soft swell of her breast beneath the tightly-laced basque, and his lips moved ever downward, raining kisses on the warm flesh.

'Please . . .' She gasped the word. 'Please wait . . .' It was the reaction she had wantonly provoked, but panic was rising within her. She was losing control of the situation, and that had never been part of her plan.

He took no heed, but slipped the other side of her bodice from her shoulder, and his lips moved further down across the swelling cleavage as his body welded itself to hers. His fingers were working feverishly at the lacing at the back of her bodice, and his breathing became more obvious, almost keeping time with the erratic beating of her own heart.

Finally, summoning all her strength, she pushed against him and succeeded in putting a small space between her body and his. A flush of perspiration had broken out on her skin, causing her face to glow in the lamplight, and cried out, 'No, Red, please, not yet . . . Not like this. No gentleman would force himself upon a lady against her will!'

His arms gripped hers, prising her body away as he glared into her upturned face. 'That, my dear Aimée, as I told you before, I have never claimed to be!' He gave a bitter laugh. 'In fact, there's hardly a soul in the whole of this doggone County would credit a Redmayne with that title! No, my dear, I may be many things, but I ain't no gentleman! And coming here like this, if I may say so, makes you no lady!'

She could feel herself shaking in his grasp as she fought to control her breathing. 'That, sir, is a despicable thing to say! I—I came here tonight to seek your help—not to have to fight off your unwanted embraces!'

'Unwanted, Aimée? Unwanted?' His laugh rang out in the silence of the room, the mockery in the blue eyes all too plain to see. 'I think not! You came here tonight, whether you're aware of it or not, to use your undoubted attractions to charm yourself into my home, if not into my life. But, luckily for you, I am not so stupid as to allow it. It is tempting, yes, more tempting than I can say . . . But it would be wrong. Wrong for me—and, more important, it would be wrong for you.'

His eyes remained locked into hers until she was forced to lower her gaze with a defeated sigh. Never could she get the better of this proud, enigmatic man. 'Then tell me what to do, Red. Please tell me? I have nothing . . . no one else . . .'

'But you do. You have the man you're still betrothed to. Don't throw that, and all it means, away for the likes of me, my dear, I'm just not worth it. Oh, sure, I know I'm worth a dozen of him. But not in this here County, honey. Here the MacDonald name has a certain "cachet" about it that no other name can ever have —not in our lifetime, anyway. Go right ahead and marry ol' Charlie-boy, Aimée. You'll be the envy of every gal in Craven County if you do!'

Her fingers loosed their grip and her arms fell to her side as she stared at him, wild-eyed. 'You're telling me to go back—to marry that—that rat?'

He gave a deep sigh, and his voice sounded as though he were trying to explain something to a recalcitrant child. 'Honey, I'm telling you to go back to Four Winds and become its mistress. You'll be far better off doing that than staying here any longer, as mine!'

Slowly she backed away from him, a look of loathing contorting the delicate features of her face. 'No, I can't do that. I won't do that! You say you're not ready to take a wife, but I never asked you to marry me. And anyway, even if I did, you can't make the estate the excuse. Wildwood doesn't demand your attention half as much as it demanded that of your father, and he married your mother, didn't he? That didn't stop him!'

'My father paid dearly for asking of his wife more than she could give!' His voice dropped to little above a whisper as he turned to a large oil-painting above the mantelpiece.

Aimée's eyes turned to follow his, resting upon the shadowy picture of a young woman in an off-the-shoulder ballgown. It was too dark to make out her features, but there was something about the proud tilt to her head that spoke instantly of the man standing before her.

'She was a French Creole from New Orleans,' he said softly. 'Marie-Claire de Maupassant. The whole of Louisiana society was scandalised when she ran off with my father. No one could credit how the beautiful, talented daughter of one of the town's richest bankers could fall in love with a penniless Irishman. But she did—and paid dearly for it. Carving a living out of these virgin red hills took its toll on her first three children, who never survived their first few years, then finally it killed her, just before my fifth birthday. She was only twenty-eight. Pa never got over it.'

And neither had he. Aimée could see that very clearly. 'Times have changed, Red,' she said quietly. 'Any woman would be honoured to live in such a place as this is now.'

His eyes moved from the picture to look at her. 'Not any woman, Aimée. You remind me too much of her . . . Beautiful, talented, headstrong . . . Born and raised in a fine city. But totally unused to the type of life we live here. It wasn't just the physical discomforts that killed my mother. I'm not really talking about that—it was the mental anguish of leaving a way of life, and people and places she once held so dear, that was as decisive in her early death as any other reason. I can sense the same unease in you.'

She started to shake her head, but he cut in quickly. 'No, don't deny it, Aimée. Don't deny what you probably don't even realise yourself. I look at you, and I see the Marie-Claire de Maupassant of a generation ago. I cannot—I will not—repeat the tragedy of my father!'

There was something about the finality in his voice that brought a chill to her heart. 'You've thought about this before, haven't you, Red?' she said softly. 'You haven't just made up your mind about this tonight.'

He walked towards her, and even in the semi-darkness, she could make out the burning glow in the deep blue eyes. His hand came up, behind the thick fall of blue-black hair, to rest on the nape of her neck, before drawing her to him. His lips were only inches from hers, his breath warm on her face, as he bent towards her.

'You're right, Aimée, so very right. I have been thinking about almost nothing else since the first moment I set eyes on you. You got under my skin, darn you, in that first instant, and you have remained there ever since.' He gave a wry laugh as he shook his head. 'But we must never confuse physical longing with love, Aimée: the two are very different. To confuse the two is to throw caution to the wind and do things, especially at night, on impulse, that you may regret later in the cold light of day. To love and to be wise are two different things, my dear. I remember reading somewhere, in one of my mother's French books: "At eighteen, we learn to adore a woman in a moment; at twenty, we love her; we yearn for her at thirty; but at forty we consider whether she is worth the trouble!" Perhaps this applies to me . . .'

'Can you not tell by my name that I also am no stranger to the French outlook? I can only presume you are now nearer the last of those four ages, and have come to the conclusion that I am not worth the trouble!' She could feel the suffocation of tears in her throat as she threw the words at him. Drat the man—he was actually grinning at her! Her hand shot out to slap the mocking smile from his face. 'How dare you make fun of me!'

He caught her wrist just before she made contact with his cheek, but the infuriating smile remained. 'I told you before, never—never try that with me! You may look even more beautiful when you're aroused, but I don't take kindly to physical assault from any man, let alone a little woman like you!'

He let her hand drop and made for the study door. 'I guess I've said too much already tonight—much too much.'

She watched in silence, too choked by conflicting emotions to utter a word as he opened it, then stood aside waiting for her to walk through. 'I'll arrange for my carriage to take you back to Four Winds,' he said quietly.

'Please don't bother! I would rather make my own way. There is nothing I shall ask of you, Daniel Redmayne, ever again! Now just leave me . . . Leave me, please.'

She turned her back and repeated the words, this time in a much louder voice, then after a few seconds the door closed with a soft click. He had gone. Out of the room—out of her life.

A tremor ran through her and she sank to the floor in front of the fireplace, feeling nothing but a deep emptiness. She should never have come here. She should never have exposed herself to what had taken place in this house tonight. If he had to send her away—to humiliate her like this—did he have to say all those other things? Did he have to torture her? And to send her back to Four Winds—to Chas! She shivered even more violently at the thought. But what choice had she?

CHAPTER SIX

FOR TEN MINUTES she sat there, biting back the tears of anger and frustration that welled in her throat. Why could he not be like other men? It was not as though she had made a habit of throwing herself on the mercy of virtual strangers. She had sensed in him a kindred spirit, someone as much out of tune with the cant and hypocrisy she had encountered in this society as she was. She knew he was attracted to her—he had made that very obvious from the look in those dark blue eyes from the very moment they had first met. But was all that implicit flirting merely a way of annoying the man he loathed more than any other—Chas, her future husband? She sighed deeply. It seemed very much like it. Perhaps that was part of the truth he had told her, about not wanting to repeat the mistakes of the past, comparing her with his mother and telling how this land had broken her . . . But she was not Marie-Claire de Maupassant—she was Aimée Fitzwilliam, and made of much sterner stuff. No, she would teach Daniel Redmayne she was no sheltered little Creole beauty but a red-blooded English woman with, in her veins, the blood both of kings and of revolutionary France. With such a combination, how could she fail?

The earlier anger and humiliation gave way to a feeling of pride and determination as she got up and straightened her clothes. She seemed to have been emotionally assaulted from all sides since arriving in Georgia, but they would not get the better of her—none of them—and that included the master of Wildwood as much as Chas MacDonald himself!

She expected to have to feel her way out of the darkened house, but to her amazement when she emerged from his study, the lamps in the entrance hall had all been lit. Her eyes darted nervously about her as she walked across the marble-tiled floor. Unlike Four Winds, there were very few portraits on the walls, but the furniture was exquisite—the finest Louis Quinze —and, from what she could tell, it was genuine, no doubt chosen by the beautiful Marie-Claire before her untimely death. But there was no time to admire the furnishings; all she wanted to do was to get out of this place, and away from Daniel Redmayne, as quickly as possible.

Her mare was still standing at the foot of the steps, but next to it stood a shiny black carriage complete with two high-tailed greys and a tired-looking black-faced coach-man. He jumped down from the carriage as she approached, but she shook her head determinedly.

'No, thank you. The carriage won't be required. I'm afraid your master has misinformed you. I'll be riding my own horse home tonight.'

'Oh no, miz! Them woods be too dark fo' lady like the missus!'

The horror in the old man's creased face was evident, but she would not be put off. 'Fiddlesticks! I'll be perfectly safe. Tell Mr Redmayne I've made my own way, won't you? I would like him to know I accepted no favours before taking my leave!'

The coachman scratched his grizzled beard, then nodded uncertainly. 'If yo' say so, miz. Ah'll tell massa.'

Aimée threw him a small but triumphant smile, and unhitching her mare, clambered up into the saddle. It would take her the best part of an hour to get back to Four Winds, and the thought of the return journey through the forest appalled her—but anything—yes, even that—was better than staying here for one minute more!

The following hour proved to be every bit as nerve-racking as she had anticipated, although this time she succeeded in keeping to the right track. Her only real moment of panic was when a wildcat scampered out of the undergrowth and made the horse shy, sending her sliding from the saddle to the hard-baked earth. Luckily she managed to keep hold of the reins, and after a few seconds spent in pacifying the startled mare, she remounted without too much difficulty. Her daily rides in Rotten Row while she was waiting for her passage on the boat had stood her in good stead, although a silk-skirted evening gown was not the ideal riding-habit!

When, eventually, the trees began to thin and the Four Winds mansion appeared like a spectre out of the swirling mist that had crept up from the river in the few hours since she had left, she felt a shiver of gooseflesh creep over her skin.

The slave quarters were just behind the trees—the rows of wooden huts as silent as the grave: the overseers saw to that. It meant a certain beating for any slave found outside his own cabin after sundown. That was just one of the little facts of life she had discovered since her arrival, and she could still recall the horror with which she received the information. How naïve they must all have found her! The memory of her first and only visit to that awful place made her shudder once more. Would she always feel like this? Would she ever come to terms with what she had learned in her short time in this very foreign place?

Her legs were shaking beneath her flounced skirts as she slid from the sweating animal's back and handed the reins over to one of the stableboys, who had stumbled from his straw bed by the door of the tack-room at the sound of the approaching hooves. The child's dark eyes stared at her, the whites glowing in the darkness as he pondered the dishevelled sight of his new mistress.

The colour rose in her cheeks. No doubt this would be all over the slave quarters by morning! But, thank God, no one had any way of knowing where she had been. She deliberately avoided going in through the kitchens at the back; that would be simply asking for trouble. It was almost impossible to retain some privacy in a house full of servants—and slaves, at that—but she was slowly learning to live with it. As her slight figure slipped round the side of the great house, she glanced up, drawn by the faint yellow glow of the lamplight in the tall wide windows that straddled the side and front of the building. Chas's room—he was still awake!

Her heart pounded in her breast as she crept silently up the front steps and pushed open the door. If she was very quiet, and Lady Luck was on her side, she would not disturb any of the house servants. The hall was dark, except for one solitary moonbeam that stretched its ghostly finger through one of the tall windows, alighting on the longface clock at the foot of the staircase. It was well after midnight.

Please don't let anyone see me, please! she prayed silently, as her slippered feet climbed the curving stairs. Even the rustling of the watered silk of her skirts seemed to be terrifyingly loud. She was aware of holding her breath, as though the very act of breathing might awaken the sleeping household, as she crept along the polished floorboards of the upstairs landing. Then, suddenly, the cathedral-like silence was broken by a high-pitched giggle. A woman's giggle. She stood stock still, her hand clasped to her thumping heart. The sound had come from Chas's room.

'Please, no, not again . . . Not tonight, of all nights!'

Throwing caution to the winds, she slipped past her own door to stand breathless and nauseated outside his. So this was what she had come back to! She leaned back against the wall, her ears straining to catch every sound from within the room. The giggle sounded again—much louder this time, freezing her blood. She felt an almost uncontrollable impulse to throw open the door and confront them both, but, instead, she did something she had never done in her entire life. Kneeling down, she peered through the brass keyhole. The aperture was tiny, but big enough to reveal all that was required to confirm her worst fears.

Two bodies were writhing on the rumpled cotton sheet. Two bodies: one as pale and white as the bed-

linen itself, the other black as the night beyond the tall
windows. As black as Chas MacDonald's heart, his
bride-to-be thought bitterly as she rose unsteadily and
walked stony-faced back along the corridor to her room.

She had no right to feel self-righteous any more, she
knew that. She had ridden to Wildwood and all but
offered herself to Daniel Redmayne. But it was not
self-righteousness she was feeling, for, as her hand
found the doorknob to her own room, she realised with a
sinking heart that she felt absolutely nothing—nothing
at all—for Charles MacDonald, the man she was supposed to love and who was supposed to love her above
all others. The man she was to marry this very summer
was in bed with another woman—a slave—and she no
longer cared. The whole world had gone crazy—and she
along with it!

'This is the South, Aimée Fitzwilliam,' she told herself
bleakly, pulling off her mittens and throwing them on to
the waiting bed. 'So you'd better get used to it!'

Aimée moved sleepily on the damp sheet as the soft
splashing of water being tipped into the hip-bath at the
foot of the bed broke into her consciousness. It had been
a hot and humid night—what little was left of it by
the time she had finally slipped between the cotton
sheets—and now the maids were already preparing her
morning toilet.

With a long yawn she pulled herself up on the pillows,
blinking and rubbing her eyes against the bright rays of
the sun that streamed in. Pansy, the youngest maid, had
pulled back the floral drapes from the tall french windows of the balcony. The two white-turbaned figures
were going about their respective businesses in silence,
laying out the clean turkish towels and her special soap
and flannels for her to complete her ablutions before her
personal maid arrived to prepare fresh undergarments
and the appropriate morning dress for the hours ahead.
Her blood froze at the thought. If it was Tizzy who
appeared at her bedroom door with that supercilious,

all-knowing smirk, she didn't know how she would deal with it.

The two girls stood at the foot of the bed, one armed with the previous day's dirty linen, the other with the empty pails and pitcher, their dark eyes staring unblinkingly at the young woman in the frilly-bibbed cotton nightdress. Aimée's cheeks coloured. Why did they all seem to look at her like that—as if they knew things she did not? It unnerved her, but the secret was not to show it, and she must not let it upset her. She must retain her dignity and composure. Flicking her braid of dark hair over her shoulder, she nodded curtly. 'Thank you. That will be all.'

They turned and left the room immediately, and the door was barely shut behind them when she could have kicked herself for her lack of thought. She should have told them to send Sadie to help her to dress! She swung down from the bed with an annoyed grimace, and pulled the nightdress over her head, tossing it on to the camphorwood chest at precisely the moment that the door opened.

Tizzy stood in the open doorway, her face as proud and sphinx-like as ever. The two faced one another across the sunlit room as the dark eyes of the slave ran the length of her mistress's ivory-skinned body. Aimée's cheeks flamed scarlet. The woman had deliberately timed it to embarrass her like this! Tizzy was bent on humiliating her in as many ways as possible!

Maintaining as much dignity as she could muster under the circumstances, she made no attempt to cover herself, but walked sedately to the tub and immersed herself in the clean water.

'I'll have the blue forget-me-not sprigged muslin today, if you please!' Her voice was as cold and clipped as she could possibly make it, and she could not bring herself to use the maid's name, or even to look at her.

Tizzy walked to the wardrobe and removed the appropriate dress, shaking the creases out before hanging it in readiness on the outside of the rosewood door. Aimée tried to reconcile the tall cotton-clad figure with the writhing form she had witnessed in Chas's bed last night. The whole thing was a charade. Life in this sumptuous prison was nothing but a charade—and a mighty inglorious one, at that! But it was a charade that all Southern women had to learn to live with, and if she was intending to stay, she had better get used to the idea, no matter how much it appalled her. One thing was certain, though; she could not face Charles MacDonald over the breakfast-table. That would be asking the impossible of what little pride she had left.

'What time is your master eating this morning, girl?'

Tizzy turned. The deliberate use of the derogatory form of address did not go unnoticed, and contempt flashed in her dark brown eyes. 'Massa done gone to Charlotteville.'

'Charlotteville?' Aimée exclaimed, before relief flooded her furrowed brow. 'Of course, there's a market there. He did say something about it the other day. What's for sale there? Anything that might interest me?' The thought of a day out in one of the small market towns that dotted the valleys to purchase some new dress-material or such like suddenly appealed very much.

The tall, dark figure looked down at her with a look of incredulity mixed with scorn. 'Ah don' know that, miz. They sell slaves in Charlotteville . . . Folks like me an' mah chillun!'

'Good God!'

There was no further word spoken for the next twenty minutes, while Aimée's mind whirled. If only she could break through that reserve and talk to this woman as a fellow human being. That was what she was, after all. Despite what this peculiar institution they called slavery did to the likes of Tizzy and her mother and sisters, she was a woman just like herself. A woman with feelings, with loves and hates, with hopes and fears. But incomers like herself had been ostracised for attempting such a thing: Fanny Kemble, for example. Everyone knew what had happened to her!

'Dat be all, miz?'

Aimée glanced into the mirror at the dark face looking over her shoulder, and pushed the last hairpin into her net-covered chignon. She sighed deeply. At present, she had not the energy to be a rebel of any kind—the events of the past couple of days had seen to that. 'Yes, Tizzy, that'll be all. Thank you.'

She had said 'Thank you'. She had actually expressed thanks to her future husband's mistress! There was no doubt about it—she had been right last night. The whole world had gone crazy—and she along with it!

It was another scorching day, when even to sit beneath a parasol on the veranda seemed to melt her skin beneath the lightest of summer frocks. But that was exactly what she was doing when the glistening black stallion came into sight.

A hot, swift current surged through her, tingling every nerve-end as she leapt from the bentwood rocker. The delicately-painted fan fell from her fingers as her hand flew to her mouth. How could he? How could he come here like this after what had been said between them last night? And what if Chas saw, and suspected that it wasn't him he was here to see—because it couldn't be, she was certain of that. It was akin to the Seventh Cavalry riding unarmed into an Indian encampment!

'Why, Mr Redmayne, this is a surprise!' Her voice was as deliberately cool as she could make it.

He was attired in a beautifully cut grey riding-jacket, with darker grey trousers tucked into the shiniest black boots she had ever seen. His white lawn shirt was ruffled down the front, but instead of the fashionable cravat, it was open at the neck to reveal a cluster of dark curling hairs beneath the bright red bandanna knotted carelessly round his neck.

'Miss Fitzwilliam!' His wide-brimmed silver-grey felt hat was doffed with a dramatic flourish as they addressed one another with respectful formality.

Aimée knew she should be distant—be determined
not to let her guard slip for a single moment—but all the
anger and humiliation she had felt the night before
seemed to evaporate into the hot morning air. He drew
the stallion up at the foot of the veranda and leapt down,
hooking the reins over the rail before striding up the
steps to join her.

'You shouldn't have come!' She found herself almost
hissing the words from between narrowed lips, as she
glanced nervously about her.

He was standing before her now, smiling down at her
as one would at an anxious child. 'Calm yourself, honey.
Ol' Charlie-boy's at the auction at Charlotteville. I
know—I checked!'

She gave a relief sigh. Of course he was! 'Won't you
take a seat!' She must at least observe a modicum of
sociability, she thought frantically. To do otherwise
would surely look even worse than requesting him to
leave immediately.

Angel, one of the table-maids, appeared at the door,
and her mistress summoned her over. 'Will cider suit,
sir?' Her green eyes turned to the man now seated by her
side.

'Suits me just dandy!'

When the maid retreated, Aimée glanced over at her
unexpected visitor, her eyes falling, for the first time, on
a brown paper parcel by his feet.

He picked it up and handed it to her, setting it on
her lap. His blue eyes gleamed as he smiled across at
her puzzled face. 'If you hadn't left such a conspicuous
calling-card, I would have thought of some other reason
for seeing you again, any ol' how.' The grin grew
broader. 'I must admit, though, most young ladies of my
previous acquaintance have made do with a lace
handkerchief or the like!'

Daylight dawned. 'My cloak!'

'And all your worldly wealth tied up real dainty in that
shawl in the pocket.'

He had noticed! Her cheeks flamed, and she slipped the parcel under her wide, flounced skirt. 'It—It was good of you to return them so soon. I'm sure I would have noticed their absence before the day was out.'

'Why, my dear Aimée, you mean you hadn't even missed them? And here was I breaking my neck—and that of my good old horse—to ride straight over to the enemy camp to return them.'

Her back stiffened, and consciously avoiding his eyes, she stared across the sloping lawns. 'You may recall, sir, that I had rather more important things to think about when I took my leave of you last night.'

He was prevented from answering immediately by the maid, who had returned with a jug of cider and two long glasses on a silver tray. They watched in silence as the refreshments were set down on a small bamboo table between them, and the drinks were poured.

'Thank you, Angel. That will be all.'

'You've made up your mind, then?' He threw the question at her directly the girl had disappeared inside the house once more.

Their eyes met as they reached for their drinks, and the intimacy of his gaze caused her to look away immediately. 'I'm going to take your advice. I'm going to marry Chas, as I originally intended.'

The emphatic answer was intended to shock him into a reaction, but it served only to dismay herself, as a quiet smile came to his lips. Slowly he raised his glass in a silent salute before taking a long drink. 'Here's to you both,' he said softly. 'May your future life bring you everything you would wish yourself, my dear!'

There was an ambiguity about his words that they were both aware of, but she was determined not to allow him to embarrass her. 'I thank you, sir!'

He was studying her closely, his blue eyes watching her mouth for any tell-tale sign of regret at her announcement, but her smile remained fixed firmly in place, and her eyebrows rose in anticipation of his next question. It came within seconds.

'And when will the wedding take place, may I ask?'

'As soon as possible.' It was her turn to watch him now, aware that they were playing a verbal game of cat and mouse, but each equally determined not to be caught out. 'You will come, won't you? I'm sure it wouldn't be the same otherwise!'

She expected an immediate cheerful acceptance, but instead he sat back in his chair and stared out over the rolling hills and the blue mountains beyond. 'I never promise what I can't deliver, my dear.'

'And what exactly is that supposed to mean, pray?'

He turned to look at her once more, the smile gone from his lips. 'It means—maybe I will, and maybe I won't. There's no way of tellin', right now. Anyways, I may be in New Orleans. I go there two or three times a year on business.'

'And it would probably prove most convenient to be there on the day I get wed.'

'Yes, my dear, it would. I reckon it would be best for both of us, don't you?'

She looked straight at him. The laughter of a moment ago was gone from his eyes. In its place was a most curious expression that sent a shiver over her skin. It was almost the same expression she had witnessed the night before, when she had pleaded to be allowed to stay. And, whatever it was, it was not the expression of a mere disinterested neighbour. She could feel her heart beating beneath the tight basque of her gown, and a delicate sweat broke on her brow—a sweat that had nothing to do with the scorching heat of the morning sun.

He got to his feet, their eyes still locked in what she could only think of as a visual embrace, and as he turned towards the steps, she rose quickly. 'No, Red, please . . . Don't go!'

He turned back, his hand clasping the restraining one on his arm, before he lifted it to his lips. Very slowly, very gently, he kissed each finger in turn, then turned her hand over to place the most tender of kisses in her moist palm. Then, without another word or look, he strode down the steps and mounted his horse.

She stared after him, and despite the humiliation she had felt last night, every part of her yearned for him to stay—or to take her with him—to do anything but leave her. But she could not utter a word. She was Charles Stuart MacDonald's bride, not his. And the knowledge tore at her heart.

He did not even look round—not once—as he rode off in the direction of Wildwood. She screwed up her eyes against the blinding sun until he was a tiny black dot disappearing into the heat haze at the foot of the distant hills.

As she sat down again on the rocker, the maid re-appeared, as if by magic, to remove the refreshment tray. Aimée looked at her dully. How many of them were watching unseen from the tall windows behind? Was absolutely everything to be public knowledge? The thought that every moment, every precious moment, she had spent with the man that had just ridden out of sight had been witnessed by others gave rise to an irrational resentment. Stooping to retrieve the parcel from the veranda, she placed it under her arm, and with her head held high, walked into the house, letting the door close with a heavy thud.

That night, in the drawing-room, Chas seemed genuinely pleased by her suggestion to arrange the wedding for the following week. 'Sure, honey, sure! There's ain't no good reason why not. I'm sure the Reverend Mr Thomas can fit it in just as easily next Friday as the one after. It's not leaving our guests too much time to rearrange their plans, though.'

She looked at him apprehensively over the *gros-point* cushion she was embroidering. 'I—I wanted to talk to you about that,' she said quietly. 'Does it really have to be such a big wedding? Do we really need the whole County attending?'

Chas's eyes narrowed. 'Now, honey, you know that ain't fair! There'll be no more than fifty at the actual

ceremony here in the house. The rest are only attending
the wedding breakfast on the lawn afterwards. You can't
deny all our well-wishers a little celebration on our
happy day! Anyways, we won't be required to stay for
that part, not if you don't have a mind to. We can leave
directly after we tie the knot right here in the house, if
that's what you really want.'

She nodded. 'Thank you, Chas. That's what I really
want.'

He looked down at her curiously. His buddies had said
that gals often acted kinda funny just before they got
hitched. It was nothing to worry about—just part of
their little ways, being female and all. 'Yeah, well, that's
the dandy ticket! I'll see everybody's notified to that
effect right away . . . One week from now. Landsakes, it
ain't long to go!'

He was right, for the next week passed in a feverish haze
of preparation. Luckily she had brought her wedding
gown and most of her trousseau from London, so all that
was left was to help Aunt Effie to order and supervise the
food and flowers for the big day. Not that she was able to
contribute much to that side of things, for the old lady
much preferred to be left to do things in her own way.
Aimée was consulted, of course, but it was hard to
change the habits of a lifetime, and the younger mistress
of Four Winds found she had not nearly as much to do as
she had anticipated as the final nerve-racking days ran
their course.

The wedding morn dawned, like every other that
summer, hot and humid, with the sun streaming in
through the open windows of her balcony. She spent
longer than usual in the tub, for her waist-length hair had
to be thoroughly washed and dried, then rolled tightly
on the long rags, while still slightly damp, to produce the
cascade of ringlets that would decorate the scooped
neckline of the ivory satin dress in which she would
become Mrs Charles Stuart MacDonald.

The religious ceremony itself was the part that she had

not allowed her thoughts to dwell on. She had spent long hours planning what flowers she would wear in her hair, and have pinned to her gown, and what food she would prefer to be offered to the guests—what wine she felt right for the toasts, and a million and one other small items; but never had she allowed herself to think of the most important thing of all. Today she would commit herself to one man, in the sight of God, for the rest of their natural lives. And that one man was not the man she was in love with. That man—the man of whom she was now thinking more than any other—the man who was in her thoughts night and day—would probably not even be at the wedding. Daniel O'Connell Redmayne.

'Oh, Red—where are you?'

Her hands gripped the balcony rail as she stared out over the sun-dried landscape beyond the well-watered lawns. There had been neither sight nor sound of him since he had strode from the veranda just nine short days ago. Sometimes, in her dreams, she would imagine him charging over those very lawns on his black stallion, to snatch her from Chas's grasp, just before the minister could pronounce them man and wife. But then she would wake to find herself bathed in perspiration in the same, lonely, rumpled bed.

At a rustling sound from inside the bedroom, she turned to see Tizzy, accompanied by Sadie, arranging her wedding gown on a hanger on the wardrobe door. A cold, sick feeling numbed the pit of her stomach as her eyes lingered on the form of the taller slave. What would this coming life at Four Winds hold in store for them all? By this time next year she could have given birth to an heir to this magnificent mansion and the plantation surrounding it. She could have given birth to the half-brother or -sister of that very woman standing in front of her arranging her wedding gown! And—dear God—how would she feel if Tizzy was to have another of his children?

A shudder ran through her, and she leant back against the rail to steady herself. The whole balcony seemed to be spinning in a mad carousel round her shaking form. She closed her eyes, and brilliant lights spun crazily in the darkness of her head. Several minutes later, she regained consciousness on her bed, with Sadie's slim fingers dabbing a cold flannel over her brow.

'You done swooned clean 'way, miz!'

Aimée managed a weak smile. 'It's the heat, I expect . . . and the excitement. I'll be all right in a moment, I'm sure.'

In fact it took almost another hour before she felt able to proceed with her toilet. And, even then, she could only sit like a rag doll on the satin-padded stool in front of the dressing mirror while the two maids worked on the elaborate ringlets that fell from the crown of her head. Her hair was swept back from her face and very full on the crown; but where less fortunate ladies were obliged to supplement their own meagre locks with a false roll, the future Mrs Charles MacDonald had hair enough for the most fashionably high crown that Craven County had ever seen. A red and a white rose, plucked fresh from the garden that very morning, adorned the completed coiffure, just above her left ear.

Her gown would be the talk of the neighbourhood for years to come, and as she pirouetted gracefully before the full-length mirror by the window, she had no doubt about the correctness of her decision to buy the finest to be had in the whole of London's West End. The ivory satin set off her pale skin and dramatic dark hair beautifully. From her handspan waist hung delicate châtelaines of myrtle and orange blossom, and the wide skirt was flounced with bouffants of tulle and the finest Honiton lace. The short train was of antique moiré, the tiny silver threads matching exactly the exquisite embroidery on her ivory satin slippers. Her head turned slowly, first one way and then another, as she examined the flawless skin of her throat and shoulders above the scooped neckline. The décolleté had been rather too revealing for a bridal gown, so she had added a tiny frill of lace, which covered just enough of the firm swell of her breasts to be considered entirely decent.

The tinkling chimes of the ormolu clock on the mantelpiece struck a quarter to twelve as she stood back from the glass with a satisfied sigh. Fifteen short minutes to go! They were all waiting downstairs for her now; the elegant hall decorated to perfection with banks of red and white roses, and her favourite arum lillies from the garden. MacDonald friends and relatives from miles around would now be seated in uniform rows facing the black frock-coated figure of Jebediah Wilks at the harmonium. Its wheezy, haunting strains were already to be heard up the wide sweep of the staircase, to send an anticipatory shiver down her spine.

The maids had left fully five minutes ago, and she glanced anxiously once more at the clock. What on earth was she going to do for the remaining few minutes? Butterflies cavorted wildly in her stomach, then her eyes alighted on the brown paper bundle still on top of the cabinet where she had placed it the week before. At least unwrapping that would stop her being consumed entirely by nerves before she made that awesome descent downstairs to join her future husband and the assembled company. Without further ado, her fingers tore at the paper, then undid the knot of the paisley shawl beneath. One by one, she extracted the articles and put them away in their places. Then came the jewellery, the few pieces she possessed of any worth not given to her by Chas. As she gathered them up, her eyes fell on a small box in white leather. Her brows furrowed as she prised off the lid and gazed in curiosity at the contents. Inside, on a bed of midnight-blue satin, lay a gleaming gold chain, hanging from which were two interlocking gold hearts. A small gasp escaped her lips as she lifted it out—the tiny gold links of the chain shimmered in the sunlight as they slipped between her fingers. Red must have put it there! Her heart lurched wildly at the knowledge.

Her eyes sparkled as she walked back to the mirror and held it up before the bare pale skin of her throat. She would wear it. She would wear it hanging there next to her heart. And no one would ever know—not one single person down there waiting for the wedding to begin would know from whom it had come and what it meant, but her. And only one other person could guess what it would mean to her as she stood there and pledged her life to another. But that one man would not be here today.

'Thank you, Red,' she whispered softly in the silence of the sunlit room. 'Thank you, with all my heart.'

CHAPTER SEVEN

MRS CHARLES STUART MACDONALD glanced across at her husband of two hours and attempted a smile befitting a new bride. She could not eat a single morsel of the wedding breakfast, the remnants of which the servants were now so busily tidying away. She had been persuaded to partake of some of the wine, though. It would have been almost impossible to refuse, with so many toasts to be drunk. But the effect was not good.

'You feeling all right, honey? You're looking a mite pale, to my way of thinking!' Chas's pale brows furrowed as he joined his new wife by the open veranda door.

'I'm just a trifle hot. I'll be all right—don't worry.' She dabbed a lace-trimmed handkerchief to her damp brow as her eyes strayed across the lawns to the great white marquee by the edge of the lake. The whole of the grounds in front of the mansion seemed to seethe with colour, from the gaily fluttering bunting to the outfits of male and female guests alike. Aimée had never seen anything like it.

'You looking for anyone in particular, honey? If so, they're all here—anyone that matters in Craven County, anyhow!'

She shook her head. 'No . . . No one in particular . . .'

She had lied, of course. But he was wrong—so very wrong. The only one who mattered, really mattered, was not here. Neither did she expect him to be. Had he not told her that he would probably be in New Orleans?

'Well, it's doing you no good standing here melting in this heat. What do you say to getting out of all that finery and making a start to our honeymoon?' He leaned forward as he spoke, his voice low and intimate, his hand grasping her elbow. 'It's been too darned long since we've had some time alone!'

Even his touch made her recoil inwardly now, but she succeeded in forcing a smile to her lips. 'Yes. That suits me very well. I'll go up straight away and change.'

It took almost an hour to divest herself of her wedding gown and put on the simple sage-green taffeta day dress that she had chosen for travelling. Its matching cloak was of the finest woolcloth lined with matching cloak was of the finest woolcloth lined with matching green silk, but she declined to fasten it round her shoulders, feeling she would be sure to melt if she did. No one at home had warned her that Georgia could be as hot as this in midsummer, and the thought of the long coach ride ahead filled her with dismay.

She had succeeded in extracting from Chas the information that they would be spending their first night in Charlotteville, then continuing the following day to Atlanta, but of their destination after that, she had simply no idea.

In a strange way she could not wait for their honeymoon to begin, so that it would soon be over and they could return to Four Winds. The thought of being alone with him for the planned fortnight was almost more than she could bear. Of course she had heard many tales over the years of how unbearable such a time could be for new brides, but it was not the physical side of their life together that worried her as much as the emotional. This would, without doubt, be the greatest test of her ability as an actress. As far as her new husband, and the world at large, was concerned she was deeply in love with the man she had married.

'Dear Lord, forgive me—and help me!' she pleaded as she fastened the green ribbon of her bonnet beneath her chin in a neat bow. 'Help me to prove a good wife. Help me, please . . .'

The equipage that awaited them at the foot of the front steps was the finest Aimée had yet seen. Certainly she had not encountered the splendid uniforms of the

two coachmen before. Since they were to use their own
carriage and attendants for the major part of the
journey, Chas was determined it would be seen to be
befitting the master of Four Winds and his new bride.

It seemed that the whole multitude of guests flocked
round the carriage and four as they took their leave, and
she was able to pick out only a few familiar faces amid
the crowd of well-wishers. Happily, one of the faces was
that of Becky Madison, who positively beamed at them
through the small window. She had caught the bouquet
of red and white roses that Aimée had deliberately
thrown in her direction after the ceremony, and now
she held it aloft with great glee as she waved her
goodbyes.

Aimée sank into the plush upholstery with a sigh of
relief as the last guests disappeared from view and the
carriage continued down the drive and out through the
wide gates. She glanced across at Chas. To her astonishment, he was slumped against the opposite window,
already fast asleep. Unlike her, he had not restricted his
drinking to the toasts, and the result was now all too
obvious.

The road wound ahead past the cotton fields, now a
sea of pure white blooms where vigilant negroes in-
spected the crop for the detested boll-weevil that could
devastate a whole field in a matter of days. At the end of
every six rows an overseer stood, whip in hand, for any
sign of flagging. She averted her eyes. To do anything
else was far too upsetting, and she knew that if she was to
make any type of life here, she must simply close her
eyes—and her heart—to so many unspeakable things.
Whether she would succeed, only time would tell.

By the time they had reached the outskirts of
Wildwood, Chas had begun to stir, straightening up in
his seat, as though to pretend that he had never been
anything other than wide awake. There were still cotton
fields here, but, to her amazement, there was not a negro
in sight, and the workforce seemed to be comprised
entirely of whites. She stared out at the blooms that

seemed to stretch to the far horizon, then turned to her husband.

'Where are the slaves, Chas? They are all white people out there. Who on earth are they?'

Chas looked profoundly bored. 'Poor white trash, honey—just poor white trash.'

'I beg your pardon?'

He yawned, and slumped back in his seat, pulling the blind of his window down with a sharp tug as if to blot out the offensive sight from his consciousness, but she would not be deterred.

'Are they slaves—or what?'

'Hell, no! He pays the critturs all right. Got rid of his slaves when ol' man Redmayne joined his maker some time back, and brought in Irish immigrants to do their work. The guy's plain crazy, if you ask me, but then he never would ask my opinion on anything. Too full of his own importance, that one!'

With that, he brought the conversation to an abrupt halt by clasping his hands over his stomach and closing his eyes. 'Wake me when we get to Charlotteville, honey. I could do with a little shut-eye after that wedding breakfast!'

Aimée removed her eyes from his recumbent figure and stared out of the one remaining window. They were nearing the entrance to the drive up to the Wildwood mansion now, and even being in the vicinity of the Redmayne home brought a tingle of suppressed excitement that made her grip the edge of her seat as she leaned forward for a better view. Of course it was silly—he would most probably be miles away in New Orleans—but her heart raced nevertheless, and her teeth bit painfully into her lower lip as her eyes scanned the dusty road ahead.

They had barely gone another five hundred yards, when, to her consternation, a tall figure on a black horse came riding into view. Her breath caught in her throat as she craned her neck in an effort to see past the clumps of wild roses that edged the path. It was he. It was Red, dressed immaculately in a white ruffled shirt, the sleeves rolled up to the elbow, and close fitting dark grey pants tucked into the now familiar black shiny boots.

As soon as he saw the equipage, he drew the horse into the side of the road and watched, transfixed, as it approached, its wheels sending up a cloud of brick-red dust. For one split second their eyes met and held, and then the carriage rattled past. It was all Aimée could do to stop herself from throwing open the door and running back along the road to join him. Every promise she had made to herself to be a good wife to the man by her side seemed a total mockery of her true feelings. There never was—and never could be—a man that stirred feelings within her that disturbed her as profoundly as did Daniel Redmayne. And how, as Mrs Charles MacDonald, she was going to cope with that fact she could not begin to contemplate.

For the remaining twelve miles of the journey to Charlotteville she gazed listlessly out of the now dusty window, vainly attempting to occupy her mind with the luxuriant beauty of the passing scenery. Between the gently rolling hills, rivers meandered—their beds now dried out in places under the scorching, relentless summer sun. Where the water still flowed freely, it was a dull red, and willows, which during the spring rains could trail their foliage in the rushing torrents, now stood aloof and dry-leafed in the yellowed grass of the banks. Occasionally a wild orange and Chinaberry could be seen, while flaming azaleas and wild honeysuckle added splashes of vivid colour. All this had enchanted her when she had first arrived—and indeed it still did, but there was a heaviness about her heart that no amount of beautiful scenery could lift. When eventually the carriage rolled into Charlotteville at a little after five o'clock, she obediently reached across and shook Chas by the arm.

He snorted twice, then roused himself to an irritable semi-consciousness. 'What is it? Wha's a matter?'

'I do believe we're here,' she said brightly, sporting a

lightness of tone and expression that she did not in the least feel.

Charlotteville, like its bigger sisters Augusta and Savannah, was built in the midst of a beautiful forest. Or so it seemed, for the public buildings were arboured in foliage, and the inhabitants, on the whole, were as well turned out as their homes and offices. None, of course, was as fashionable as the swells one encountered in the bigger cities, but Aimée found a curious comfort in knowing there was such a pleasant little town less than two hours' drive from their home.

They were booked into the Lake Michigan Hotel on Main Street, so named because the proprietor hailed from its southern shore. That, however, did not prevent him from being more virulent in his support of Secession than any true-born Southerner she had yet come across.

'It's all to do with pride, ma'm,' he informed her, hooking his thumbs into the armholes of his waistcoat and standing back with a satisfied expression as they signed the registration book. 'There ain't no Northern upstart gonna tell the likes of me and your good husband there how to run our lives. Why, this town would go to the dogs in five minutes without them there slaves!' He owned twelve slaves, and maintained he could not possibly run at a profit without them, notwithstanding the fact that he thought them a shiftless lot of good-for-nothings!

The oldest of them carried the trunks up to their room, and Aimée made a point of pressing a dime into the old man's hand—only to have it snatched back by an irate Chas. 'What in heaven's name are you playing at, woman? You'll have every last one of them demanding tips after this! The very idea! Be off with you, boy!'

The 'boy', who was at least seventy, backed out of the room as if in fear for his life, and Chas MacDonald turned to glare at his young wife. 'Landsakes, Aimée, have you no shame? How could you do such a thing to me? Lose all respect for their betters, these varmints do, if you go round doing that sort of thing! You've a lot to learn, gal, and the quicker you start learning, the better for all of us—especially me!'

It was not the start to their honeymoon she had anticipated, and when he refused to talk to her for the next half-hour, she announced she would take a breath of fresh air before dressing for dinner. He did not demur—but merely looked at her sullenly from the chaise-longue by the window as she retied the ribbons of her bonnet and picked up her parasol from the stand by the door.

It was a relief to be out in the fresh air. Even if her bridegroom had been in a better humour, the inside of the hotel was suffocatingly stuffy. Outside, however, the blistering heat had gone out of the sun, and a fresh breeze made the still oppressive warmth bearable as she set off down the tree-shaded main street. Birds gossiped cheerfully in the dense green foliage, through which the sun cast mottled patterns of light and shade on the narrow sidewalk, and she set off in what she took to be the direction of the river.

There was a levée of a sort some eight hundred yards away, and she sat down on a vacant bench to watch a succession of wagons and drays off-loading a consignment of casks from the open deck of a barge. A group of negroes worked in line, heaving the heavy cargo on to the quayside, their sweating bodies glistening almost blue-black in the late afternoon sunshine.

After a time her presence became the object of comment from a few young bushwhackers lounging idly on the next seat, and she was forced to continue her walk along the riverside. Apart from a large warehouse, the only building of any note was a single-storey white-painted shack that announced itself to be the booking office for the river paddle-steamer service that plied the waterways all the way down to the Gulf.

Her eyes were immediately drawn to a colourful poster depicting the city of New Orleans. So that's where he goes, she thought to herself, remembering with a grimace where Daniel Redmayne had hinted he might be on this very day. She took in the romantically pictured, white-painted French and Spanish colonial houses, their window-boxes and courtyards spilling over with flowers of every hue. Even the name New Orleans seemed to possess a magic all of its own. But then, being part French, she could just be a trifle prejudiced in that regard!

Next to it was another smaller notice, still relating to New Orleans, advertising 'The Pleasure Palace—the finest night-time entertainment to be found in the whole of the Gulf'. The information was superimposed on a picture of bevy of beautiful girls, and her interest was immediately aroused as she read: 'Everything the weary visitor to our Queen of Cities could wish can be found within our walls. Beautiful girls from every land, including the most celebrated dancers and songstresses from the European stage, are here for your entertainment and pleasure. In residence at the moment we are proud to present, straight from Gay Paree, the French capital's most popular soubrette, the lovely Françoise "Fifi" Boulanger!' Beneath was a small picture of a pretty blonde-haired young woman with a particularly pert smile.

Aimée stared at it for a moment or two, then gasped, 'Fanny Baker!' If that was Françoise 'Fifi' Boulanger —then she had not that very day become Mrs Charles MacDonald! So that was where the little minx had ended up! A wry smile curved the corners of her mouth as her mind went back to her early days at the Gaiety Theatre in London. Fanny Baker had been her understudy on more than one occasion, when the freckle-faced youngster had just arrived as a gauche but keen fifteen-year-old from the green fields of Kent. Just what her family had been, no one could say for sure, because Fanny never told the same story twice, and it was only Aimée's judicious intervention on more than one occasion that had kept the hapless youngster out of the arms of the law. Likeable though she undoubtedly was, the would-be actress with the cheeky grin had a definite penchant for pretty pieces of jewellery—particularly other people's. Twice the manager had threatened her with the police unless the missing items were returned, and they always had been, until the day when a bag of gold sovereigns was missing from the main booking-office at the front of the house. Fanny was missing on the same day—and neither was ever heard of or seen again—until now!

Shaking her head, Aimée give a wistful sigh as she continued her way back to the hotel. All that seemed a long time ago, and a long way away now—as indeed it was. It sometimes seemed as if her old life had never happened—as if she had never been a fairly successful actress, and, if the truth were known, quite an accomplished singer into the bargain. She had thought long and hard when the chance came to give it all up and travel across the Atlantic to become Mrs Charles Stuart MacDonald. Of course, there had been other proposals of marriage before that—plenty of them. But there had been something about the idea of starting afresh in the New World that appealed very much to her as she neared the ripe age of twenty.

And oh, he had been gallant—so very gallant! Never had a girl received so much attention as Chas MacDonald had lavished on her. Roses by the armful and jewellery beyond her wildest dreams, as well as the very best seats at all the best shows in the West End. Oh yes, it had been a magic time, and faced with the same choice, she would probably make the identical decision again. It was so easy to be wise after the event.

She turned the corner into Main Street and glanced up at the Lake Michigan Hotel. He would be up there now—her husband—slumped in a drunken stupor, most probably on the chaise-longue by the window. 'Love, honour and obey' the preacher had said a few short hours ago. And she would do her very best to adhere to the last of those promises—but the first two . . . Oh dear, oh dear!

Chas continued to snore for another hour while she

busied herself preparing for dinner. When he finally awoke, she was already attired in a light taffeta gown of salmon-pink, tied at the waist with a deep rose-pink sash.

'Mighty pretty, honey! Mighty pretty!'

She turned from the oval mirror to smile her appreciation. 'Thank you, Chas! I kept it specially for today.'

He got up clumsily and lunged towards her, trying in vain to appear quite sober. 'Time to kiss the bride!'

His hands landed heavily on her bare shoulders as his lips headed for hers, only to land halfway down her chin. He straightened up and gazed down at her, giving a faintly sheepish smile. Then his eyes fell on the delicate gold chain round her neck. Her heart stood still as his fingers reached down to lift the pair of intertwined hearts. His forehead, beneath a stray lock of fair hair, wrinkled for a moment, then he let the tiny pendant drop. 'Ah'll get you something much prettier than that to wear, honey—just see if Ah don't!'

The dinner in the plush dining-room passed off quite well, although Aimée found she had not regained her appetite. To her obvious distress, Chas insisted on finishing two bottles of best French claret on his own, while she sat helpless and disapproving, nursing her cup of coffee.

'Don't you worry 'bout me, honey! Ah'll still be as capable as any man-jack you care to think of when it comes to performing my nuptial duties tonight!'

She winced, staring past his leering smile towards the open door of the room. The thought of rising from the table and climbing those stairs with him was almost too much to bear. 'I have no fear on that account, my dear!' she replied in as sweet a voice as possible.

'Spoken like a trooper!' To her horror, he got up from the table, knocking over his half-full glass in the process. Her eyes moved from the spreading red stain on the white cloth to meet his. 'Right, Mrs MacDonald—we're going to finish our wedding day in style!'

His arm came out and made a grab for her wrist, hauling her unceremoniously from the chair. She stumbled after him, attempting to salvage what little dignity she could, as they continued out of the room and on up the staircase. The door of their room slammed behind them and he pulled her roughly towards him. The sweet, sickly smell of the wine on his breath made her avert her head, until a resounding slap on her cheek forced her to look at him once more. 'That'll teach you to screw your nose up at me, madam!

Her hand flew to her smarting skin as her humiliation was compounded by the hot sting of tears. His face was twisted into a grimace such as she had never seen before. The man before her was not her husband, but a stranger—a drunken stranger!

'Come here, bitch!' He snatched her hand from her cheek and twisted her wrist back as he dragged her towards the bed. 'Take this darned thing off!' His fingers ripped impatiently at the lace-trimmed neck of her dress, ripping the bodice.

'No!' Bitter tears were streaming down her face as she attempted to wrench herself free. It wasn't going to be like this. Please God, don't let it be like this!

But he was roused now—the twin passions of anger and desire burning with a wild fire in his eyes as he lifted her bodily and threw her on the bed. He tore at the hooped cage beneath her skirts, pulling it roughly down over her wildly kicking legs before throwing it across the room, where it landed grotesquely on top of a brass oil lamp on the dresser.

'Bitch! This is what you've been dreamin' of, ain't it? This is why you got so het up over poor Tizzy! Your namby-pamby English dandies were too darned gentle for you! It's a red-blooded Southerner you need! And that's what you're gonna get!'

The mention of the slave's name burst the dam of anger within her. 'Defiler! Slave-defiler!' She screamed the words, her eyes staring wildly at the ceiling, as she fought to remove his massive weight from her body.

'Don't touch me! Don't dare to touch me! Damn you, Chas MacDonald—I'm not your slave!'

His hand came down hard over her mouth to stop the assault on his ears, and she bit deeply into the soft flesh, causing him to let out a yelp of pain, and jerk backwards. The moment's release was all she needed to scramble from under him, but he caught the flounce at the hem of her skirt and hauled her back to the bed.

'So you're not my slave, are you not?' His grey-blue eyes cut through her like the finest steel as he pinned her to the mattress and glared down at her. 'You're right, madam! I have slaves enough to bed when I've a will. Tizzy is my slave . . . But you are my wife. And it is the duty of both of you to pleasure me when and how I feel like it!'

His words sent a chill to her heart, which was beating wildly beneath the torn bodice of her gown, and she could feel his breath, warm and cloying, on her flushed face. She was tired, so very tired, and her head ached every bit as much as the wrists he had pinned behind her thrashing head.

'Do I take you by force—or do you submit like a lady?' He sat up, towering above her, as she lay pinned to the mattress, wedged between the strong, saddle-muscled thighs in the grey plaid trousers. The question was put in a soft, almost intimate, voice that made its query all the harder to take.

'If you are an example of a Southern gentleman, sir, then I will never claim to be a lady!'

A slow smile spread across his pale face, as, savouring the anticipation of what was about to occur, he slowly removed his frock-coat, throwing it to the floor, before unbuckling his leather belt. 'So be it, then, my dear. So be it . . . I will be no gentleman to you tonight!'

Aimée lay staring into the darkness. Her husband of twelve hours lay beside her on the dishevelled bed, naked but for a heavy film of sweat that glistened in the pale moonlight filtering in through the open window.

She was shivering, although it was as hot and humid as every other night of this long summer. Across her pale body livid red weals were appearing where he had forced her to submit to demand after demand, until, his lust finally satiated, he finished the bottle of brandy he had brought from the bar earlier in the evening, then collapsed into a drunken sleep.

It had been worse—much worse—than she had expected. She had fought him off until there was not an ounce of strength left in her body. And, what was hardest of all to take, he had relished it. Every sob, every scream, every plea that she had uttered only served to increase his brutality—his almost manic intent to prove that she was his to use, or misuse, as he willed. Over the past hour, lying in the darkness beside his prostrate form, she had cried and cried until there was not a single tear left in her. And, as the night progressed, a cold resolve hardened within her heart. She would cry no more tears over Chas MacDonald. No, never again.

It had been a mistake—no, worse than that, it had been a tragedy to leave London and come out here to this unknown land to marry this man. She had done a terrible thing by standing up there in the presence of all those people today and giving herself body and soul . . . She buried her face in her hands at the memory. She had not given herself in body tonight. He had taken her—and taken her more brutally than she could bear to recall. But she was still in possession of her soul. Charles MacDonald would never own her soul!

She sat up and drew her hands through her tangled hair as a plan formed in her mind. Even to think in such terms brought a cold sweat to her naked skin and a tight knot of nerves to the pit of her stomach. But her mind was made up. She would leave this man—and leave him now. She could not bear to refer to him as 'her husband' even in her own private thoughts.

Almost sick with fear at the enormity of her decision, she slipped from the bed and pulled on her chemise and matching lace-trimmed drawers. Finding it impossible to wedge herself into the tight back-lacing corset without help, she decided to do without, and pulled on the light-weight hoop with its petticoats, so essential for the voluminous skirted dresses that fashion demanded.

Dressed once more in her green travelling outfit, she closed her trunk, sitting on the top to press the catches into position. Her heart was in her mouth as she dragged it across to the door. Were he to waken now and discover what she was up to, all hell would be let loose. To her enormous relief, Chas moaned once and thrashed an arm across her empty pillow, but his eyes remained firmly shut as she stealthily opened the door and pulled the trunk out on to the landing.

Fortunately the proprietor was not at his usual post behind the reception desk in the downstairs hall. Had he been there, it would have made her task doubly hazardous, for he would surely regard it as his sworn duty to alert her husband. After all, Charles MacDonald was a much respected gentleman in these parts.

Her only hope was to find a coachman who would be willing to take her away from this place . . . But where? Her mind went blank, and she pressed herself into the shadows against the landing wall. Good heavens, she didn't even have any money—Chas had it all! Just when the problems of escape seemed insuperable, she clasped her hands in despair, and her fingers touched her favourite gold and jade bracelet. Her jewellery! She surely had enough pieces to get her as far as a bigger town where, with a little luck, she might find some work. It could take forever to save enough to get back to England, but she would scrub floors or do anything to get away from the situation she was now in.

Aimée scanned the darkened street as she slipped out through the front door. Light and laughter were still coming from a saloon bar opposite. Perhaps, if she waited by the door long enough, someone would come out—someone who could help her to get away from this place before daylight. It took less than five minutes for her wish to be granted. There were three of them—young men of about her own age, who, by their look, had indulged in rather too much of the raw bourbon that the landlord passed off for the best Scotch when his customers were too far gone to know the difference.

She approached with caution; then, when she feared they would disappear into the darkness too quickly, she ran down the street after them and gently tugged at the elbow of the tallest one, who was lanky and redheaded.

'Well, what have we here? Look, boys, a real li'l honeychile on the lookout for a good time! What'll it be, honey—a dime a time? Or are you one of them fancy dames who expect half a dollar?' His arm swung round her waist as his mouth came pressing down towards her.

She averted her face as the whisky-laden breath filled her nostrils and his lips caught her left cheekbone, his single front tooth bruising the soft skin. 'I'm not a—a goodtime girl . . . You must believe me!' With a desperate shove, she sent him staggering back on the sidewalk as she looked pleadingly at his companions. 'I—I'm no harlot, believe me! I'm looking for transport, that's all—someone who can get me out of this place tonight.' She blurted the words out in her anxiety to get her message across.

'And just where would you be thinking of heading, ma'm?' It was the smallest of the three who spoke; a stocky young man who slurred his words as his eyes looked her up and down with an unmistakable leer.

Aimée shrugged helplessly, her eyes darting back to the hotel across the street, certain she would see an irate Chas emerge at any second. 'I—I really don't mind, sir . . . Somewhere on the coast, perhaps. Somewhere convenient for getting a boat back to England.'

'England, is it?' The redheaded one had regained his composure and was walking round her as though examining some circus exhibit. 'Well, now, Ah hears tell them English misses are real classy like! You some kinda lady or somethin', ma'm?'

As she began to shake her head, the short stocky one

intervened. 'Sure she is—look at these here clothes! How much would it be worth—jest supposin' we has transport available? You got plenty of bucks on you, ma'm? It's real late at night to be catchin' a stage, y'know. We'd have to make special arrangements, wouldn't we, guys?' He glanced round at his two companions, who voiced their agreement with a loud, slurred, 'Yeah, we sure would!'

A sudden panic gripped her. There was something about the three of them that told her, drunk or sober, they were not to be trusted, but the memory of what had just occurred in that hotel room across the street made her desperate. 'I—I've got no money, I'm afraid, only this.' She took off the jade and gold bracelet, and held it before them. 'It's worth at least fifty dollars, I swear.'

'Fifty dollars!' The middle one, a fair-haired, spotty youth who had not spoken before, snatched it from her fingers. 'That'll buy us one helluva lot whiskies, agreed, boys?'

The bracelet was thrown from one to the other as they danced round her. She stood in the middle of the circle, tears of frustration and indignation welling in her eyes. 'Please—Please stop!' She turned to each in turn as the mad dance went on, and she was grabbed first by one and then another, their hands groping clumsily beneath her cloak as she was thrown between the sets of outstretched arms, until finally she was spun so hard that she was sent sprawling into the red dust of the road. She lay there in helpless rage after they had run laughing and whooping down the dark street, disappearing round a corner, their shouts still echoing in her ears.

'Are you all right, ma'm?'

She looked up into the eyes of an elderly man in a dark frock-coat and a tall hat. He held out his hand, and she took it gratefully to get to her feet, and gazed down at her dust-covered cloak. 'Yes, I am, thank you kindly, sir.'

'Do you live hereabouts? I'd be happy to escort you home.'

She attempted a casual smile. 'That—That's very gracious of you, but I live just across the street—in the Lake Michigan Hotel.'

When he had gone, she stared bleakly after him. Perhaps it was meant. Perhaps it was a stupid idea that she could run away in the middle of the night like this. She was a married woman in a strange country, with no money. Slowly, very slowly, her feet started walking back across the street and in through the hotel door. But as she re-climbed the stairs and dragged her heavy chest back into the bedroom, her determination hardened, and she turned towards the snoring figure of her husband. 'I've come back to you, Charles MacDonald, in body—but you will never possess me—not ever again—neither in body nor soul. I shall be your wife in the eyes of the world—but in no other way—not now—not ever . . .'

As she spoke the words, the figure on the bed groaned and moved fitfully on the rumpled sheets. He had heard nothing tonight, but as soon as he was awake, she would leave him in no doubt of the vow she had made and meant with all her heart to keep.

She fell asleep eventually, curled up on a chaise-longue, to be awakened only by the insistent knocking of the maid, at a little after eight, with hot waffles and coffee. She staggered to the door and took the tray with a murmur of thanks.

'Wha'sat, honey?'

The thick, slurred voice from the bed made her turn to see Chas pull himself up from the tangle of sheets and peer at her through half-open eyes.

'It's breakfast,' she announced stiffly, setting the tray down on a side-table by the bed. 'Serve yourself if you want any.'

'You're my wife—you do it!'

She glared at him. 'I may be your wife, Charles MacDonald, but I'll never be your slave! You'll never make me that!'

'What are you talking about, woman?' He swung his

bare legs over the edge of the bed and ran a hand through his dishevelled hair. 'Just hand me my breakfast, will you?'

'Get it yourself!'

'Damn you, Aimée, what the hell's got into you? What kinda start is this to our honeymoon? What do you think you're doing, talkin' to me like this?'

'What I'm doing, Chas, is exactly what'll I'll be doing every day of our marriage from now on—retaining my self-respect!'

'And just what is that supposed to mean?' He reminded her of a petulant small boy as he frowned at her from beneath furrowed brows.

'It means that if I'm to continue for one day more as your wife, it will on my own terms. You couldn't bear it, could you, if I walked out on you on your honeymoon? Just think of the shame of going back to Four Winds alone! What would all your drinking buddies—and all the neighbours—say?'

She poured coffee for herself from the silver-plated pot and looked at him steadily over the top of the fine porcelain cup. 'No, my dear husband, if I am to return to Four Winds with you, it is on the understanding that we are husband and wife in name only. You will never enter my bed again until—or if—you are invited to do so.'

'You bitch—you sassy little bitch! Do you really believe I could agree to that?' He jumped up from the bed, his naked figure incongruously pale in the bright sunlight that filtered in through the open curtains. 'What do you take me for, a meek little mouse, who would agree to such a thing?'

'Not a mouse, Chas—a rat! A rat who would sleep with a slave while his bride-to-be lay only a few yards away along the corridor, and who would rape that same bride on the first night of their honeymoon.'

'Rape, my eye! You enjoyed it—women always do! It's only natural that they like a man to be a man!'

'Oh, that's what you were being, was it—a man?'

He pulled his dressing-robe from his open trunk and

slipped it on, knotting the belt round his waist, as he threw her a contemptuous look. 'I guess that's just the trouble—I'm too much of a man for the likes of you, Aimée! What would you prefer—one of those foppish dandies you left back home in London?' His eyes narrowed as he searched her face for a reaction. 'Or is it the likes of that no-good Irishman Daniel Redmayne, that you hanker after?'

Colour flared in her cheeks. 'Leave him out of it, if you don't mind!'

'Oh, I've struck a raw nerve there, have I? I thought so! Don't think I don't know when you entertain him in my own home behind my back!'

'I—I don't know what you mean.' She could feel her face flush, and she deliberately avoided the look of triumph in his eyes as she replaced the cup on its saucer and toyed with the knob on the lid of the coffee-pot.

She was on the defensive now and he could sense it—sniff it out as well as the hounds he kept in the compound behind the slave quarters to track down those foolish enough to attempt an escape. 'Do you really think you can get away with anything in my own home behind my back—with my own niggers serving you in your deceitful little pursuits?'

The maid—she must have mentioned it to Tizzy, who had passed it on to him. Her mind whirled with a million excuses, but he gave her no time to open her mouth.

'And, before you protest, I'm not just referring to that morning on the veranda. Oh no, my dear little wife, I'm talking about the nights you took off on your own on horseback in the direction of Wildwood. Explain that if you can!'

Dear God, he had even found out about that! They glared at one another across the table-top, then Aimée turned abruptly and walked quickly to the window, unable to bear the cold scrutiny of his gaze. 'I have nothing to explain,' she said coldly. 'Even if I had, would it not be a case of the pot calling the kettle black? At least you don't have to suffer the indignity of a herd of little Redmayne bastards running around the place!'

'Bitch!'

The slam of the door a few seconds later told her he had left the room—gone down to get a new bottle of brandy from the landlord, no doubt. She sighed deeply and sat down heavily on the bed. It was not the most auspicious of starts to a marriage, no one could claim that, and she had the most awful sinking feeling that things would not be getting much better in the future.

Their honeymoon lasted only another four hours—just long enough for Chas to get really drunk and summon a carriage in a fit of pique to take them back to Four Winds.

'There ain't no sense in continuing this jaunt with a block of ice for a companion!' he hissed through gritted teeth as he threw the last of his clothes into his trunk and slammed down the lid. 'No, my dear, I'm darned if I'll spend a single cent more on this little caper. Most gals would give their eye-teeth to have had the honeymoon I had lined up for you—but there ain't no way you'll be seeing any of it, no siree!'

Aimée looked up from the chair by the window where she had been seated, already dressed for departure, for the past half-hour. If he really felt he was making her suffer by refusing to go on with their trip, then so be it. It would do no harm, and might even do some good for him to believe that he had won the first battle, but the war between them was not over yet—not by a long way. 'If that's how you want it . . .'

'Darned right that's how I want it! Now, if you're ready, it's time we were going. That coachman has been sitting down there waiting for the past hour.'

She glanced out of the window once more, to where the equipage he had ordered was waiting. 'The only reason the poor man has had to wait so long is because you've been too busy finishing that bottle!'

She gestured to the half-empty bottle on the table

beside him, and he threw her a scathing look as he shoved it into the pocket of his cloak. 'Let's just get going, huh? It'll take the best part of the day to get back to Four Winds, and another minute stuck in this room with you is more than I can bear right now!'

They walked in silence down to the waiting coach, while the old slave who had served them on their arrival staggered down behind them with the trunks. 'Thank you, Cyrus.' Unable to give him any money, she had at least taken the trouble to find out his name, and made a point of smiling her thanks as he heaved them on to the back of the coach. The subsequent glare she received from her husband made the little attention even more worth while. He would not break her spirit, she told herself as she climbed into the well-upholstered interior. He would never turn her into someone like himself—never!'

They spoke little as the coach bumped along the dusty roads back to Four Winds. By the time they got within ten miles, and the earth outside the carriage had once more turned to the familiar brick-red clay, the brandy bottle was finished and tossed casually through the window, to land with a dull thud at the roadside. 'Whata we gonna tell 'em? About cuttin' short the honeymoon?' His slurred words awoke her from a shallow doze as he leaned over to prod her with the silver top of his Malacca walking-cane.

She blinked at him out of sleepy-heavy eyes. 'Tell them anything you wish . . . I really don't care.'

'Yeah, that just about sums it up, don't it? You don't give a damn!' There was a sulky sneer to his mouth as he glared at her from the other side of the coach. 'Now, if it was that no-good Redmayne who was askin' the question, that would sure be a different story!'

At the mention of Red's name, her glance darted out of the carriage window. They were passing Wildwood land! Her heart leapt in her breast, but she was determined he should not notice the quickening of her breathing as she settled back in her seat. 'You're becoming boring, Chas. Daniel Redmayne means nothing to me.'

They sat in frozen silence for another two miles, and her declaration repeated and repeated in his head. His eyes remained riveted on the land outside the window —Redmayne land. Then suddenly he let out a roar that made her jump violently. 'We'll see about that, my dear little wife! We'll see about that, all right! Coachman, pull up the horses!' He stuck his head out of the window and roared out the command once more before the carriage drew up to a creaking halt. With a look of triumph he threw open the door, then turned to Aimée. 'He's right over there—that no-good sonofabitch—you can tell him yourself, in front of me, that he ain't your fancy man! See how you like that!'

CHAPTER EIGHT

CHAS REACHED OUT and snatched at Aimée's wrist, pulling her out of the carriage on to the dusty roadside beside him. 'He's over there, your fancy man! Let's shout him over huh? Let's settle this thing once and for all?' Cupping his mouth, he turned towards the cotton field and yelled, 'Hey, Redmayne, come here, will ya? There's something my wife wants to tell ya!'

Panic gripped her as, screwing her eyes up against the glare of the sun, she gazed out over the field. His eyesight must be better than hers, she thought, for she would never have recognised Red at this distance. But, as he drew nearer, she felt her heart lurch as the familiar features became clearer. He was dressed in black riding-breeches and the habitual black leather boots, his white lawn shirt open almost to the waist. The bronzed skin of his chest with its curling dark hair glinted with perspiration as he crossed the edge of the field towards them with long, easy strides.

'You want something, MacDonald?' Before Chas could answer, Red had turned to Aimée, and he bowed to her. 'Real nice to see you again so soon, ma'm. You enjoyed your honeymoon, I trust?'

His eyes locked on to hers and she flushed, but had no time to answer because Chas intervened. 'I reckon my wife's got something to tell you, Redmayne. Ain't ya, honey?' He pulled her forward by the wrist and stared at her accusingly. 'Go on, then—cat got your tongue?'

'There is nothing I wish to say to Mr Redmayne at the moment.' Her chin lifted defiantly as she spoke.

'Well, if you won't, then I sure will! I know your little game, Redmayne—running after everything in skirts in the neighbourhood. Well, nobody does that to my wife and gets away with it . . . I'm warnin' you!'

'You're warning me—nothing!' Red's right hand shot forward and grabbed Chas's necktie, wrenching him half off his feet as he glared at him. 'I want nothing of yours, Charlie-boy, nothing! But, even if I did, a lily-livered bastard like you wouldn't stop me from taking it—if or when the time came!'

'Irish peasant!'

The blow that was delivered straight into Chas's open mouth sent him staggering back to sprawl spread-eagled on the hard-baked earth. As Red took another threatening step towards him, Aimée put out a restraining arm, clutching at his sleeve.

'No, don't, Red, I beg you! He's drunk, that's all . . . He—He doesn't know what he's saying!'

'He knows all right!' His blue eyes glinted like steel as they glared down at the man at his feet. 'A MacDonald never said or did anything without an ulterior motive. I can't imagine what possessed you to marry such a guy!'

'Can't you?' She turned to fix him with an incredulous stare, as her voice turned to ice. 'Perhaps I went to the wrong people—or person—for advice.'

He had the good grace to glance away, and for a moment she was sure she could detect a fleeting look of embarrassment on his face. But a moan from the earth beside them made them look down to see Chas scrambling to his feet.

'Bastard! You won't get away with this! I'll make you pay for this, Redmayne. By God I will!'

'I doubt it.' The three words were accompanied by a look of total contempt before he turned and strode back to his waiting field hands.

The fact that the episode had been witnessed by the workers doubled the indignity, and Chas's eyes positively bulged as he stared after him. 'Well, what are you standing about there for? Let's get outa here!' His order to Aimée was positively spat out, then he picked up his Malacca cane and whacked it in frustration against the wheel of the carriage.

For the remaining few miles of the journey he sat with

fists clenched, muttering oaths beneath his breath of what he would do to Daniel Redmayne before he was finished with him. He did not once speak to, or even look at, Aimée.

But, as the coach trundled up the sweeping drive of the MacDonald mansion, she felt it was time the ice was broken. 'I—I'll tell everyone it was my fault we had to abandon the honeymoon trip. I'll say I was taken unwell after arriving at Charlotteville and felt unable to continue.'

'Say any damned thing you want!' He stared sullenly out of the window, and when the carriage eventually stopped and the coachman opened the door, he leapt out, throwing a handful of gold coins at his feet before bounding up the steps and in through the front door.

Aimée stared after him in embarrassment. 'If you care to leave the trunks by the steps, I'll see that one of the servants carries them in,' she said by way of apology, as the poor man scrabbled in the dirt for the money.

The house seemed enormously large and empty as she made her way in through the front hall and on up the great winding staircase towards her room. They were not expected, so there were no servants to rush to her beck and call, and as she threw open her door, she was all prepared to throw herself on her bed when the sight that met her eyes made her drop her parasol in astonishment.

Tizzy was standing in the middle of the floor dressed in her ivory wedding gown, complete with head-dress and silver antique moiré veil. For a moment, as she twirled in front of the dressing-table mirror, she did not see her mistress, but then she caught sight in the glass of the incredulous eyes staring at her from the open doorway, and let out a shocked gasp.

'Get it off! Get that dress off!' Aimée's command was issued through gritted teeth as a great anger surged within her. All the hurt—all the indignity and humiliation—she had suffered at the hands of Chas MacDonald was now here in front of her, symbolised by the incongruous figure of this woman—this slave—dressed in her own wedding gown.

'Get that gown off!' Picking up her fallen parasol, she rushed across the room and lashed out at the tall dark figure.

But Tizzy was too quick for her and too powerful as she snatched at it and tore it from her grasp, flinging it across the room, where it landed with a crash on the glass top of the dressing-table. The noise made by the scattering objects caused Aimée to glance round just long enough for Tizzy to flee out of the open door, slamming it loudly behind her. Aimée stared at it as it shook on its hinges, then settled into silence. Only then did she realise that she was shaking from head to foot, but she could not cry. She felt only a cold, hard anger.

Her eyes fell on the pile of Tizzy's discarded clothes lying by the bed. She picked up the red rough cotton blouse, fingering the cheap material between her forefinger and thumb. She felt like ripping it to shreds as the vision of her in her wedding gown still burned in her brain. Then, as she continued to stare at it, for one crazy minute she had the almost uncontrollable urge to try it on. Perhaps it was the actress in her, but something was urging her to dress in the slave clothes that lay at her feet. How would it feel to be even more confined to this place and its master than she was at this moment?

She shook her head as she tossed the garment back on the floor. In many ways she was as much a slave as the owner of those clothes. Her jailers were this gold ring on the third finger of her left hand and the piece of paper that told the world she was married to Charles Mac-Donald. They tied her to this place and this man as surely as a ball and chain round her ankle, for no woman could walk out on a marriage, especially here in the South, and expect to hold her head up in decent society again. Could she really blame Tizzy for taking the opportunity of her absence to try on the wedding gown?

Who knows, if she had been in her place, she might well have done the same. When the cat's away . . .

But the revulsion she felt had little to do with the actual act of someone trying on her clothes, it was the knowledge that the woman who had done it was already the mother of her husband's children, not once but several times over, and would always be here as a constant reminder of that fact. Her jaw clenched as her fingers gripped the edge of the wooden shutters. There was nothing for it; Tizzy had to leave her personal service. There was not room for both of them in this house. She could go back to the fields with the others. There was no reason why not. No overseer would dare to lay a finger on her, knowing she was Chas's mistress. Yes, that was the answer. Her mind was made up, and she would make that very clear to Chas at dinner tonight.

As the dinner-gong sounded, however, she felt her resolve begin to flag at the sight of the hard-set face at the other end of the table. She had dressed with particular care, choosing a blood-red flounced satin gown that she decked out with fresh white roses from the garden, but the stunning effect was lost on her husband, as he slumped moodily in his chair.

She had not seen him since their arrival earlier in the evening, but hoped fervently that he had got over his humiliation at the hands of Red. It was important to have him in at least a fairly good mood before venturing to bring up the subject of Tizzy. Although Aunt Effie joined them for the main part of the meal, she left before the liqueurs were served along with the coffee, and Aimée found herself alone in the room with him, apart from the invisible presence of Ebenezer and the other two liveried servants in the background.

'I—I had rather a disturbing experience when we got home today . . .' She began falteringly, unsure of quite how to word her complaint, as she took her first sip of the hot, dark coffee. On no account must it seem like a deliberate attack on Tizzy. He would never stand for that. Her voice quavered slightly as she continued, 'I surprised one of the servants in my wedding gown. Can you imagine, Chas? In my own wedding gown and veil!'

His face showed no surprise, or any emotion, and he continued to stare moodily at her over the top of his brandy glass.

'I—I really don't like complaining about the servants, Chas, you know that, but I think, this time, things just went too far. Why, I'll never be able to think of that gown or look at it again without imagining her in it! If you'd seen her, you would know what . . .'

'I saw her.' The flat, unemotional statement interrupted her flow, and she stared at him in confusion. 'You're talking about Tizzy, ain't you? Well, I saw her, and she looked real nice—real nice indeed . . .'

The lecherous tone that had come into his voice and the curl of his lip froze her blood to ice-water. 'You —You saw her, and didn't do anything about it?'

'Oh, I did something about it, all right!' The leer was broader now, as his blue-grey eyes fixed on hers. 'I figured the good Lord smiled on me this evening, my dear. If the first little gal to wear that gown didn't live up to the obligations that went along with it, then he sent me another dressed in it to do just that!' He flicked his cigar in the vague direction of the crystal ashtray and stuck it back in the corner of his mouth as he paused, as if savouring the memory. 'And my oh my, did she live up to expectations!'

Aimée rose to her feet, white-faced, and pushed back her chair. 'You're telling me you made love to that woman—that slave—this evening while she was wearing my wedding gown?' This was really too much to take!

'You said it, honey, not me.'

'Do you know what you are, Chas MacDonald? You're depraved—really depraved! How do you expect me to live here as your wife when you treat me with such contempt?'

'Stop your whining, woman! You're treated every bit as well as any other lady hereabouts. Marrying me has given you a beautiful home, and as many fancy gowns and shiny baubles as any woman could wish for. More important than that, you're accepted into the best society in the South. It's beyond what someone of your background has a right to expect. There are too many people around here trying to be what they're not! That bastard we ran into this afternoon that you're so fond of is another. It's a pity you didn't get hitched to him!'

'Do you know something, Chas? I think that's the truest thing you have ever said in your life!' She threw the words at him, then hitched up her skirts and flounced out of the room. But even as she ran upstairs to her room she knew it had been no victory. She had accomplished nothing. Tizzy was still her maid, still a permanent thorn in her flesh to torment her with her husband's unfaithfulness. And, perhaps worse, she had fed his suspicion and jealousy of Red.

She kept her door locked that night, and the following night, and every night for the remainder of the summer until he often did not bother to try the handle as he made his way along the landing to his own room. Appearances were kept up, of course: invitations were extended to, and accepted by, all the best families in the County and they, in their turn, were invited to all the great houses for miles around. No one could afford to ignore Charles MacDonald's new bride, although Aimée could feel the undercurrent of disapproval, especially among those ladies of the older generation who felt it was still beneath them to become too intimate with someone who had begun her adult life on the stage.

At almost every reception Red was present—a constant brooding presence in the background, whose eyes seemed to be riveted to her face whenever she plucked up the courage to glance in his direction. He seemed to sense her desire that he keep his distance, and he restricted his encounters to a perfectly executed bow and the odd enquiry after her health. During the dance evenings, however, she often regretted bitterly his sense of propriety that forbade him from filling in his name alongside those of the other handsome young neighbours on her card. To see him swing round the floor with another attractive belle in his arms caused a bitter-sweet sensation that did not lessen however often it happened.

As the heat of the summer gave way to the cooler evenings of autumn, she took to walking down to the river, where she would sit and gaze across to the distant hillside that signified the beginning of Redmayne land. She had never had the courage to ride out that way again, feeling that the ring on her finger weighed too heavily for such a risky venture. If only she had someone in whom she could confide, to share the turmoil in her mind. The news that the Madisons were selling up and moving out of Magnolia Mount merely added to her unhappiness. Becky was one of the few really friendly faces in the neighbourhood, and the thought that she might soon never see her again seemed symbolic of her growing emotional isolation.

As the fall drew to its golden close, preparations for the coming Thanksgiving Balls proved a welcome diversion. The biggest one in the neighbourhood was to be held almost twenty miles away at the home of Judge Amos Carmichael and his wife, and guests travelling from further afield than fifteen miles were invited to stay the night. The week before, Chas had announced that they would be taking up the invitation to be house-guests.

'I want you to wear something real special at the Judge's, honey. I understand there are to be some mighty important people there. In fact, I heard tell the Governor himself and quite a few Senators have been invited. I can't have you letting down the MacDonald name by wearing some ol' thing that's already been seen at some previous soirée.'

She smiled wryly at the memory as at five o'clock on Thanksgiving Eve she placed the sparkling emerald aigrette in her hair over her left ear, and feathered the

curling white ostrich plume into position over her cascade of ringlets. They had told her it was impossible to
have a new gown made up in less than a week, but her
seamstress had done the impossible and produced the
most beautiful gown she had ever possessed. Made of
the finest emerald tulle and edged with snow-white
velvet, it set off her eyes and complexion perfectly, and
she smiled in satisfaction as she fastened the matching
white velvet cloak round her shoulders.

Even Chas could not disguise his admiration as she
descended the staircase to join him for the journey to the
Carmichaels'. 'Real pretty, honey, real pretty! You'll be
the belle of the ball, if I say so myself!'

She took his arm and politely smiled her thanks.
Perhaps tonight would mark a turning-point in their
relationship. It was the first night she had spent away
from Four Winds since their aborted honeymoon, and it
would be a relief to have a change of surroundings and
faces, even if only for a few hours.

Egremont, the Carmichaels' elegant home, stood in
gently sloping woodland, so that the house itself was
visible only from halfway up the mile-long drive. The
drive itself was almost packed with carriages, and they
had to take their turn in being set down at the front door.
Aimée recognised quite a few familiar faces among the
crowd on the steps as they made their way up through
the small knots of chattering guests into the brightly-lit
hall. But it was one face in particular that made her heart
stop beneath the tight emerald bodice of her gown.

Red was standing at the foot of the main staircase, his
tall figure clad in a midnight-blue velvet evening coat and
immaculately-cut off-white trousers. In the dark blue
silk necktie under the collar of the fine lawn shirt glit-
tered a diamond stickpin, but its sparkle could not match
that in his eyes as they fell on her approaching figure.

'Ignore him!' Chas's voice hissed in her ear as they
glided slowly across the marble floor in his direction.

'Mrs MacDonald, may I say you look particularly

beautiful tonight.' His voice caressed her hearing, making her catch her breath, before Chas's abrasive tone cut in.

'Cut it out, Redmayne! A MacDonald no longer acknowledges scum like you—and Aimée is a MacDonald. You should know that by now.' The words were inaudible to all but the three of them as Red stood, legs astride, on the bottom step, blocking the way.

Chas's pale eyes looked deliberately past him, but Aimée could not resist glancing at the darker blue ones a few inches above her own. There was a look in them that she had not seen since that first moment they had met on the path by the slave quarters behind Four Winds. It was a devil-may-care look that seemed to dare her to avoid his gaze. A gaze that held an intimacy that could not be denied.

Sensing it, Chas turned, and after fixing him with a contemptuous glare, snarled, 'I'm warning you only once, Redmayne. Keep clear of my wife!'

'Charlie-boy, do you really believe I'm so stupid as to make a move before your beady little eyes? If so, then you're an even bigger fool than I took you for—and that's hardly possible!' Then he murmured something that only Aimée could hear, and watched his fair-haired neighbour turn puce before his eyes as Chas marched his wife on up the wide sweep of the staircase.

She stumbled on the thick carpeting, and her irate husband pulled her roughly by the arm in his endeavour to put as much space as possible between himself and the mockingly smiling face of Daniel Redmayne. 'What the hell was that supposed to mean, Aimée? What did he say, for Chrissake?'

What the eye doesn't see, the heart cannot grieve over, she repeated to herself with a quiet smile. 'I really can't imagine, Chas dear! I didn't quite catch it, I'm afraid,' she murmured, hurrying to keep up. But a furtive glance behind her at the grin still on Daniel Redmayne's lips belied her words before they had even left her lips.

*　　*　　*

The dinner-table was laid out in the very best tradition of Thanksgiving, the silver plate gleaming on the damask cloth alongside the fine Royal Worcester dinner service; even the floral decorations were a work of art. Crystal chandeliers, glittering with the lights from a hundred candles, illuminated the faces of the exquisitely attired guests as they moved in a sedate line to their allotted positions.

To Chas's delight the place-cards announced that they were to be sitting only three places down from the Judge himself. Such things were important, and he turned to beam his pleasure at Aimée. 'You can see how they rate us, can't you, honey?' he whispered in her ear as she sat down on the high-backed chair, adjusting her crinoline beneath her as neatly as the table would allow.

The delight was short lived, however, as Daniel Redmayne pulled up a chair almost directly opposite. His blue eyes smiled a greeting to all those already seated and quickly passed Chas's grimacing face to linger on Aimée's just slightly longer than the rest.

'How in heaven's name did he get seated there? You see who that is next to him? It's Pierre Beauregard—one of the Army's best soldiers and from one of the very best Louisiana families, to boot. I can't think what the Judge was thinking of to place him next to that galoot Redmayne!' Chas hissed into his wife's ear, his pale eyes staring deliberately past those of the Irish-American opposite.

Aimée feigned a complete lack of interest as she kept her eyes averted in the other direction. 'I expect the good Judge had his reasons . . .' Red had Betty-Jean Munro on his other side, and that, to her mind, was a much greater cause for concern. Betty-Jean was one of the prettiest girls still available in the whole of the county, and by the adoring looks the willowy blonde was giving to the dark man by her side, she for one was obviously delighted with the placings.

The ladies, however, hardly got a look in during the conversation as the meal progressed. The talk, as usual,

was all about Secession, and while there was not a man
present who was not whole-heartedly for the Southern
cause, Red being no exception, Chas made a point of
disagreeing with every opinion he uttered.

'I still maintain we would do well to diversify our
economy down here. They are making far more money
per head of population up in the North than we are
here. You can't have only one half of the country
industrialised—it ain't natural.' Red pressed his point
emphatically, shaking his head as he drained his glass of
the last of the fine claret, but Chas was quick to
intervene.

'That's bull, Redmayne, and you know it! Are you
trying to tell us King Cotton is dying? Why, in the past
ten years the average yield has soared from two million
bales to well over five million! You can hardly call that
an economy in decline!' He laughed in derision as he
looked around the table for support. 'I reckon, if you'd
kept your slaves and not had to rely on that collection of
white trash you've got working for you, you'd know
what a good yield really was!'

Red's jaw clenched and his lips narrowed. 'At least my
cotton is not tainted with human blood, MacDonald,
unlike some I could mention!'

'Are you getting at me? If so, I'll have you know that
there are no happier slaves in the whole of the County
than mine!'

'Really? Then that poor guy who died under the lash
last week at Four Winds just happened to be passing by,
did he? And that overseer who administered the beating
had nothing to do with you?'

Aimée's head, until then lowered over her coffee,
looked up, incomprehension in her eyes. 'I think you
must be mistaken, sir. There have been no slave deaths
since I've been at Four Winds, except by natural causes,
I can assure you.'

The dark brows across from her quirked. 'Beggin'
your pardon, ma'm, I wouldn't be too sure of that. One
hundred lashes across the back hardly rates as natural

causes in my book . . . Have a quiet word with your
husband, if you doubt mine.'

All eyes in the vicinity turned to Chas, whose pale skin
had turned paler still. 'I'd be obliged if you would stick to
your own affairs, and your money-making down in New
Orleans, Redmayne, and keep your nose out of decent
folk's business.'

Chas's fists clenched beneath the tablecloth as he
continued, 'You're beginning to sound to me like one of
those lily-livered Abolitionists from up North, and we
sure don't want one of those varmints supping at the
same table as decent Southern folks! Ain't that right?'
His eyes darted first to the left and then to the right, to be
greeted by a succession of nods and murmurs of agreement from the guests within earshot. 'A plantation with
a high yield—a successful plantation like mine—speaks
for itself. Unhappy niggers wouldn't work, it's as simple
as that! How much cotton does any one of your white
trash workers pick in a day, tell me that? Go on,
Redmayne, come clean, we're all listening!'

All eyes turned to Red, who took a slow sip of his
claret and replaced the glass thoughtfully on the table. 'I
don't mind telling you—or anyone—Charlie-boy! I've
got nothing to hide. I reckon my workers average something over two hundred pounds of cotton a day.'

'Two hundred pounds!' Chas laughed scornfully.
'What the deuce are they doing—picnicking between
the rows? If my overseers can't get at least three hundred
pounds a day out of each last one of 'em, then I'm right
down there wanting to know why!'

'I wouldn't bring your overseers into it if I were you,
MacDonald. If there was any justice in this land, then
every man-jack of them would be up before the courts. It
ain't just the clay in the good earth that colours your
furrows red, sir, it's blood—negro blood!'

'Come now, Redmayne. You're not saying decent
white men simply doing their jobs should be brought to
trial just because the occasional nigger happens to pass
away during field work?' It was the Judge himself who

intervened, his shaggy white brows rising as he regarded
Red over the top of his wine glass. 'I reckon my job is
hard enough without decent citizens being brought to
trial for the occasional nigger death!'

Red sat back in his seat, his fingers toying with the
delicate stem of his glass. 'I guess that just about sums up
what I am saying, Judge, and I make no apologies for it. I
don't reckon any man has the right to work another to
death—black or white. No crop is worth that price, not
even cotton!'

'And there, gentlemen—and ladies—is the reason
why Mr Redmayne here will never be as successful a
plantation-owner as the rest of us!' Chas looked triumphantly round the table. 'He would prefer that his
workers hardly broke sweat—and would free all our
slaves into the bargain! I reckon some folks just ain't cut
out for proper work. You'd be better off staying down in
New Orleans, where you seem to spend so much of your
time anyway, Redmayne. You'll never fit in around here
with half-baked views like that!'

An embarrassed silence followed, but there was little
doubt that the universal opinion at the table agreed with
Chas. Sensing it, he sat back in satisfaction and drained
the red wine from his glass.

Aimée glanced across at Red. His expression was
entirely neutral as he sipped his coffee, but the blue of
his eyes had turned to steel. If there had been victory at
the table tonight, it had gone to Chas, for the simple
reason that Red had felt it *de rigueur* not to disagree with
the views held by the host, Judge Carmichael himself.
Had he been on neutral territory, however, he would
have had no such scruples, she was sure. And that was
why he would never be entirely accepted by these
people.

Pierre Beauregard eventually broke the silence that
had fallen by turning to Red. 'Speaking of New Orleans
reminds me, Red. Next time you're down our way, you
must look in and see us. My family are always on at me
about seeing too little of you!'

Aimée glanced across at her husband, to see his jaw clench in irritation. So his arch-enemy was also an old friend of the Beauregards . . . Somehow, his victory would not taste quite so sweet, she was certain of that.

By the time the meal had finished, the small orchestra was already tuning up in the hall and she had a difficult task to persuade Chas to join the other couples on the floor for the first waltz. Another drink was what he needed most of all, but he finally acquiesced. When they took the floor, his face remained frozen in a frown, and as they circled and swayed alongside the other gaily swirling dancers, his back remained ramrod straight and his eyes stared fixedly into the middle distance.

Normally she would have made an attempt to lighten his mood, but not now, not after what she had just learned. She had heard nothing of the slave death that Red had spoken of, but could not bring herself to doubt his word. The knowledge horrified her, but she dared not raise the matter with Chas under the present circumstances. She could feel the animosity within him, in every tensed muscle, as his mind dwelt on the tall figure that now stood at the far end of the hall, a quiet smile on his face as he surveyed the circling couples.

'Hey, Chas!' Abe Anderson, one of the Anderson twins from the Carlton plantation, by Charlotteville, waved a hand from the side of the floor as the music for the waltz ended. 'Can I have a word with you for a minute?' He caught up with them, his round, boyish face flushed, and he nodded a perfunctory greeting. 'Evenin', ma'm,' he said to Aimée, then fixed his attention back on Chas. 'One of the guys is organising a hand of poker in one of the other rooms. Care to join us?'

Chas glanced at Aimée.'

'Oh, I wouldn't worry about your little lady—there'll be plenty of folks around to see she doesn't weary! You won't mind us borrowing him, will ya, ma'm? It just wouldn't be the same without Charlie here!'

She shrugged her shoulders. 'Under the circumstances, how can I refuse? See you don't go gambling away all that profit you claim we're making, though, Chas!'

Despite the smile on her lips, the pointed barb did not fail to make its mark, and he grimaced as he disentangled his arm from hers. 'Enjoy yourself, honey . . . I surely intend to!'

She watched him stride across the crowded floor with the Anderson boy. In one way it was a relief, but in another she also felt cheated. Almost all the other young women had partners, and the thought of having to spend the rest of the evening either sitting out the dances or taking the floor with the few wheezy, bourbon-smelling old men that were left did not appeal in the slightest. Suddenly, out of the corner of her eye, she saw Red take the floor with Betty-Jean Munro. As they swung past, his hand encircling her neat waist, he caught her eye and succeeded in throwing her a conspiratorial wink before they were lost in the swirling crowd.

Aimée's face flushed, and she fluttered her fan in front of it and turned her back on the floor. Why did it upset her so much to see him in the company of another woman, especially a young, pretty one like Betty-Jean? The orchestra was playing a particularly sentimental popular tune, and he was probably singing the words in her ear! She winced at the thought. It was ridiculous, but she could not stay and watch from the sidelines like a wallflower for one minute longer. Picking up her skirts, she ran through the small knots of guests lining the edge of the dance-floor, only slowing down as she reached the cool of the veranda. It was not cold for late fall, but she shivered nevertheless as she grasped the balustrade and gazed out over the moonlit gardens.

Judge Carmichael was known for his beautifully-kept grounds, and she could just make out the curves of the rose bower in the distance. Without making a conscious decision, she began to walk towards it, down the broad steps and across the soft springy grass until the heady smell of the roses assailed her nostrils. It was a relief to get into the fresh air, away from that crowded hall with all its laughter and noise, and the heightened tensions that always occurred when neighbours gathered in any great number. As she wandered slowly through the rose-scented pergola, she could see the stars twinkling in the midnight-blue velvet of the sky in the spaces between the branches. At times like this, she thought, away from people and all their problems and petty rivalries, she could almost begin to believe in the magic of the South —the old magic that had so enthralled her for the first few days after her arrival at Four Winds.

'Penny for them . . . Or are they worth at least a dollar?'

She swung round to see her way blocked by the broad shoulders of Daniel Redmayne. He had appeared as if from nowhere, his footsteps silent on the soft grass. He must have followed her out, and her pulse quickened as she gazed up at him. 'You—You startled me!' she began. 'I thought . . .'

'You thought I was content to spend the rest of the evening in the gardenia-scented company of li'l Miss Munro, is that it?'

Although she could not see clearly, she could tell from his voice that he had that mocking smile on his lips that she knew so well. 'It never crossed my mind.'

'Cross your heart and hope to die?'

She laughed, the tenseness in her lessening as he took her arm and placed it on his, and they continued the walk through the bower. 'You followed me out here, didn't you,' she murmured. It wasn't put as a question, but as a statement of fact.

'Do you mind?'

'I . . .' She shook her head. What could she answer to that? 'I really don't know, Red—and that's the truth. One part of me says keep away from you—stay well away . . .'

'And the other part, Aimée? What about the other part?'

There was a husky intensity to his voice that made her steps slow to a stop. 'I look upon the other part as the devil in me,' she said softly. 'And the devil we must renounce at all costs.'

'Get thee behind me, Satan—and I'm to be Satan from now on, am I?' He was smiling down at her, but there was a seriousness beneath the laughter in his eyes. 'I'm no angel, Aimée, I've never claimed to be that, but neither am I the devil . . . I'm a normal man, with a normal man's good points and failings. I've done a few things in my life that I'm proud of—and some that I'd give everything I possess to change. But, then, we all make mistakes.'

'You are fortunate, sir. You have made yours in private—some of us have made ours in public!' She walked on in front of him, her head bowed, her lace-mittened fingers twisting the gold band on the third finger of her left hand. 'Some of us were unfortunate enough to take advice that we have come to regret bitterly.'

As she said the words, she faced him, her eyes blazing in the darkness. 'You told me to marry him, Red. You—You were the one I came to, and you sent me back to him—to that man!'

He stared at her silently, then the broad shoulders in the velvet frock-coat shrugged. 'Don't torture yourself, Aimée. As I said, there are some things I'd give my all to change . . . But I can't play God.'

'Can't you, Red? But isn't that what you all do—all you men here in the South? You're so all-powerful —whether it's with your women—or your slaves! I believed you at dinner, when you accused Chas of having that slave killed. But is that so very different from what you've done?'

The bitterness and frustration of the past months welled as hot tears in her eyes, but she blinked them back, determined not to break down in front of him. 'You condemned me to live my life tied to a man I not only no longer love but whom I actually detest . . . I detest everything he stands for! I hope, if this war that you're all hoping for does come—I hope that your precious South is defeated, so that perhaps its slaves, and, God forgive it, its women, will be able to hold their heads up with dignity!' She hardly recognised her own voice as she threw the words at him.

When she made to run back towards the house, he was too quick for her, catching hold of her arm and pulling her roughly towards him. 'You have it all figured out, don't you, Mrs MacDonald? I'm the one to blame for forcing you into marriage to Charlie-boy there, and everyone in this whole darned country is tarred with the same brush. We're all wife-abusers and slave-beaters just because your experience with one man has soured you of life here in general. Well, I've got news for you—nobody but yourself made that decision to become Mrs Charles MacDonald! And we ain't all slave-killers, or even slave-owners, round here! And, just occasionally, we get a little tired of know-all foreigners, whether from the North or from England, coming here and telling us how to live our lives!'

'You're lucky you've got a life to live!'

'Meaning you haven't? Do you really believe that? Is life really that bad at Four Winds?' The anger faded from his voice as his eyes searched hers in the moonlight.

But the last thing she wanted now was his sympathy. 'I've made my bed, and I must lie on it.'

'Must you, Aimée?'

His hands found the bare skin of her shoulders, the touch of his fingers warm against her cool flesh, and she attempted a derisive laugh. 'Actually, no. No, I don't have to lie on it—at least not with him! I made that very clear since the very first night.'

'You are no longer lovers?' His question was hushed, his head bent to hear her answer.

'Lovers? We have never been "lovers"! My dear husband would not know the meaning of the word!'

'But you would.' His words, so softly spoken, sent a shiver through her, as his fingers increased their pressure on her shoulders. 'You would know the meaning of that word, wouldn't you, Aimée?'

Suddenly the perfume of the roses had given way to the musky, masculine scent of the man before her, with his head bent nearer to hers. She opened her mouth to answer, but no words came, and her lips were smothered by his.

She should resist, she knew that, but as his hands moulded her body to his she felt powerless in his grasp. She was a prisoner, but a willing prisoner. His arms enfolded her in their velvet embrace, pressing her ever closer, and sensations rose within her that she had first experienced that night in Wildwood and had relived so often in the silence and privacy of her lonely room at night, knowing that her husband was only yards along the corridor making love to his slave woman. But never, not even in dreams, was it ever quite like the reality, as his hands moved with increasing urgency over her shoulders. His lips whispered her name as his kiss became deeper, and she found herself responding, her body losing its tenseness as it reacted, touch for touch, breath for breath, with his own.

His mouth moved from hers, raining kisses down the pale curve of her throat, until his lips touched the tiny interlocking gold hearts that hung in the deep swell of her breasts. Slowly his head lifted to look at her, his fingers caressing the gleaming pendant. 'Every time I have seen you since that night, you have worn this,' he said softly. 'Is it only because it is a pretty decoration, Aimée? Is that the only reason?'

She shook her head, fighting to control her breathing. 'Don't ask that question, Red. It is one I have not even dared to ask myself.'

For a long time they stood looking at one another, their eyes asking silent questions that their lips could never utter, then his arms enfolded her again. 'Let your lips give me the answer,' he murmured, as his mouth moved slowly down towards hers.

'No . . .' She gasped the word, pushing herself away from him. 'If I do that, there's no turning back. It's not a road I can afford to go down—not now—not ever.' She shook herself free and stood facing him, her face flushed. She could feel her heart beating erratically in her breast. Her every nerve-end seemed to be vibrating —pleading for his touch once more, but she had to be stronger than that. If he would not make it easy for her, then she must not weaken. She was a married woman now—Mrs Charles MacDonald—she must never forget that fact. This man was her husband's enemy. She was playing with a fire that could blaze up and consume them both if she allowed it. She must stifle it now, this very instant, before it was too late. It was far too dangerous to give in to mere physical sensation. 'You shouldn't have followed me out here. It was wrong, very wrong.'

'But I did, Aimée. I have confessed to you that I am no angel . . . When I saw you disappear out of the door, what could I do? Are you really telling me you did not expect me to follow you?'

The colour in her cheeks intensified. 'You—You think I came out here to lead you on?' This really was too much!

'Didn't you? Are you denying that each time we meet there is something that happens—something that passes between us—that needs no spoken words to transmit the message?'

He was telling the truth. Dear God, he was telling the truth . . . 'Perhaps . . . But we are not animals, mere physical creatures, Red. It is the power of reason that differentiates us from them.'

'But what if I have decided I am no longer a reasonable man where you are concerned?' The huskiness in his voice sent a fresh shiver down her spine, but she was determined he must not know.

'Then, sir, I would say that is your problem, not mine, and you must strive to overcome it as best you can!'

She did not look at him—she dared not—as she spoke the words, and had already turned and started to run back through the banks of roses before he could reply. She did not stop until she reached the mansion, and at every step she expected to feel a restraining hand on her elbow. It did not happen, and when she turned to glance back over the moonlit lawn, she could see no sign of him.

A wave of disappointment flooded over her. Why did life seem to consist of being forced into decisions to do the last thing on earth that she wanted? If dreams could come true, he would ride across that lawn at this moment, on the back of his black stallion, and brushing her protests aside, sweep her up into the saddle and ride off with her to somewhere miles away from all these people and their small, gossipy lives. But dreams rarely did come true—not in real life—did they? Especially not for respectable married women, who already seemed to have everything they could possibly want out of life.

Her teeth bit painfully into her lower lip as her eyes strained for a glimpse of the tall figure. He denied her the satisfaction, and frustration engulfed her as she shook her head and turned slowly to mount the steps back into the ballroom. The night was yet young, but for her, she knew it was already over.

It was after five o'clock the following morning when Chas staggered into their shared room. She was still awake, and could tell he was even more drunk than usual because he made no sound other than the occasional moan as he made his swerving way across to the bed. He collapsed on it beside her, still fully clothed, and fell immediately into a deep, noisy sleep.

She left him there, still snoring loudly, when she dressed a few hours later and made her way downstairs for breakfast. It was served at separate small tables in a long, sunny room overlooking the veranda. To her consternation, Red was already seated at a table with two others nearest the window. Three other seats were free at his table, but she deliberately avoided it, pretending she hadn't noticed, as she sat down at the one nearest the door and nodded 'Good morning' to the couple already there.

Her appetite was non-existent, and she could only

pick politely at a small buckwheat cake, declining a plate of hot eggs and bacon. She could feel his eyes on her throughout the fifteen minutes she sat there sipping her coffee, but tried desperately to look away. She knew she was being ridiculous, for she was thus making it all the more obvious to him that their meeting the night before had had a disturbing effect on her. But the alternative was to look straight into those fathomless blue eyes and feel her face flame a beetroot-red in front of all these people. No, she would retain her dignity, excuse herself early, and go straight back upstairs to rouse Chas for the journey home.

To her relief, Chas was awake and at least half sober when she got back to the bedroom. She sat on the window seat while he shaved and dressed, and listened to him relate the details of the card game of the night before. He was almost two hundred dollars in pocket—a fact which, thankfully, did much to improve his mood from when she last saw him. For once, Daniel Redmayne had receded from his mind, and she found herself praying that the tall Irishman would already have left by the time they themselves were ready to depart.

But her prayer was not to be granted, for while they stood on the front steps waiting for their carriage, to her consternation Red came striding across the drive towards them. He had obviously come, and intended returning, by horse, for he was dressed in the same burgundy riding-coat, black breeches and riding-boots that he had been wearing when they first met. She clutched at Chas's arm defensively as he drew nearer, his tanned features smiling quietly as he doffed his hat and bade them both a very pleasant 'Good morning'.

'Push off, Redmayne. We've got nothing to say to the likes of you!' Chas's lips barely moved as he hissed the words out.

'Now, ain't that just the type of right neighbourly thing I've come to expect from you?' Red grinned. 'But, actually, Charlie-boy, it's your good lady I want a word with.'

Aimée's heart lurched crazily and her fingers clutched Chas's arm more tightly. 'Really, sir?'

He had that quirky, lopsided grin on his lips as he turned to her and nodded emphatically. 'Yes, indeed. I was thinkin', ma'm, after I retired last night. You remember that road you were talking of . . . the one you thought you could not possibly travel down?'

Her brow furrowed, then a faint panic gripped her as she remembered her words to him—'It's not a road I can afford to go down—not now—not ever.' Swallowing hard, she nodded uncertainly.

'Well, as I said, I gave it a lot of thought after you'd gone last night, and I reckon there is only one answer.' He paused, glancing with a quiet smile at Chas's irate face, before continuing quietly, 'If there is a particular road you wish to travel, then I will do all in my power to make that possible!'

With that, he placed his hat back on his head and bowed politely to her before, still smiling, he walked back casually towards his waiting horse.

'What's all this talk about roads and stuff?' Chas turned to Aimée in exasperation. 'What in tarnation is he on about?'

Still staring after the retreating figure, she shrugged helplessly, and called upon all her past acting talent to say convincingly, 'Oh, I wouldn't worry about it, my dear. If I remember rightly, we were only having some silly sort of argument over rights of way between our land and his . . .'

Chas snorted. 'Well, I sure hope you put him right. That guy would steal every last inch if we gave him the chance! I hope I can rely on you to stand up for our rights in a case of land-grabbin', if that's what he's got in mind. If he can't match us for cotton production, then I wouldn't put it past him to have an eye to filchin' some of our forest land. You put him right on that account, I take it, Aimée? You didn't let the varmint off with any nonsense?'

Her eyes narrowed, her heart beating faster, as she

watched the tall figure on the black stallion disappear down the drive in the distance. 'Of course not, Chas dear. Of course not.'

'If there is a particular road you wish to travel, then I will do all in my power to make that possible.' She repeated the words under her breath as she took his arm and descended the steps to their carriage. One innocuous little sentence, but it could mean so much . . .

CHAPTER NINE

'IF THERE IS a particular road you wish to travel, then I will do all in my power to make that possible . . .' Aimée stood at her bedroom window repeating the words that Red had felt it so important to say to her before they left the Carmichaels' that morning. She shivered and went back to bed, slipping in beneath the smooth cotton sheets. What was he trying to tell her—that she should leave Chas and run away with him? Or even that she should leave Four Winds and move into Wildwood? She shook her head. That would be unthinkable, particularly in the South where the greatest store was set by propriety.

It was a question that was to haunt her all that night and all the nights that followed up to Christmas. She thought it might help that she saw nothing of Red between Thanksgiving and Christmas week, but she soon learned to her cost that out of sight did not mean out of mind. Missing him became an almost permanent ache, and she longed for even a sight of him riding the hills above Wildwood on his beloved black stallion. It never happened, and as Christmas drew nearer she pinned her hopes on an invitation to one of the neighbouring houses in the hope that he might also be there. But none came. The Madisons had already moved to Charleston, and with Secession now almost a reality, most of the others were postponing their seasonal celebrations until the New Year, in the hope that they could combine them with a party to celebrate the expected break from the Union.

In her desperation, she even thought of arranging an 'open house' at Four Winds for Christmas Eve, but Chas had been so moody recently that she did not dare raise the subject. In fact, life in general in the great house had been strangely tense of late. Tizzy had disappeared from her personal service not long after they had returned from honeymoon, and as far as she knew, was back on field work, but she dared not ask Chas the reason for this. Perhaps he had simply had second thoughts, deciding that if he was ever to get back into his wife's bed again, he should not antagonise her by the constant presence of his mistress in the house.

Sadie and Pansy, however, were proving able substitutes, and she had succeeded in building up a feeling of trust with them that she hoped extended beyond the normal mistress–slave relationship. But when they woke her with the jugs of hot water and warmed towels on Christmas morning, they were strangely subdued in their response to her cheerful 'Merry Christmas!'

'Is anything wrong . . . Sadie? . . . Pansy?' She looked at each of them as she sat up in bed, feeling with one hand on top of her bedside cabinet for the special little presents she had especially wrapped for them. 'Whatever's the matter? You look hardly full of the Christmas spirit, the pair of you!'

The two girls looked from one to the other, as if loath to be the one to speak first, then Sadie said quickly, 'It's Tizzy, ma'm. She done hab baby.'

'What?' Aimée pulled herself up further on the bed, her eyes staring at their downcast faces. 'A baby?' She looked at each in turn. 'When? When did this happen?' Disgust welled in her stomach as the sight of another little half-caste MacDonald flashed into her mind's eye. So that explained Tizzy's absence from the house—and to think she had never even suspected!

'Jest now, miz. Mebbe half hour since.'

'Good God! Does the master know?' She felt her face flame as she voiced the question, but she had to ask.

At that, Sadie burst into tears and they fled from the room, leaving their mistress sitting white-faced on the bed. It was a most peculiar reaction by the maids, but they obviously felt embarrassment for her at yet another permanent reminder of Chas's unfaithfulness. Probably the whole of the plantation knew by now! They had all probably known about the coming birth for months, and humiliation was to be heaped upon humiliation. There was only one thing for it—she had to see for herself.

Throwing the covers back, she leapt out of bed and pulled on her red quilted dressing-robe, then snatched her cloak from the back of the door. It might not be the done thing to go out dressed in such a fashion, but she was in no mood for a leisurely toilet. Besides, the maids had already vanished downstairs and there would be no one to help her with her stays and gown.

As she opened her door, she was astonished to see Aunt Effie hurrying along the passage towards her own room. Since it was useless to call out because of the old lady's profound deafness, she ran after her and clutched at her arm. To her surprise, there were still wet tears on the old lady's cheeks.

'What's happened, Aunt Effie? Has something happened down in the slave quarters this morning?' She mouthed the words as clearly as she could to make her understand.

'Ay, lass, it has that! But you'll better no ask me about it. You'll better ask that husband of yours!'

With that, she was gone, hurrying down the corridor, her lavender-scented handkerchief clutched tightly in her hand. Aimée stared after her. What on earth was going on? Pulling her cloak round her, she sped down the passage and on down the stairs. She did not stop running until she reached the dirt-track that led into the slave compound. A strange silence hung in the still air, a tenseness broken only by the occasional muted sound of sobbing from a hut here and there. Surely a birth—even a mulatto one—could not cause such an atmosphere, and such strange behaviour from everyone?

Tizzy must be in the medical hut, she thought, as she hurried along the dusty path. Aunt Effie usually insisted that all confinements took place there. Did she know that the child she had probably just seen being born was as much a MacDonald as her nephew himself? Was that the cause of her distress? The old lady's reaction puzzled her. Surely she had seen Chas's illegitimate offspring born before this? She must be well used to it by now. As she approached the long log cabin that served as a makeshift hospital, her pulse quickened and her steps slowed at the sight of the small crowd of women who had gathered outside the door. Almost all were in tears, but there was also an anger in the air that Aimée could feel as she neared the group. They watched her approach with hostility in their dark eyes, so that when she spoke, her words came out in an embarrassed rush.

'I understand Tizzy, my former maid, has had a child this morning. Is she in there?' She indicated the closed door of the hut they seemed to be so jealously guarding.

No one spoke, and only when she repeated the question did they begin to move aside reluctantly to allow her to enter. She opened the door, blinking at first as her eyes became accustomed to the dim light. There were about a dozen beds in the one long ward, filled mainly with old slaves, and the occasional child, but at the far end, one bed had been partitioned off with a rudimentary screen.

Looking straight ahead to avoid the inquisitive stares from the other beds, she walked quickly down the ward and pulled back the rough sacking. Tizzy lay on a straw mattress on the iron bedstead looking straight back at her, and in her arms was a newly-born baby. But it was no MacDonald. It was as jet-black as though it had newly arrived off one of the African slave ships that very morning.

Aimée stared, speechless, at the babe and then at the mother, as Tizzy clutched the child defensively to her breast. She had been crying—that much was obvious —and she averted her face from the curious gaze of the young white woman at the foot of the bed.

'That's your child, the one that was born this morning?' At last Aimée found her voice.

Tizzy nodded, her swollen eyes still fixed on the bare floorboards at the side of the bed.

'May I ask who the father is?'

At that, two large tears formed in the dark, liquid eyes and trickled slowly down the coffee-coloured cheeks as she looked at her mistress. 'Please, miz, save him! Please save Jonah . . .' There was no sign of the haughty superiority that used to infuriate Aimée as the broken voice implored her help.

'I—I don't understand . . . Who is Jonah?'

'Jonah—my man. Don't let them kill him. Oh, please, miz, don't let them kill him!' With a lurch, she reached forward and clasped Aimée's hand, pulling her round to the side of the bed. 'He's a good man, miz—a good man. Don't let massa kill him!'

Aimée attempted to pull her hand from Tizzy's grasp. 'Don't be silly! No one is killing any one—least of all the master. This is Christmas Day—people don't kill each other on Christmas Day!' She succeeded in extricating her fingers as her brows furrowed. 'Who is Jonah, anyway? Is he this child's father?'

Tizzy nodded miserably, silent sobs shuddering up through her body, and tears continued to pour down her damp cheeks. 'The massa, him say he kill mah man, Miz Aimée . . . Oh, please, save him!'

Comprehension began to dawn in Aimée's mind . . . Sadie and Pansy's behaviour this morning; the looks on the faces of those women at the door of the medical hut—and this child, this little coal-black child . . . They all knew only too well what their master's reaction would be to his slave mistress giving birth to an all-black child. 'Don't worry, Tizzy,' she said quietly. 'I'll see to it that nothing happens to your child's father. There'll be no one killed on this plantation—least of all today, I can promise you that!' Even as she uttered the words she knew it was a promise that she could give no guarantee of being able to keep.

With a last look at the sleeping child and the distraught mother, she turned and went quickly up the ward. The huddle of women outside the door moved aside furtively as she appeared, and she glanced desperately at the sullen faces. 'Where is the master? Tell me, please, I've got to know!'

There was no response, and she repeated the question in her most authoritative voice. 'Please, I must know! You, girl, tell me! If you have any regard for that child's father's welfare, you will tell me now!' She directed the command at the youngest of the group, a girl of about fifteen, who from her blossoming voluptuous looks could have been Tizzy's younger sister.

She glanced nervously at the others, then nodded in the direction of the back of the huts. 'Massa at the whipping tree, miz. Him took Jonah!'

The whipping tree! Even the name brought a sick feeling to the pit of her stomach. Without stopping to thank the girl, she clasped her cloak more tightly round her and set off at a run in the direction the girl had indicated. She had never been as far as this into the slave compound before, but obviously something was happening here this morning that was wrong—very wrong.

It did not take her long to find out. About a quarter of a mile behind the huts she came to a clearing in the trees, dominated by a tall elm in the centre. As she approached, she could see very little of what was happening because of the group of male slaves that had either been forced to attend, or had gathered of their own accord, round the tree. She pushed her way through them to the front, to her horror finding herself bearing witness to the scene she had been dreading.

From one of the stronger, lower branches of the elm, a young naked black man hung by his wrists; his back no longer the gleaming ebony of the rest of his powerful body but a bloody red, as the leather whip wielded by his white master struck lash after lash on the open wounds.

'No, Chas, no!' Heedless to the shocked gasps of the spectators, she dashed forward and attempted to wrench the whip from her husband's hands.

'Le'go, Aimée, damn you, le'go!' Chas MacDonald stepped back, his sweating face white with fury as she

grappled with him, holding the whip aloft out of reach of
her seeking fingers.

But still she persevered, tugging at his rolled-up
sleeves, until, in frustration, he lashed out with his arm
and sent her flying on to the red dust. 'Get her outa here,
will ya, Hector!'

An old slave bounded up at the snarled command and
picked his mistress up from the ground, while Chas
turned back to the work in hand. As she watched
helpless, restrained now by the sinewy hands of the old
man, another whiplash cracked out, sending another
spray of blood from the open wounds on the hanging
man's back.

'Stop it! You'll kill him! Dear God, you'll kill
him!'

'Then it'll be no more than he deserves!' Another lash
found its target, but no sound was emitted from the lips
of the young man. His shining black face shone like
polished ebony with the sweat that trickled down from
his brow in rivulets, but his half-open eyes showed only
the whites as his face turned heavenwards.

She started to scream at the stark horror of it all—the
grim pleasure on Chas's face as he administered the
beating; the looks of mute, helpless misery on the faces
of the spectators; and, worst of all, the poor, bloodied
body that swung grotesquely from its ropes less than ten
yards from her.

'Get her outa here!' There was not a single second's
let-up in the methodical crack of the whip as Chas
barked the order. 'Willie-boy, give Hector a hand!'

A young man leapt out of the crowd to take hold of her
other arm, and, still screaming, she was led away down
the path in the direction of the big house. 'You go home,
miz . . . You go home now.' The older slave looked at
her imploringly as she attempted to shake herself free.
'It be no good for Jonah if you here . . . Massa already
angry. It only make him worse.'

She glanced back helplessly in the direction of the
elm. 'I—I promised Tizzy,' she said in a defeated voice.

'I promised her I wouldn't let the master harm Jonah.'

The old man shook his head sadly. 'Jonah no harmed now, miz. Him wid the good Lord.'

'No!' She stared at him, aghast. 'No! The master wouldn't kill him. He can't be dead!'

'Him not dead, miz. Him across Jordan now . . . Him free!' There was a look almost of envy on the old man's face as he said the words. He had seen it all before. His suffering was still going on—but Jonah was already free, in the arms of his Lord.

'This is an awful place! Dear God in heaven, forgive us! Forgive what has happened here this day!' She sank to her knees, her hands clasped in front of her. It was Christmas Day—Christ's birthday. She shook her head as she covered her face with her hands. 'Just go. Just leave me—please!'

They left her alone, kneeling on the dry, red dust of the path, staring with sightless eyes into the clear blue of the heavens. 'I have to go. Dear God, I have to go . . . Help me to leave this awful place before it turns me into one of them!'

She did not go back to the big house straight away, but hid in the scrub that edged the clearing until it was all over and they had cut Jonah's dead body down from the branch of the elm. It lay on the ground, in its own blood, until someone fetched a piece of sacking to cover it to prevent the vultures from finishing the job. Then she walked slowly back to the home she shared with his killer, and shut herself in her room.

After half an hour, she succeeded in composing herself enough to pick up a pen and write:

Chas—
    When you find this note, I shall be gone. Do not try to find me. I should never have come to this place or agreed to be your wife. The fault is mine. May God forgive me for my mistakes —and you for yours.
Aimée.

It took her a further half hour to dress in a travelling gown and pack her biggest trunk with a selection of her clothes. Sadie appeared as she pressed the last gown into the chest and fastened down the lid and, without explanation, she instructed the puzzled girl to order the buggy. 'I'll manage it myself today. Please don't bother with a driver.'

The journey to Wildwood took her the best part of an hour. There could be no question of going anywhere else. She could not spend another minute in the home of Charles MacDonald, and Red was the only person in a position to help her. And help her he must.

Nevertheless, her heart was beating rapidly as the wheels of the buggy rattled up the wide oak-lined drive to the Wildwood mansion. She pulled it up in front of the main steps and hooked the reins over the balustrade.

To her consternation, her tug at the bell was answered not by Red but by the housekeeper, a small white-haired Irish woman, who regarded her curiously out of shrewd, brown eyes. 'Yes?'

'Is—Is Mr Redmayne at home?'

Her nod brought enormous relief. If he had been in New Orleans on business, whatever would she have done? 'I'd be obliged if you would tell him that Mrs MacDonald is here to see him—Mrs Aimée MacDonald.'

Red listened in silence to all she had to say, his dark brows drawn into an irregular line as he paced the floor in front of the roaring log fire in the drawing-room. When she had finished and had sat back exhausted on the plump satin cushions, he looked down at her for a long time before finally saying, 'Well, honey, it seems you have finally burned your boats!'

'I can stay, then?'

'Don't you think this is the first place he will come looking for you?'

'Probably, but I really don't care any longer.'

'What if I said I was leaving here myself tomorrow?'

'Then I'd simply ask to come with you. I presume you will be going back to New Orleans on business—or at least to some other town from where I can make my way back to England?'

He nodded slowly as he regarded her thoughtfully. It was impossible to tell what was going on behind his sleepy-lidded gaze as he said quietly, 'You've really made up your mind this time, haven't you? Well, far be it from me to try to persuade you otherwise . . . I'll be passing through New Orleans before going on to my grandfather's home, if that suits you. I usually spend a few days with him at this time of year. Christmas isn't quite the same on your own.'

'Good heavens, it's still Christmas Day!' It suddenly seemed like some absurd joke.

'Perhaps we should drink a toast then, Aimée?' He walked to a round rosewood table and poured two generous glasses of port. 'What'll it be, then? What would be an appropriate salutation?' He handed her one of the glasses and looked at her enquiringly over the top of his own as he said softly, 'How about—To you, my dear Aimée?'

She felt herself blush as she looked down into her wine. 'It is your home . . .' she whispered back. 'I should return the compliment. How about—To you, Daniel Redmayne?'

He walked towards her and touched his glass to her. 'In that case, my dear, it seems like it has to be—To us . . . Here's to us, *ma belle* Aimée!'

'To us,' she whispered in reply, as a strange sense of foreboding overcame her.

'New Orleans! This is really New Orleans, Red . . .' Aimée turned to the man by her side, tingling excitement running through her as they leaned against the rail of the *Queen of Cities*, as she pulled gracefully into her berth in the great Gulf port. In a curious way it was almost like coming home. After all, hadn't the family of her great-grandmother, the beautiful French actress

Marguerite Duval, come from the original historic town of Orléans in France?

Her green eyes scanned the bustling levée, narrowing against the brightness of the winter sunshine. Everywhere were black bodies, as slaves sweated to heave the great bales of cotton on and off the waiting steamers that crowded the wharves. Beside the cotton stood barrels packed with pickled foods, rum, tar, rich aromatic coffee and salted meat and piles of tobacco, hemp and animal skins. Dealers called to one another in the rich Creole patois, and she strained her ears trying to decipher this strange hybrid of the French language.

As they moved slowly down the gangplank, her head rang with the clanging of countless bells, the constant clatter of the drays that waited at the water's edge for their heavy loads and the mournful sound of the slaves' songs. Red's reassuring hand was on her elbow, although they spoke little because of the noise. He had been strangely quiet over the past twenty-four hours —distant, almost—but, in a way, it was a relief. It would make her task that much easier once they arrived in the city itself.

She had been deliberately vague to him about her immediate plans on arrival. It was too embarrassing to admit she did not have sufficient funds to book her passage home to London. Many times she had felt he was on the verge of questioning her on her intentions, but something had held him back. It was as though everything that had seemed to exist between them had been a figment of her imagination. His resolve that they must let love and happiness be their guide seemed bitterly ironic, now that her life was to be dictated by the lack of money. There was nothing for it, she had decided on the boat; she must rely on the hope that that poster she had seen all those months ago in Charlotteville was not too old and that Fanny Baker was still in New Orleans. She would find the Pleasure Palace and apply for a job like Fanny's, and work there until she could save enough money to make her way back to England.

But Red must never know. She did not want his sympathy, and her pride would not allow her to take his money.

'You're sure you won't change your mind and let me see you safely into a good hotel? You're being very mysterious, Aimée . . . I don't like it. I feel responsible somehow.' His blue eyes looked down in concern as he took her elbow once more and moved her out of the way of a rolling bale of cotton.

'There's really no need for that, Red, I can assure you! I'm a married woman now—remember? I'm perfectly capable of taking care of myself.' Her voice was light, and she deliberately avoided his eyes as she adjusted the ribbons of her bonnet.

'Well, give me your address, at least—somewhere I can reach you and satisfy myself that you're all right.'

'I don't think that would be a good idea, somehow.'

'Why, Aimée, why?' His hands gripped her shoulders, forcing her to look at him. 'Grant me that much at least! You can't just disappear out of my life like this.'

'But I can, Red, and I must. I would not be doing you any favour by staying in contact with you—nor you with me. We both know that. The best thing we can do for each other is to fade quietly, and quickly, out of each other's life.' She laughed light-heartedly as she pulled away from him. This had to be one of her finest acting performances.

He said nothing more, but his face remained a frozen mask until eventually they were able to claim their trunks. 'You'll at least allow me the satisfaction of seeing you safely into a cab, then?' A nerve twitched at the side of his clenched jaw as he waited for her answer.

'I really don't think so. I'd prefer it if you went first—honestly I would.' On no account could she allow him to overhear her request to be taken to the Pleasure Palace.

They stood facing one another on the crowded quay. Why did he have to look at her like that? She felt as if those eyes were touching her very soul. With an enormous effort she succeeded in keeping her lips frozen in what she hoped passed for a casual smile as he took her hand and raised it to his lips. 'Regrettably, this is finally *adieu*, then, monsieur.'

'No, *ma belle* Aimée, not *adieu*—never *adieu*—just *au revoir*. This world is not so big that you can run away and hide from me so easily.'

She threw back her head and gave a light laugh. 'Are you telling me you intend coming to seek me out as soon as I disappear? This is no child's game of hide and seek, sir!'

'No, that is true, and we are no longer children. But, when the time is right, I shall find you again. When that day will be, I cannot say. When this coming war is over, perhaps . . . I do not know for certain, but you will look up one day and find me there. I promise that.'

She made no reply, but the smile on her face had melted, and fearful of what her features would reveal, she turned abruptly and walked over to a nearby cab. In as low a voice as possible, she instructed the driver to take her to the Pleasure Palace.

Red stood silently watching as, once her trunks were loaded on board, the cab disappeared. There was so much he could have said—perhaps should have said, but the situation was almost impossible. He could never have taken Aimée—Charles MacDonald's wife—back to Wildwood with him. They would have crucified her. He had done the only gentlemanly thing possible in letting her go. With an impatient wave of the hand, he gestured for the next cab in line to draw up and load his baggage. Life had to go on, and there was a lot to be done before this coming war was upon them.

Before Aimée settled in her seat, she leaned forward and called out to the driver, 'You wouldn't happen to know who runs the Pleasure Palace, would you?'

The driver, a little old Irishman, chortled, showing the stumps of a row of decayed teeth. 'Sure and I would

—there's not a better known face in the whole of Basin Street than that of Sadie Fitzgerald!'

There was something about his manner when she mentioned the Pleasure Palace that sent a shiver of unease through her, but she pressed on nevertheless. 'In that case, you wouldn't know if she still has a singer by the name of Fifi Boulanger working for her?'

The old man chortled once again. 'Now there's a pretty filly, an' no mistake! She's about as French as my Aunt Sally, but she's popular with the boys, all right! You a friend of hers?'

Unwilling to give too much away, she fell silent for a moment. 'We—We met some time ago in London. I thought perhaps I might look her up.'

'You'll not get her—or any of 'em—up at this time o' day. But I wish ye the best o' luck! You should get Sadie around, though.'

Aimée's unease grew. Just what sort of theatre did this Sadie Fitzgerald run?

She was soon to find out.

The cab drew up outside a tall white building, and the driver got down and lifted her heavy trunk from the back shelf. She sat silently, her eyes transfixed on the heavy walnut door with its brass knocker in the shape of a naked Venus. Before she could make a move, the door opened and the liveried figure of the doorman appeared; red-coated, white-gloved, and with a black top hat which he removed with a flourish as he opened the cab door for her to get out.

As she turned to pay the driver, the cold, sinking feeling she had felt earlier, then dismissed, returned in full measure. 'It—It's not a bordello, is it?' she whispered to the cabbie in as low a voice as possible.

'You'd best ask Sadie that, m'dear. You'll be meeting her soon enough!'

Still quaking, she followed the doorman through a marble-floored foyer, in which stood a life-size alabaster statue of the same naked Venus as on the knocker, then on into an elegant hall, its high ceiling a superb elliptic dome from which hung a glittering crystal chandelier.

A young male mulatto slave, about her own age, carried her trunk, waiting silently behind them as the doorman handed her over into the charge of an equally elegantly liveried servant. 'You prefer to speak English or French, madame?'

'Oh . . . English. It—It doesn't really matter,' Aimée replied, glancing round her uncertainly.

The man smiled indulgently. 'Your name, then?'

'Aimée—Aimée Fitzwilliam!' She did not mean to lie. It came automatically. She could never think of herself as Aimée MacDonald.

'I'll inform Madame Sadie of your arrival.'

Within minutes she was ushered into a room that was the last word in rococo luxury. Although it was still only late afternoon, the windows were discreetly covered with a red silk material beneath rich red velvet drapes that gave the room a restful rosy glow. In one corner was a magnificent grand piano, and along each wall stood overstuffed sofas, plump with elaborately embroidered cushions. On rosewood side-tables between the sofas stood gleaming brass ashtrays and small alabaster statuettes of nudes in various reclining poses. The remaining furniture, which was gilt and obviously French in origin, stood on multi-coloured Indian carpets, and the walls seemed to consist entirely of gilt-framed plate glass mirrors, which made the room seem much larger than it was. Above the marble fireplace hung a magnificent oil reproduction of Botticelli's *The Birth of Venus*. It was all of twelve feet high, and Aimée's eyes were drawn immediately to the creamy-white skinned nude with the long golden hair.

'Beautiful, ain't she?'

She gasped, her head swinging round in the direction of the voice. She had no idea there was anyone else in the room. The voice, which was female and still retained a slight Irish brogue, came from the direction of the thick, tasselled drapes that shaded the wide veranda windows.

'My fella always said the dame in that picture reminded him of me, so he got an artist pal of his to paint a
replica. When he died, he left it to me in his Will . . .
Along with a good bit else, I'm happy to say!'

The speaker was a small buxom woman in a flounced
black moiré gown. She was heavily made up, with hair
that Aimée imagined had been once golden—the same
shade as the Venus in the Botticelli painting—but was
now dyed a brilliant orange and heavily padded out
with a platform of false ringlets at the back. 'Sadie
Fitzgerald's the name—pleasure's the game!'

A plump beringed hand was extended as she came
forward from the shadows and Aimée shook it politely.
The older woman's pale blue eyes regarded her curiously. 'I understand you asked to see me. What can I do
for you? Have you come here to bawl me out about a
wayward husband, or are you after a job?'

Her bluntness took Aimée's breath away, but she
found herself warming to this overblown rose of a
woman. 'A—A job, actually . . . If there's one going.'

Sadie Fitzgerald's pale brows rose half an inch as she
looked her up and down. 'You done this sort of work
before—as a *fille de joie*?'

'A *fille de joie*?' Aimée exploded, pulling herself up to
her full height at this polite French euphemism. 'Don't
you mean "whore", ma'm? Are you asking me if I'm a
whore?'

Sadie's brows knitted for a moment, then a smile
creased the ageing face. 'Now, now, don't go gettin' on
your high horse! I didn't think you looked like the usual
dolly-mops I get coming here begging me for a job. What
do you do then, Miss Aimée Fitzwilliam—for that is
your name, ain't it? The foyer flunkey said you were a
Fitz like me. That's half the reason I told them to bring
you in here—I don't usually agree to see any old person
off the street without an appointment, you know. My
time's much too valuable!'

Aimée's colour subsided, but she retained her dignity.
'I certainly haven't come here to beg from anyone,' she

said coldly. 'I understood you employed entertainers
. . . I've obviously been misinformed.'

Interest flickered in Sadie's eyes. 'An entertainer, eh?
And just what do you do, Miss Fitzwilliam?'

Aimée ran a smoothing hand over the green taffeta of
her dress. 'I—I'm an actress, but I've done a little
singing in the past.'

Sadie tapped her closed fan on her ample bosom and
looked pensive for a moment. 'Ah, a little songbird!
And from London, too, by the sound of it. I swore I'd
never employ another from that darned place after that
flibberty-jibbet Fifi, but you look a more sensible gal.
Right, Miss Aimée Fitzwilliam, let's be hearing
you!' Her potential employer motioned her to a seat
at the grand piano in the corner. 'You do play, I take
it?'

'A—A little.'

'Know any of Burns's songs?'

'One or two.'

'My man was from Scotland . . . Give me "My Love is
like a Red Red Rose", it was his favourite.'

Aimée took a deep breath, the words of the old love
song returning to her memory as she spread her fingers
on the keys. She got to the end of the last verse:

    Till a' the seas gang dry, my dear,
    And rocks melt wi' the sun,
    And I will love thee still, my dear,
    While the sands of life shall run.

At that point, Sadie's tears were spilling down her
rice-powdered cheeks, and, to her consternation,
Aimée's own eyes were sparkling as the old love song
plucked at heart-strings still too painful to be exposed in
public like this. The two woman looked at one another,
each searching in the voluminous folds of their skirts for
a handkerchief.

'Looks like you got the job, honey! You can start

tonight. Marcus will show you to your room. We always have a couple of spares. There's always one of my gals taking off with some sweet-talkin' fella or other.' Sadie's pale eyes darkened at the thought, then lightened again. 'Mind you, most are back within a couple of days—when the money runs out! But that's neither here nor there. You just concentrate on getting yourself done up for our customers tonight. They pay good money to hear the likes of you entertain them, so you'd better be good!'

Sadie's words were to echo in her head over the next hour as she sat in the plushly furnished bedroom she had been allotted at the back of the three-storey house.

From what she could gather from Marcus, the mulatto slave who showed her to her room, the Pleasure Palace itself was a theatre-*cum*-restaurant next door which acted as a front for the real business of the redoubtable Sadie Fitzgerald. Madame Sadie was, in fact, the most notorious—and most expensive—Madame in the whole city. Not that she approved of being referred to as such: let anyone dare to utter the word 'bordello' in her hearing!

But whatever her private thoughts about Sadie Fitzgerald, Aimée resolved, that remarkable lady was now her employer and she must attempt to live up to the trust invested in her by doing her best by the customers who would be paying tonight to hear her sing.

From what she could gather, it seemed that Fanny Baker—the incorrigible Fifi—had disappeared the week before with one of the young well-heeled stage-door Johnnies who queued backstage each night with an armful of roses for their favourite act, and Sadie had been desperately seeking a replacement. Aimée knew that, with a bit of luck, she could be the one, and, if so, it was more than she had ever dreamed of. To top the bill at the Pleasure Palace was to earn more than any other entertainer in all New Orleans—and to become the toast of the town into the bargain. Her heart leapt at the prospect.

CHAPTER TEN

THE CHEERS RESOUNDED the length and breadth of the theatre as the pale, dark-haired young woman walked back slowly to the stage and then halted in the centre of the small flight of steps that led up to the platform. The rustle of the skirts of her watered silk gown could be heard by the small groups of soldiers sitting at the tables nearest the stage, and a faint whiff of French gardenia perfume tantalised their senses, making them raise their voices even louder in the shout that went up from the capacity audience: 'Lorena! Lorena! Lorena!'

The chant continued, causing Aimée to raise her hands as if in benediction to the gathered multitude. Her eyes scanned the elegant theatre, with its gilt carved balconies and handsome Doric columns. The place was home to her now, and had been for the past sixteen months. Yes, it was all that time ago since she left Red standing on the levée after they had disembarked from the *Queen of Cities* and she had set eyes on New Orleans for the first time.

She had intended being back in England by the time war broke out, but events had overtaken her. When the first Confederate shot was fired over the Union-held Fort Sumter just ouside Charleston harbour, no one doubted that South Carolina had lit the spark which would soon set the whole of the South ablaze. The outbreak of war came as a surprise to no one, but as the months dragged on and the cheering died to an echo in the memory, patriotic fever gave way to a starker reality. Fathers, brothers, husbands and sweethearts were dying out there, and as tragedy touched every home, a closeness came into every community. From the smallest village to the great bustling cities, the citizens identified with their boys in grey. As for the soldiers themselves,

the memory of the girls they had left behind became
embodied in the songs that were being sung and in the
singers of those songs, as they congregated in the music-
halls and burlesque-houses during their precious respite
from the battlefield.

Never in her wildest dreams, either in London's
Gaiety Theatre, or at Four Winds as Chas's wife, could
she have imagined that one day she would become the per-
sonification of all those missing sweethearts for so many
men. New Orleans had taken her to its heart. Within
days of taking over from Fanny as top of the bill at the
Pleasure Palace, they had claimed her as their own. 'The
Belle of New Orleans' the billboards proclaimed her,
but very soon that title had given way to another as she
became identified with one of the most sentimental
ballads of lost love to come out of the war that now raged
around them—'Lorena'. Aimée Charlotte Sophia
MacDonald—née Fitzwilliam—from London had been
turned into 'Lorena—the Belle of New Orleans'.

But, somehow, to be adored by the multitude was
never quite enough; there was always something—
always someone—missing. When the applause rang out
in the auditorium night after night, she continued to scan
the sea of faces before her. Every night for sixteen
months she had done the same. Sometimes her heart had
even leapt in her breast at the sight of a dark, curling
head of hair and a pair of bright blue eyes, only to sink
again in disappointment. It was never him. Never once
at all those hundreds of performances had she set eyes
on Daniel O'Connell Redmayne.

Her net-mittened hands fluttered in the air once more.
'Not that one again, please! I've sung it four times
already. I'll do one more verse of any other, then that's it
for the time being!' Her gaze fell on a dark-haired young
man at a table in the front row, with the same thick
curling hair that she had pictured so many times in her
dreams. 'What about you, young sir? What would you
like to hear?'

' "Juanita", ma'm,' he stammered, rising to his feet.

'It's my girl-friend's name. I'd like to hear "Juanita".'

'Then so you shall, but only one verse, mind! I've already overrun my time!' She smiled down at him, then turned to her accompanist at the piano. 'Let's do one verse of "Juanita" for the soldier, Maurice!'

A hush descended, and as her eyes found those of the Zouave soldier seated before her, she sang the sentimental ballad especially for him. Tears were sparkling in the young man's eyes as she finished, and in many more around the crowded theatre, as, after curtsying deeply to the audience, she stood up and blew kisses in three different directions, then turned and walked quickly backstage.

Emotions had been running high in the city recently. Rumour followed on rumour, each one more alarming than the last. The more faint-hearted—or plumb-crazy, Aimée was never sure which—were declaring that King Cotton was dead and any day now the city would fall to the Unionists. But as the cheers died to an appreciative buzz in the Pleasure Palace, there were few in the city that night who realised how close was the end as far as the Confederate hold on the city was concerned. The sight of the Union navy ships off the levée sent the population into a state of immediate panic. Those brave souls who ventured down to the waterfront area reported that the whole place was ablaze—ships, steamers, coal, cotton and property were alight in one huge conflagration.

As the news swept along Basin Street, the inhabitants of Madame Sadie's Pleasure Palace grew increasingly restive with excitement. Throughout her stay, Aimée had attempted to maintain a discreet distance between herself and the *filles de joie* in the other part of the building, but it was impossible not to be affected by the prevailing mood, which, was now verging on hysteria. Many, with beaux fighting for the Confederacy, were panic-stricken at the thought of not being able to receive any more visits now that it looked as though the Unionists were in charge.

Aimée's own heart sank as the news came in. New Orleans was falling, she had no doubt, and it seemed that the whole of the South was doomed. Her chances of running into Red again were diminishing by the minute. She was sure he would be in the Army by now, and even if he were lucky enough to obtain leave of absence, he would never, wearing the Confederate grey, dare to show his face in this city. If he were still alive, that was! The thought that this might be the last show she would give to their own men only made matters worse as she flicked through her wardrobe of gowns for the late performance.

Her fingers finally settled on a blood-red satin, heavily flounced in fine white silk tulle around the hem, and she would wear fresh white roses in her sash and in her hair. White for honour—to honour all those boys who had come to hear her sing over the past year and were probably lying in a muddy field somewhere, wishing the cruel war was over.

'When this cruel war is over . . .' She murmured the words of the popular song under her breath as her eyes misted over. Yes, she would sing that song for them tonight. And if there were Unionist soldiers already there and they arrested her for it—then let them! But it had been a Northern song originally, hadn't it? Didn't someone tell her they had changed the words, so that they applied to the boys in grey?

She gave a wistful sigh an hour later as she peeped out behind the heavy velvet curtains that draped the stage. A lost love was as keenly felt in New Jersey or Illinois as in Alabama or Louisiana. She would be singing for them all tonight—for every young man in uniform, whether grey or blue. She let the curtain drop back, a tremor ran through her body. She was nervous. For the first time in over a year, she was actually nervous! As always, being top of the bill, she went on last and sang for an hour. But she had the distinct feeling she would not get away quite so quickly tonight. Her audience was clinging to an era that was passing in the life of the city. If it was true that tomorrow belonged to the North, tonight still belonged to them—and the South!

The lamps on either side of the platform dimmed and then flared into a blaze as she walked to the centre of the stage to be met with the most rousing applause of her career. The whole audience stood waving their hats in the air and calling, 'Lorena! Lorena! Lorena!' Tonight, more than ever, she was the embodiment of every sweetheart, every wife, from whom they were now parted, and knew they might never see again.

They were all so young looking. Despite the luxurious sidewhiskers, moustaches and fine beards, most of them were little more than boys. And tonight they were her boys, as she sang favourite after favourite, their massed voices joining in the choruses until there was not a dry eye in the house. As the last notes of the last song ended, hanging in the air like a haunting memory in the heart of every man present, there was complete silence. No one moved; no one spoke; no one cheered; no one dared break the spell. Except for one man.

Out of the darkness at the back, one man walked slowly forward. A tall man dressed in dark evening clothes, a black scarlet-lined cloak round his shoulders, his shiny black top hat held in a white-gloved hand. He walked slowly and deliberately down the centre aisle, his eyes fixed firmly on the young woman in the centre of the stage.

When he got to the foot of the steps, he extracted a single red rose from his hat and walked on slowly up the steps, the rose held before him. Not once did his blue eyes blink or waver for an instant from those of the young woman.

'Red!'

'I warned you I would find you, didn't I? I said I would come back.'

'Red . . .' Aimée could only repeat his name once more.

He handed her the rose, then lifted the fingers of her other hand to his lips. The curtain came down immediately, but neither was aware of anything or anyone as his eyes smiled down into hers. 'You were good, Aimée—darned good!'

'Thank you, sir.' She was glad he had not called her 'Lorena'.

He offered his arm, and she took it as they walked slowly backstage towards her dressing-room, quite oblivious of the whispers and stares of those around. They did not speak on the short journey, and by the time he closed the dressing-room door, the whole thing had taken on a curious dream-like quality. She entered the room first, and caught her breath sharply when he quietly turned the key in the lock before turning to bathe her in that faintly mocking smile.

'Red . . . I—I can't believe it's really you!' His face swam before her, the bronzed features gloriously near as she feasted her eyes on the deep blue, slightly hooded eyes and the quirkily smiling mouth. Surely she had to be dreaming . . . after all this time?

'You're not dreaming, Aimée,' he said quietly, as though he had read her thoughts. 'It really is me. It's taken a long time, but I'm back.'

She longed to ask for how long, but dared not. 'But the war . . .' Her eyes flicked over the immaculate broadcloth of his evening suit. 'Aren't you fighting?'

An enigmatic smile played at the corners of his mouth. 'I'm doing my bit. I'm actually down here on business —Confederate business.'

'You're not in the army, then?'

'If I had to categorise myself, I guess I'd say the navy, more like . . . But even that wouldn't be quite true.' His eyes searched hers, as though he were unsure how much to divulge.

She sensed his dilemma and said quickly, 'Of course I don't mean to pry, if it's something that shouldn't be discussed.'

He took her hands in his, his thumbs caressing her slim fingers. 'It's not that, honey, but I would be grateful if you kept it under your bonnet when I'm gone. You see, the South needs supplies—badly—and I'm just one of the guys trying to arrange it.'

Her eyes widened as fear gripped her heart. 'You mean you're blockade-running?' She had heard of those men who were risking life and limb to run the gauntlet of the Federal navy to get the cotton across the Atlantic to the empty mills of Lancashire and bring much-needed supplies back to the South.

Amusement showed in his deep blue eyes. 'Well, you can give it any fancy name you care—but it's a job that has to be done.'

'But why you, Red? Why are you doing that dangerous work? You don't actually sail on the boats yourself, do you?' This was more than she could bear.

He shrugged his broad shoulders. 'Sometimes it's required, sometimes it ain't. More often than not I'm simply the organiser. I know that east coast like the back of my hand. To be honest, that's really why I was landed with this job. Pierre Beauregard remembered from our days together in Florida and Louisiana that I had a pretty good aptitude for finding my way about all those creeks and inlets round there.'

Aimée's eyes widened even further, her thoughts flying back to that night at Judge Carmichael's so long ago. 'Pierre Beauregard! You mean you really are an old friend of the General?'

He laughed once more—the title obviously amused him. 'Yup! I have been for more years than either of us cares to remember! We were at West Point together, but he stayed in the Army and is now one of our finest officers. It was at one of the Confederacy's first high-ranking pow-wows that he thought of me. Everyone knows the quickest way to bring the South to its knees is to stop the flow of cotton to England and stop the flow of essential supplies coming the other way. Ol' Pierre knew High Command needed men who know a bit about the cotton business—and who know that coast pretty well—so he got in touch. Simple as that!'

Aimée blenched. It wasn't simple—anything but!

Blockade-running was a highly dangerous occupation, and the thought that he was actively involved in it made her blood run cold.

'New Orleans should never have fallen, you know!' A frown creased his brow. 'It's the biggest blunder the South has made—neglecting its navy! Anyway, I've been working with an ol' sea-dog who really knows his stuff, and now it's up to the likes of men like myself to try to make up for it, but, God knows, it ain't gonna be easy!' His fists clenched and unclenched before he turned to look her straight in the eyes. 'But enough about me, Aimée . . . What of you?'

She made a hopeless gesture with her hands. Where did she begin? There was so much to say, but somehow the words stuck in her throat. She had dreamt so long about this moment, but now that it was here, she was completely at a loss.

'Your running out on ol' Charlie-boy sure caused some tongue-wagging around Craven County, I can vouch for that!'

She smiled, her cheeks colouring. 'I expected it would. I've never regretted it though, Red—not for a minute. The only regret I have—and I shall carry it to the grave with me—is in marrying him. But I am paying dearly for my mistake. In many ways it is worse than being a widow. At least then one may have the memory of a genuine love to look back on, and perhaps the chance of another in the future, with no stigma ever attached to a new liaison . . . But what have I? Nothing but bitter memories and no future!'

She shook her head. Just seeing him like this, standing before her, the living, breathing embodiment of all she could ever pray for in a man, was simply too much. Why had he come? Why must she be tortured like this? Even if, by some miracle, he felt the same—they could never marry. There could be no future for her with any man, let alone with Daniel Redmayne.

He came over and took her hands. 'The mistake wasn't yours, Aimée . . . it was mine. I've thought a lot about what happened at that time, and I should have seen it would never work with you and Chas. But I was sure, once you got used to Southern ways, you could be happy at Four Winds. I guess I didn't bargain for things turning out quite the way they did with that . . .'

'No, don't say it! Don't talk about it!' she interrupted quickly. He must not mention that awful episode of the killing of the slave; it had haunted her dreams ever since that terrible day. 'I had no idea Chas owned any slaves before I came over here! He never mentioned it, and somehow it never crossed my mind.' She paused, looking him straight in the eyes, as she said with a wry smile, 'If I had been more intelligent, perhaps I could have found myself an eligible Southern beau who did not feel it necessary to own other human beings.'

He dropped his eyes and gave a dry laugh. 'Do such creatures exist?'

'Why, sir, I do believe I'm looking at one!'

Their eyes met and held. Then he took a step towards her, but she moved aside, walking quickly to the door, where she stood with her back pressed against it. Things could get out of control, and it would be all her fault. She wasn't prepared, wasn't ready for this—not yet, not like this. 'I—I'm tired, Red . . . I'm sorry.'

He touched her cheek with his fingertips. 'I'm the one who's sorry. Aimée. I've turned up out of the blue like this, when you've just been through an exhausting hour-long act. I'll go now, but I'll be back tomorrow, and I'll . . .'

A sharp knock on the door prevented him from finishing the sentence, and she moved aside quickly to open it.

'Beggin' yo' pardon, ma'm, but Madame Sadie—she want an extra performance tonight. Them customers —them no goin' home, no, ma'm! So Madame Sadie, she tell 'em you do one more encore.' Marcus, the mulatto slave, stammered the news out, his eyes darting apologetically from her face to that of the man behind her.

'Like hell she will! She's tired—can't you see that! Tell your darned Madame that Lorena's finished for tonight!' Red's eyes blazed as he made to slam the door in the man's face, but Aimée prevented him.

'No, Red, wait!' She squeezed herself between Marcus and the door. 'Tell Madame I'll be right down, Marcus.'

As he hurried back along the passage in the direction of stage, she turned to Red. 'I can't let them down, Red, not tonight. I'm not doing it for Sadie, but for all those boys out there. With the Yankees in charge, I might not be able to do it for much longer.'

'But, Aimée . . .'

'No, Red, please . . . Tonight is for them.'

'And tomorrow for us?'

She did not answer, but tiptoed up to place a quick kiss on his cheek before hurrying down the lamp-lit passage in the direction of the waiting crowd.

> The years creep slowly by, Lorena!
> The snow is on the grass again.
> The sun's far down the sky, Lorena . . .

She was never to reach the end of the song, for Lorena —every soldier's favourite belle of New Orleans—had swooned and was carried from the stage before the end of her last encore.

In a city already rife with rumours of all sorts, by the next morning the news had penetrated even the elegantly-appointed dining-room of the St Louis Hotel less than a mile from the Pleasure Palace. The tall dark man seated in the alcove by the window sat up, straining his ears to hear the hushed conversation of the two waiters at the breakfast buffet table behind him. To his acute frustration, the one who was talking turned his back, deliberately lowering his voice so as not to disturb him. With an embarrassed cough, Red leaned over and touched the young man on the sleeve. 'Beggin' your pardon, but did I hear you mention something about Lorena?'

The black-moustached face turned towards him in surprise. 'Why, yes, sir. I was just telling Jean-Paul here—it was my night off last night and I managed to get a ticket for the Pleasure Palace. The place was packed, and the audience just wouldn't quieten down. They were yellin' for encore after encore. It was sure no surprise the little lady couldn't take it no more.' He paused, shaking his head at the memory. 'I reckoned they had shot her at first—one of them damned Yankees, that is—but it seems like she had only swooned.'

Red's dark brows furrowed. 'She's all right now though, ain't she?'

'Well, I don't rightly know, sir. They brought the curtain down directly. But Madame Sadie came on right after to say Lorena would be taking a break for a few days . . .'

Before he reached the end of his story, Red got up from the table. 'Thank you kindly, young man, that's all I need to know.' A silver dollar was pressed into the astonished waiter's hand as Red made for the door. He did not even wait to finish his hot waffles and coffee, preferring instead to grab his soft felt hat and dash out into the sunlit street to hail a cab.

His fingers, in the white kidskin gloves, drummed anxiously on his knee as the carriage rattled through the busy streets. She had been overdoing things. He should have insisted that she did not do that extra encore.

Aimée was up but not yet dressed, when despite the protestations of one of the liveried house slaves, Red brushed the man aside and burst into her room.

'Red—what on earth are you doing here at this time? It's not even nine o'clock!'

She was sitting on the small dressing-stool in front of the mirror, dressed only in a pale pink cotton wrap and matching nightgown, and she whirled round in amazement at the sight of him in the glass.

When he strode across the room, she jumped up from

the seat and backed nervously against the dressing-table, but there was nothing but compassion in his eyes. 'Are you all right?'

Her hand flew to her hair, only recently released from its night-time braid. 'I—I'm fine,' she said haltingly, running a hand over the long dark mane. 'Why have you come, bursting in like this? Is something wrong?'

'You tell me!' he said tersely. 'What on earth happened on stage last night?'

She shrugged. 'It was nothing—really. I—I felt a bit faint, that's all. How on earth did you find out? You weren't out there in the audience, were you?'

'No, drat it, I wasn't! I overheard two of the waiters talking about it over breakfast this morning and came straight over.'

'There really was no need for that, I assure you. I'm perfectly all right now, really I am. People shouldn't go gossiping and spreading alarm like that over a trifling incident that could have happened to anyone.'

'Thank God they did! And it didn't happen to anyone, Aimée—it happened to you. And what happens to you ain't ever trifling to me. Anyway, it brought me to my senses! You need a break. You've been working too darned hard for your own good, and I'm going to see that you get one. I'm due at a house-party at La Terre d'Or—my grandfather's place—today, and you're coming with me. You'll enjoy it, Aimée. It's nothing imposing—just a small group of Confederacy Army officers and their wives. There'll be good food and good talk.'

She sat down on the stool again, feeling her legs go weak beneath her, and shook her head. 'How can I—a cabaret singer—go as your guest to a place like that?' She had heard of the wealth and influence of the de Maupassants in and around New Orleans, and could just imagine the type of place he was referring to.

He knelt down on one knee and took her hands. 'Precisely because you are my guest, Aimée! You are the one I wish to accompany me, and you'll be the most beautiful lady there. I can vouch for that!' He touched her cheek, smoothing back the long tendrils of dark hair behind her ear. 'It's time you had someone looking out for your welfare, and, for the time being at least, it's gonna be me!'

La Terre d'Or stood, white and stately, in the rich golden corn and cane country fifty or sixty miles below New Orleans, on the narrow strip of land that protects the Mississippi channel on either side from the Gulf of Mexico. 'The best land in the world' they called it down here, and Aimée could understand why, as her eyes took in the rivers and bayous which yielded fish and oysters by the ton, and the dark moist earth where plantation-owners grew rich on the sugar-cane, corn and rice, the fruit and vegetables which grew in tropical abundance. It was almost nightfall when they arrived, and sad cypresses and live-oak forests were casting dark shadows over the sluggish swamps as their coach rattled its way over the rough roads.

At one point, Red beckoned to her to look out the window. 'That's Contreras—the Beauregard plantation,' he said, gazing out through the dusty glass. 'That's where I first met Pierre.' But she could see little in the gathering twilight.

As the carriage turned up the long drive of the de Maupassant mansion almost an hour later, she felt the reassuring touch of Red's hand on her arm. No word was said, but she was grateful for his unspoken concern. 'How many people will be there?' Surprisingly, it was the first time she had thought to ask.

'Oh, fewer than a dozen, I guess—and a handful of wives. As regards the family, there's only Grandpa left, and Madame Edith, the housekeeper.'

She nodded. With such a houseful, she could surely fade quite happily into the background for most of the time. They were met at the door by the housekeeper, a rather formidable grey-haired woman of uncertain years. Aimée was aware of her shrewd eyes behind her pince-nez scrutinising every inch of her travel-weary figure as they shook hands, and she was conscious of a childish urge to make a favourable impression. There was little time for more than a few rudimentary pleasantries, however. Red was impatient for her to meet his grandfather.

The old man was seated in a bathchair in the library, a red plaid rug over his knees, and his eyes lit up at the sight of the two of them in the doorway. For a moment Aimée could do little but stare at the striking face and shock of white hair. It could have been Red himself forty years on.

They conversed mainly in French, and to her consternation, Red lost little time in confiding to the old man that his beautiful lady guest was in fact the popular chanteuse, Lorena, from New Orleans. But, to her delight and amazement, the old gentleman did not appear in the least shocked. On the contrary, he was clearly delighted and much amused by the news.

'You've been doing as much as many fighting men to win this war for us, mademoiselle!' he insisted, before they went out. 'Perhaps you'll do us the honour of singing for us before you return to the Queen City?'

'With pleasure, sir,' she murmured as she offered her hand to be lightly touched by his lips, acutely aware of the smiling Red by her side. It obviously meant a lot to him that his grandfather approved of her, and *vice versa*.

Her room was on the second floor, large and airy, and furnished almost completely with Louis Seize pieces that Aimée had no doubt were genuine. She had declined the offer of supper, accepting only a glass of milk and a small plate of molasses cookies, and as she prepared for bed, a curious thrill ran through her. Here she was in Red's family home, about to go to sleep in a de Maupassant bed—and he was only along the passage, less than a hundred feet away!

It was a long night, hot and humid, and she slept little, tossing and turning in the wide bed until the sun crept over the great spreading oaks that bordered the house.

She rose and walked to the window, throwing open the veranda door and wandering out on the balcony. She always thought of this as the silent hour—that time, just after sunrise, when the world was not yet fully awake and no one in the big house was stirring. Only the slaves, out of sight in their quarters, had already risen to greet the coming day.

A gentle rain had fallen. She had heard its soft spattering from her bed, and now, sparkling like jewels in the first rays of the morning sun, the droplets lay like jewels on the glossy oval leaves of the magnolia tree beneath the window. She could almost reach out and touch the blossoms—the petals as creamy-white and soft as her own skin. Their perfume wafted up to her on the slight breeze. The heady scent almost overpowered her senses as she closed her eyes and turned her face to the heavens.

It was so like Four Winds—so very like Four Winds. But perhaps all plantations felt the same . . . Perhaps it was like this at Wildwood, too, in the early hours of the day. Her eyes misted over as she opened them and gazed out over the green and pleasant land that was La Terre d'Or. She would never know. Whoever eventually became mistress of Wildwood, that beautiful place up there in faraway Craven County, it would not be her. It could never be her. She was Mrs Charles Stuart Mac-Donald, and no one could ever change that inescapable fact of life.

With a sigh that came from the heart, she turned and made her way back into the bedroom. In a few hours she must go down and meet the other guests at breakfast. It was a daunting prospect.

The others were already seated at table when she walked into the long, light breakfast room at a little after eight o'clock—nine men and four women, all older than herself. The men rose to their feet as she entered, and Red made the introductions. All were quite high ranking officers, but Pierre Beauregard had not been able to be present. He had been almost constantly employed in the fighting zones, and it seemed that even a few days' rest in his home County would not be possible for some time to come.

To begin with, the talk was of battles won and battles lost, until Mamie Johnston, one of the women, gave a polite, but very deliberate, yawn and said in a loud voice, 'Gentlemen—please! Can war manoeuvres not keep until you retire to the smoking-room? I'm sure there are more pleasant things we can be discussing right now on a beautiful spring morning! Don't you agree, Miss Fitzwilliam?'

Aimée looked up startled to find herself being addressed directly. A pink flush rose to her cheeks as she glanced round the table. 'I—I'm sure you must be right,' she said haltingly, unsure whether it was polite to agree with this reprimand of the gentlemen or not.

'Good! Now you see even the least warlike among us agrees with me!' Mamie Johnston looked triumphantly round the table. 'Now let's change the subject to more light-hearted matters! Tell us about yourself, my dear! Where are you from, and what are you doing in these parts? That accent was never from this side of the Atlantic, of that I'm sure! Unless you're from the very highest echelons of New England society, that is! You're not from Boston, by any chance?'

Aimée's colour deepened. 'No, I'm not from Boston —or New England. I came from London, England, originally.'

'Oh, really?' All eyes joined those of Colonel Johnston's wife to alight on the young English woman in growing curiosity. 'And just what brings you to Louisiana?'

Drat the woman! She was not going to be put off, that was for sure. 'I—I'm working as a governess in New Orleans at present . . .' She came to a halt, ashamed of the lie, but totally unable to tell the truth, because of the shock it might cause. Red glanced at his grandfather at the opposite end of the table, then across at her; a deep frown etched on his brow. He was annoyed that she had lied, she could see, and felt utterly miserable for the remainder of the meal. When it ended, she rose quickly and made for the open door that led to the outside terrace. All she wanted to do was to get away from the inquisitive eyes and ears of the other females. She was not one of them, and she was certain they could sense that fact and were out to embarrass her at every possible opportunity.

She wandered out across the lawn to a small pond where willows trailed their branches. It was bordered on the far side with dogwood trees, their blossoms like spring snow against the bright green leaves. Then she sat down on a garden seat beneath the luxuriant foliage of a Chinaberry tree, its spreading branches with their strange umbrella shape offering perfect shade against the bright sunshine. From somewhere above a whip-poorwill was calling and a mocking-bird answered, imitating the sound. Insects were dancing, suspended in the light, and the air droned with the sound of their humming. After the early morning rain everything was fresh, and with a contented sigh she closed her eyes and leaned back.

'Aimée, how could you? How could you embarrass me like that?' Red's voice cut through the silence like a knife, making her eyes jerk open. She sat up, smoothing the pink muslin of her skirts as she squinted at him in the bright sunshine. 'Why did you lie like that—deliberately mislead those people about what you did?' There was real anger in his eyes and voice.

'You—You know why I did it,' she said defensively. 'I didn't want to embarrass you, that's all!'

'Embarrass me!' he exploded. 'Why, in heaven's name, should you embarrass me? Don't you know I've spent the best part of my life fighting against the type of mean-mindedness that you are now endorsing? Good God, woman, didn't we both suffer from that, way back in Craven County?'

She nodded miserably. He was right. Of course he was right, but that didn't make it any easier. 'Maybe I'm just not as strong as you are, Red,' she said softly. 'Maybe I just prefer an easier life.'

He took hold of her wrist, pulling her to her feet. 'If we're to have any chance of a life together, girl—any chance at all—then you'd better get it into your head that taking the easy way out is no damned good! You've got to be strong, Aimée—strong! God help me, I can't do it alone!'

A shout from across the lawn indicated that the others were waiting for him to join them on the terrace. He glanced back at her startled face and opened his mouth to say something further, then thought better of it. 'I've got to go now,' he muttered. 'But remember what I said. For God's sake—and our own—remember it!'

She watched him go, striding over the lawn—a tall, powerful figure that she could already imagine in the grey tunic and sky-blue trousers of an officer. His words burned into her brain. Whatever had he meant by them? Surely he knew as well as she did—better than she did—that the thought of any life together was impossible—totally out of the question? A shiver covered her skin beneath the pink muslin with gooseflesh. She was sure of nothing any more . . . Not even of life itself, with this awful war raging over the land.

The rest of the day passed at a leisurely pace. She spent most of the time in the garden, walking and reading. She had always felt at ease in her own company and had known very little of it of late. She was aware of the other ladies passing comments among themselves, and could imagine at the speculation that was going on behind her back. They would be forecasting wedding bells between her and Red before the year was out—the war permitting, of course. If only life were so simple!

Conscious of her desire to keep her profession private, his grandfather did not attempt to keep her to her promise to sing for the assembled company, but when after dinner that evening a sing-song developed spontaneously around the piano in the drawing-room, she was only too happy to take part. Mamie Johnston started the proceedings with a rousing rendition of 'Dixie', then two of the other wives followed with a duet of 'My Old Kentucky Home', despite a protest that Kentucky folks had failed to show 'true grit' and had come out, albeit belatedly, in favour of the Union.

Oblivious of her other life, one of the company suggested that Aimée should entertain the company with a solo performance, but she declined with a reluctant shake of the head.

'Oh, come now, my dear! Someone of your pretty looks must be able to sing for her supper! Why, I reckon you're even prettier than that floozy they call Lorena who's so popular in New Orleans at the moment!' Seth Dupont, a Major in the Zouaves, looked around him for confirmation as he extended what he regarded as a great compliment to the attractive dark-haired young woman.

Aimée's face flamed as she caught Red's eye, and she could see by the set of his jaw that he was as upset as she was. A floozy—that's what she was, wasn't it? A floozy who had no more right to sit at the same table with these people than the slaves in the South had to dine with their masters. 'I—I'm rather tired,' she heard herself murmur as she stood up and attempted a strained smile. 'If you'll excuse me, ladies and gentleman . . .'

She fled from the room, and Red caught up with her as she reached her own door. 'Aimée—wait!'

She turned to him, her face still flushed. 'Don't say anything,' she pleaded. 'Major Dupont is right. You know it, and I know it. That's what I am, Red, isn't it—a floozy? Not only am I a wicked woman who has run away from her husband, but I'm also a cheap floozy from the most splendid little whorehouse in town!'

He grasped her shoulders, shaking her like a rag doll. 'Don't say that! Don't ever say that! You're more than that, Aimée, much more than that! You're . . .'

'What am I, Red? What am I?' Tears burned in her eyes as they searched his.

'You're the woman I love, goddamn it, Aimée— you're the woman I love!'

'No! Don't say that! Don't ever say it. Just let me be, Red, I beg you. Haven't we tortured each other enough?' She flung the words at him as she wrenched herself free, and throwing open her door, dashed inside and closed it in his face, turning the key firmly in the lock.

Her heart was beating so hard that it was almost painful beneath the tight bodice of her gown as she leaned back against the door. She walked to the window and gazed up at the moon, hanging like a gleaming silver scimitar in the night sky. He was in love with her! Red was in love with her!

A shudder ran through her body, and her fingers touched the bare third finger of her left hand where a gold band should be. Tears blurred the moon, high in the sky above. She could remove the ring from her finger, but she could never remove the heavy weight of it from her heart. She was Chas MacDonald's wife, and it would do neither her nor Red any good to forget it, even for a moment.

CHAPTER ELEVEN

'AIMÉE! AIMÉE! Are you awake?'

The insistent tapping on the oak panels and Red's voice behind the closed door roused her from sleep. 'What—What is it?' She sat up, blinking her eyes against the bright sunshine that already filled the bedroom.

'May I come in?'

Before she could answer, his head appeared round the edge of the door and he slipped into the room, closing the door softly behind him. 'I'd better be careful—we don't want to cause any scandal, do we?'

The irony in his eyes and voice was not lost on her, but she chose to ignore it. 'It's very early, isn't it?' Her eyes glanced at the small clock on the mantelpiece. It was just before seven.

'I know!' He sat down on the edge of the bed and leaned over to place the most featherlight of kisses on her brow. 'I wanted to see you before the others are up. It looks like the house-party is breaking up this afternoon, for there's just too darned much happening on the war front. I tell you, Aimée, whichever side wins, this thing will have paid one helluva price for victory!'

Fear clutched at her heart. 'You want to be there with them, don't you?'

He nodded; his features set in granite. 'It's not enough any more to be hidden away in some office planning blockade-bustin' strategy. I've got to be out there with 'em, Aimée! I've got to be there slugging it out in the mud with the rest. Otherwise I'd never look myself in the face afterwards.'

She stared at him mutely. So this was goodbye. What did she do? What did she say? 'You—You're leaving now?' Her voice was barely above a whisper.

He shook his head. 'That's why I'm here. I'm leaving with the others this afternoon. I—I thought we might take a walk up the bluff before the rest are up. It's the last chance we'll get to be alone together.'

Their eyes met and locked. There was so much left to say, yet so little time to say it. 'I'll get dressed.'

Hand in hand they headed towards the river and climbed the narrow path up the western slope of the bluff, pausing every now and then to look down at the lush green acres of La Terre d'Or.

'It should be La Terre Verte!' Aimée said softly. 'The Green Land—not the Golden! Everything is so fresh and beautifully green!'

Red paused, his arm loosely round her shoulders, as he scanned the panorama below. 'You should see it in the fall,' he said softly. 'It's golden then, all right. Standing up here at that time of year is like looking down on a cloth of gold that has been spread out as far as the eye can see.'

'Will all this be yours, too, some day? Will you be the master of La Terre d'Or as well as of Wildwood?'

She felt a tenseness in his grip as his face hardened. 'Will there be anything left to be master of when this bloody war is over? Nothing is certain right now, Aimée, nothing—even life itself!'

'No! Don't talk like that! I won't allow it!' She swung round to face him, concern and anger clouding her eyes. 'Nothing's going to happen to you, Red . . . It—It can't—not now that we've found each other again.'

He made no reply, but took her hand, and they resumed their climb. The path was steeper now. The spring rains had washed away part of it and he walked ahead, for the last few yards digging out footholds for her with the toe of his boot. When he reached the top, he swung himself on to the ledge that jutted out several inches above them, then reached out with both hands and pulled her up. For several minutes they remained, locked together, silhouetted against the endless sky, as they gazed down. Up here they were above it all—above the disapproving gaze of a society which condemned them to deny their love—above the war itself.

Behind them was a small copse of oak and hickory trees, and he led her to a patch of soft dry grass beneath their spreading branches.

'What will happen to us, Red? What will become of us?' She turned to him, her eyes pleading for him to answer the unanswerable question, as she sat down, spreading out her skirts.

He lay on the ground beside her, his fingers pulling a long stalk of bent grass from a clump at the foot of the tree by his elbow. His lips twisted cynically as he gazed out with unseeing eyes into the azure-blue of the sky. 'Life is short, a little love, a little dreaming, and then, Good-day!'

She turned to face him, her lips repeating the words, feeling the hot sting of tears in her eyes. 'You can't mean that! You can't really believe that's all there is to it!'

He shrugged and lay back, his arms behind his head. There was still a bitter smile on his lips, but his eyes were not smiling. 'Right now, yes, I do believe that. I suppose, in a way, that's why I sought you out after all that time. I knew you were someone else's wife and could never be mine, but somehow it had ceased to matter. The social niceties no longer existed—the war had changed all that. When you've lived for a whole year not knowing if you would be alive the coming week, quite frankly, my dear, you don't give a damn about social conventions! Nothing can ever be the same again.'

'So we take what we can, while we can, and to hell with the consequences?' Her voice was little above a whisper.

'I didn't say that.' He threw the blade of grass aside and sat up. 'We have to pay for everything in this life, Aimée. Nothing is free. I learned that a long time ago.'

She stared at him, her eyes brimming. 'I didn't ask to

love you . . . Must I go on paying for it for the rest of my life?'

Suddenly the time for games had past. The war had taught her that. There was no time left for charades.

'A place in thy memory, dearest, is all that I could claim . . .' His voice, huskily low, repeated the words of one of her most popular songs. 'But it's not enough, is it, Aimée? It's just not enough . . .'

She shook her head as the tears spilled over her lashes. 'No, Red, it's not.'

He was silent for a long time. His features seemed set in granite, except for a tiny nerve that twitched at the edge of his clenched jaw. She had never seen a look in his eyes like this before and her heart pounded mercilessly in her breast as she attempted to hold his gaze. She could not cry—she must not cry. But emotions were welling within her that she could no longer control.

He gently wiped away the tears that glistened like diamonds in the sunlight on her pale skin. She caught her breath as he moved closer, his fingers moving down to caress the sensitive skin at the nape of her neck beneath the thick dark hair. His eyes seemed to darken and glow with an intensity that scorched her very soul. He did not speak, there was no need, his eyes were now saying all there was to say.

Her body trembled beneath his touch as the years between melted away in the warmth of the morning sun. Everything seemed heightened—the sky more blue than she had ever seen it; the air more pure; the sunlight more golden.

'Red . . .' Her lips formed his name as his mouth moved towards hers. Then suddenly she was in his arms, her body arching beneath him as his lips blazed a trail of kisses down the pale curve of her throat to the soft swell of her breasts.

She was not aware of the shedding of their clothes, only of the searing ecstasy as their bodies met, naked and unashamed, beneath the blue infinity of the sky. All the pain, all the loneliness, was wiped away with every slow, sensuous caress of his hands on the trembling white skin of her body. Tears blinded her, and she closed her eyes as his lips kissed her soaking lashes and cheeks, and he murmured her name, 'Aimée . . .' She was hearing it for the first time, for he had made it, too, into a caress, and his breath was warm on the wet skin of her face as he breathed it over and over again.

The salt of her tears was on his lips as they found hers, and her mouth parted in silent invitation. At first he was gentle, infinitely tender, as if it was not a living, breathing woman in his arms but the most fragile creature, made of the finest porcelain. But, as his kiss grew deeper, she felt his body change; the golden skin beneath her hands turned from velvet to gleaming metal. Her hands moved up through the curling hair on his chest to his shoulders, her nails digging into the smooth flesh, and her body became one with his.

It had never been like this with Chas—never. And could never be with anyone else, she knew that now. Never had she been more sure of anything. She was no longer a separate entity but a part of him, as, breath for breath, heart on heart, their bodies melted into one pulsating whole. Time and place lost all meaning. Nothing existed but the two of them. The war and all its heartaches dissolved into the clear morning air. Touch, taste, smell were all, as he filled her senses to overflowing and sensation mounted on sensation.

Then suddenly the world exploded, and she cried his name out loud as together they came tumbling back to reality, their naked bodies glistening and exhausted on the bed of warm earth beneath the whispering trees. For a long time neither spoke, and as she lay quiet and still in his arms, her head resting on the soft dark hairs of his chest, she felt her very heart would break. He had promised her nothing, but had given her everything. Nothing in this life would ever be the same again.

They dressed slowly and in silence, as though to speak would be to break the spell that still held them enraptured. If they were to return soon to this hell they called

war, then today, together, they had for a few precious
moments known all there was to know of heaven. No
one could take that away from her—not ever. And,
when the time came for them to walk down the steep
path together to his grandfather's house, she knew if she
were never to see him again, she would have no regrets
for what had happened here today.

She left him on the terrace, staring out over the soft
green sweep of the lawn as she made her way indoors.
The housemaids were already laying the table for breakfast, but she had no appetite and asked to be excused
both breakfast and luncheon before retiring to her
room, pleading a headache. The mulatto maid brought a
little laudanum to relieve the pain, and she took it
gratefully before lying down on the patchwork quilt. The
maid drew the curtains, bathing the room in a soft grey
light before withdrawing silently to reappear several
hours later to assist her in changing into her dark blue
moiré travelling-gown.

Red had suggested she stay on longer at La Terre
d'Or, but all she wanted was to get back to New Orleans.
The thought of staying on in this beautiful place without
him was unbearable. Here they were almost untouched
by the bloodshed that was raging further north—and, if
he was willing to put his life at risk by joining the Army,
she, too, must do something. Just what, she had as yet no
idea, but at least getting back to New Orleans was a
start.

Everyone assembled on the terrace directly after
luncheon to prepare for departure, and Aimée was
astonished to see that all the men, except Red, had
changed into the smart grey tunics and blue breeches of
the Confederate Army. The officers, it appeared, were
leaving unaccompanied by their wives, and Red was
travelling with them. She watched as he took his leave of
the other ladies, his tall figure in the light grey frock-coat
bending to kiss each hand in turn. When he came to her,
she was aware that all eyes were upon them as they stood
less than a foot apart on the stone-slabbed terrace.

She could not bear to meet his eyes before his dark head bent to kiss her hand. But when he refused to release her fingers until she did so, she was forced to look up and meet his deep blue gaze. 'Not *adieu*, my love,' he said softly. 'Never *adieu*, Aimée.'

Tears sparkled in her eyes, transforming the sea-green to a deep emerald. 'Only *au revoir, mon amour*,' she nodded. 'Only *au revoir . . .*'

The cabaret was already in full swing when she got back to the Pleasure Palace, but she deliberately avoided the theatre, unable to face the gay hilarity of the comic songs, or, worst of all, the sad, sentimental ballads that rang out as the audience joined in the well-loved choruses. Instead she went straight to her room, where she threw herself on the bed and stared up at the ceiling.

Her misery was too great for tears. It was as though part of her—the most important part, her heart—had been wrenched from her body. She felt empty, incomplete. But never, not for one second, did she regret that he had come back. He had claimed her for his own, if only for a few stolen moments.

The days dragged into weeks, each one more unbearable than the last. At nights, in the theatre, it was a sea of blue she saw—not grey—as Union soldiers replaced those of the Confederacy. And they, in their turn, raised their caps and voices to call for 'Lorena' every night. But it was no longer enough. She had no quarrel with any of them, but every blue uniform reminded her bitterly of the man she had lost. The man who, she knew, was now wearing the Confederate grey.

She had heard nothing of Red since they had said goodbye on the terrace of La Terre d'Or. She was convinced he would be in the Army by now, perhaps even in action; but where, or in what capacity, she had no idea. Perhaps it was just as well, she tried to tell herself, as she went though the familiar but monotonous routine of her life at the theatre. What she didn't know, she couldn't worry about. But it was not as simple as that—in fact, it was exactly the opposite. Because she did not know where he was or what he was doing, every scrap of information about every battle or skirmish, no matter how slight, she pounced upon.

As time passed, it became more and more difficult to remain civil to the increasing numbers of Union officers who came backstage after each performance to pay their respects. They were not her enemy, but they were his, and the knowledge twisted a knife deep into her heart.

It was just after her last song of the evening on one hot, humid night in June, that she received an extra special, but deeply resented, visitor. General Benjamin Butler himself, the Union officer in charge of the city, called backstage with his entourage to pay his compliments. Like everyone else at Madame Sadie's, she had heard of the fearsome ex-Massachusetts lawyer now referred to by all and sundry as 'The Beast of New Orleans', but never had she imagined she would actually be required to meet him face to face so soon.

'So this is Lorena!' The harsh, but exceedingly articulate, voice seemed incongruously out of place in the short, stout body on the spindle legs when the General came forward to greet the young woman he had heard so much about since taking up residence in the city. A slightly sweaty palm was extended as he regarded her curiously from beneath heavy-lidded eyes. He had a high, intelligent forehead, but his lack of hair made his head appear much too large, and his free hand mopped his perspiring brow as she allowed her hand to be shaken. 'I've heard a great deal about you, m'dear. You're doing a great job for the morale of the men.'

She bobbed a curtsy, taking care to make it only a very slight one, as he looked her up and down.

'I understand you're English,' he said. 'So I guess you'll not be taking sides in this little old dispute of ours!'

Aimée flinched. He made it sound like an accusation. 'My heart is with every man on every battlefield,

General. The blood on the furrows is the same red, whether the coat be blue or grey!'

He looked at her closely. 'Well, I'll be darned! But I reckon you're right there, ma'm! Trouble is, not too many of your townsfolk here see it quite like that. Far too many of 'em take a real pleasure in seeing Union blood spilt—and often on these very streets!'

He turned to his men, and there was a murmur of agreement and a solemn nodding of heads as he continued. 'I understand there used to be a picture of your so-called President Jefferson Davis hanging behind the stage out there during the performances?'

Aimée remained silent, unsure of what was coming next.

'Well, you can deny it if you choose, but the fact is there's to be another to replace it from tomorrow. A picture of the only genuine President of this here country—Abe Lincoln—will hang there from now on, flanked by two Union flags! And you'll all be required to swear an oath of allegiance to the United States government. It'll mean a spell of Desolate Ship Island for any female who refuses! With so many of my men frequenting this type of place, I can't afford any traitorous whores—beggin' your pardon, ma'm—spreading dissent among the troops. It's either that, or we close all these places down!'

'I trust you're not referring to me in that category, sir?'

'Now, Aimée, hold your fire there!' Sadie Fitzgerald's voice cut in. 'I'm sure the good General meant no such thing.'

All eyes turned to the buxom figure in the doorway as Sadie made her entrance in a cherry-red taffeta gown, deeply flounced in white tulle, her orange ringlets as lifeless and profuse as ever on the plump shoulders. 'I heard tell you and your men were on the premises, General, so I took this opportunity to invite you all upstairs for a toast to the Union!'

Aimée stared at her in disbelief, but there was no trace

of irony in her employer's voice. Sadie obviously believed in dancing to whatever piper happened to be playing the tune—and right now that piper happened to be Ben Butler.

The General himself seemed slightly nonplussed by the suggestion, but felt honour bound not to refuse an invitation to drink to the success of the Union cause. His men, on the other hand, beamed their enthusiasm to their hostess. Unable to get out of it, Aimée was forced to follow the party upstairs to Sadie's best salon, where a choice group of her *filles de joie* were already seated on the plush sofas. The girls got up immediately the Union men entered and clustered round in a highly-perfumed cloud of rustling dresses and fluttering eyelashes. Despite their previous protestations at remaining true to the Confederate cause, they had been as keen as their Madame to encourage trade with the blue-coated victors.

With a clap of her plump hands, Sadie summoned two negro footmen resplendent in red and gold livery, who came forward bearing silver trays filled with brimming champagne glasses and handed one to each of the soldiers and ladies.

'Well, General, here's to a very happy stay in our fair city to you all!' Sadie beamed as she raised her glass to touch that of Benjamin Butler, then spread her smile around the assembled company.

'To the Union!' the General pronounced.

'The Union!' chorused his officers, before swigging most of the sparkling drink in one gulp.

Within five minutes, however, the General had excused himself, but left his men with firm instructions to inform the inhabitants of the building and the adjoining theatre of what would be required of them under the new régime. Once he had left, all pretence at official army business disappeared, and the remaining men were only too happy to pair off with their increasingly solicitous hostesses.

Aimée found herself seated next to Major Bradley

Hoskins, a short, stocky man in his sixties with a gleaming bald cranium that was compensated by a luxurious
growth of thick white sidewhiskers and a Van Dyke
beard. Feeling obliged to engage him in conversation, she asked politely if he had seen much action
of late.

'That I have, m'dear, that I have! I had the good
fortune to be under the command of two of the finest
men ever to wear a blue coat—Ulysses Grant and Will
Sherman—at Shiloh!'

Her eyebrows rose. Several weeks back the newspapers had been filled for days with the terrible slaughter
that had taken place near the small church at Pittsburg
Landing. 'I understand the losses were terrible there
—thousands dead and dying on both sides.'

The old man's brows furrowed. 'Indeed, m'dear,
indeed! It was a victory at a price, and no mistake: well
nigh twenty-five thousand dead on that battlefield! Can
you imagine it? I walked among them myself when it was
all over, and the cries of those boys will live with me till
the day I meet my Maker!'

'Twenty-five thousand!' Aimée repeated, horrified.
'And, no doubt, many thousands more wounded?'

'Uncountable, m'dear, uncountable! And almost no
one to tend 'em!'

Her face paled. 'Were there no hospital facilities?'

'Hospital facilities!' A gnarled hand was slapped on a
blue-trousered thigh. 'What hospital facilities? I tell
you, if one of those boys in a thousand saw medical care,
he was darned lucky! Field hospitals just don't have the
men—or women—to man them!'

'You mean they accept women for that type of work?'
She sat up on the edge of the padded cushion.

'They'll accept the devil himself—provided he comes
armed with disinfectant and bandages!' the Major replied with a wry laugh. 'But why the interest in all
that blood and gore? A pretty gal like you wouldn't
know anyone interested in that type of work, would
you?'

She looked him straight in the eyes as she came to a decision. 'Yes, I would, Major. I most certainly would!'

CHAPTER TWELVE

AIMÉE'S HEAD REELED. There had been so many bodies
. . . Dear God, so many bodies! Some scarcely more
than boys. Would this murderous war never end? It was
two-thirty in the morning and still the ambulance-trains
were arriving to disgorge their bloody, pathetic cargo on
the lantern-lit platform. The flower of Robert E. Lee's
army, now reduced to this!

Her eyes, red with lack of sleep, scanned the covered
wagons waiting to trundle them through the darkness to
the makeshift sanctuary of the field hospital. After
almost two years, she thought wearily, she should be
hardened to it by now! Antietam, Chancellorsville,
Vicksburg, Gettysburg . . . So many battles, so much
blood split on this beautiful land. And still it went on.

Her life at the Pleasure Palace seemed like another
world. Was it really she—the same person who now
stood dirty and blood-spattered on this station platform
—who had once spent each day dressed in the finest
gowns, the toast of the greatest city in the whole of the
South? That Major Hoskins had a lot to answer for! But,
if she ever met him again when this cruel war was over,
she would thank him. She would thank him from the
bottom of her heart.

The past two years had been harrowing, yes, and so
tiring that some days she felt she would never be able to
wake up again once her head hit the pillow of her hard
camp bed, but they had also been the most worth while
of her life.

Clara Barton and Dorothea Dix had been her inspi-
ration—two women who had shown the way for others
to join the intrepid band of volunteer nurses who moved
with the armies from battlefield to battlefield to tend the
wounded and bring what comfort they could to the

dying. She had made it her business to find out all she could about their work, and then, in the certain knowledge that what she was about to do was right, she informed Madame Sadie that she would be leaving at the end of the week.

They had all thought she was mad, but had admired her spirit nevertheless. In fact, Sadie had made quite a show of her last performance at the theatre, and Aimée had stood in the middle of the stage in tears as bouquet after bouquet of flowers were pressed into her arms; then, when she could hold no more, they were laid at her feet until she had to wade through the sea of blossoms when the curtains came down for the very last time on 'Lorena'.

Behind the desire to do something more positive, to give back in kind a fraction of the loving response she had received from all the men who came to hear her sing, was the burning hope that one day she would meet Red again. For the past two years, throughout the long days and nights as she toiled through the scorching heat of the summers and the bitter cold of the winters, that flame had never ceased to burn in her heart. And, as time went on, it had become a fire burning deep within her breast. She had heard fourth- or fifth-hand reports that he had been seen by someone, who had mentioned it to someone else . . . and so it went on. But she knew almost certainly that people were only trying to be kind. Just staying alive had become a major operation for the men who still rallied behind the now tattered flags of both sides. There was no time or energy to be wasted by enquiring after an unknown man, no matter how pretty the nurse who had begged them for the information.

In the distance a train whistled, and there was more movement on the platform. Other nurses, their blue gowns now a dull dirty grey with the dust and dried mud, bustled forward to greet their next consignment of wounded. Behind them, cavalry horses moved like ghosts in the gloom of the lanterns. This strange, unreal world was now the only one that existed. It took almost

two hours to relieve the carriages of their cargo
of human misery, as men and boys on improvised
stretchers were carried to the waiting wagons and carts
that would take them the remaining few miles to the
hospital. She gave a wry smile. 'Hospital' was a very
flattering word for the group of makeshift huts and tents
that lay spread out in the field on the edge of the war
zone.

She travelled in the last of the wagons with six of the
more seriously wounded men. Two were unconscious,
and one cried out loud every time the wheels jolted over
a particularly rough piece of ground. Part of the gunshot
was still embedded in his thigh and the discoloured flesh
was swollen and hideous beneath the ripped and
bloodied blue trousers. The youngest of them, a fair-
haired boy of little more than sixteen, refused to release
his fevered grip on her hand as they made the rough trek
up to the hospital camp. His thin fingers dug into her
own with a painful urgency that made her wince, but she
did not complain or attempt to remove her hand. Her
suffering was nothing compared with theirs.

In the opposite direction, on the way towards the
station they had just left, came a dark moving serpent. It
was a line, broken and ragged, of grey-coated soldiers,
their regimental flags waving like ghosts' wings in the
night breeze. Aimée gazed at them from the back of the
wagon. Their faces thin and dust-covered, with a week's
growth of stubble, had that strange haunted look caused
by lack of food. And their eyes, in hollow sockets,
burned like hot pitch through lack of sleep. They had
borne witness to sights no man should ever have to see.
She knew, for she had seen them, too. Her hand still
clutched in that of the young boy by her side, she leaned
back and closed her eyes. Perhaps, God willing, she
might get a little sleep tonight, once the wagons had
been unloaded and their occupants settled for the night.

Because of lack of medical supplies, it was almost
impossible to tend to all the men's wounds. She herself
no longer possessed a single petticoat—all had gone to

be torn up as bandages. It seemed that every moment of their spare time—what little there was of it—was spent in tearing up ladies' petticoats. Was there a single female left in the whole of the South with more than one to her name? She doubted it!

Morning dawned cool for early May, with a mist that lay like a blanket around the surrounding countryside. Small craft on the river in the distance rose like phantoms from the thick grey haze. There were twenty-nine ambulance carriages, someone had counted, on the train that had come in the night before, and more were expected before the morning was over. And, through it all, the walking wounded never ceased—the gaunt, forlorn backwash of battle that came in their thousands from the fields of slaughter that surrounded them on all sides as the two great generals, Robert E. Lee and Ulysses S. Grant, fought in out in the Wilderness.

'Would you care for another cup, Aimée?' Lizzie-Ellen Monihan offered the can of hot brownish liquid made from okra seeds that was a substitute for coffee, but her colleague shook her head.

'Thank you, no. I'm not that desperate! One cup will suffice.'

The two young women had been working side by side for the past three months and had proved a great comfort to each other. Lizzie-Ellen's husband, a dashing young cavalry officer, had not been heard of since the Battle of Gettysburg the previous summer. It was a subject neither of them ever discussed, but Aimée was well aware that the reason the young fair-haired girl had joined the nursing fraternity was to seek him out. Her eyes burned with the same fever as her own whenever a new consignment of casualties arrived, and they anxiously checked every wounded officer in case a beloved face was discernible beneath the dirt and stubble.

The main hospital quarters for the most serious non-infectious cases consisted of an old warehouse with barred windows, dirty floors and long rows of rude bunks, with only inches of space between each. By some miracle, a fresh supply of carbolic had arrived the previous day, and the two women set to work to boil two pails of hot water to use part of the precious disinfectant to attack the lice and other vermin that seemed to lurk everywhere. They decided to start at opposite ends of the wooden floor and hoped to meet in the middle within an hour. Lizzie-Ellen collected her bucket and headed for the back of the building, and after rolling up her sleeves, Aimée got down on her hands and knees to begin at the door.

The great swing doors were fully open, and as she bent to begin her task, a sound like rubbing sandpaper came filtering towards her on the morning air. A brigade was passing through on its way towards Richmond, a passing runner informed her. The cooks had been advised to prepare breakfast, as the men had been on the march throughout the night. It was a common enough occurrence, with so many men grouping and regrouping to try to stem Grant's advance towards Richmond. It meant more work for the hospital staff, especially the cooks, but no one minded. All knew that the approaching soldiers were much worse off than themselves. The marching feet threw up a dustcloud that obscured the sun, which had now broken through the morning mist, and Aimée stood up to avoid the worst of it. It seemed to cling to every pore, and sometimes she felt as if all the waters of Tennessee could never make her clean again.

Each man in the column wore it like a mask, their sidewhiskers, moustaches, beards and the bush of hair thrusting out from beneath their forage caps were all a whitish grey, and when one of the figures suddenly broke rank and let out an exclamation of 'Great Jehos'aphat!', she shrank back in alarm. The man was tall and gaunt beneath the grey of the major's coat and cape; his light blue trousers and black boots a uniform dustcolour. He stared down at her with that same almost half-crazed look that she had come to recognise so well.

'Can I help you, sir?'

He continued to stare, as though unable to believe his own eyes. 'Has it been so long, *mon amour*? Don't you even recognise me?'

Her legs went weak beneath her. Surely it couldn't be? Not after all this time! Not here in this godforsaken place!

The eyes, still the same brilliant blue, were now red-ringed, the whites a painful pink from the swirling dust as they stared at one another. Then suddenly she was in his arms, her tears making tiny dirt-streaked rivulets down her cheeks. 'Red! Red! Red!' She could do nothing but repeat his name, as his hand stroked her long hair, now caught in a bun at the nape of her neck.

'At ease, men! Take your rest!'

With a thankful murmur, for they were too weary to cheer, the men broke rank and congregated around the cook-house door, many pulling ill-fitting boots off their painfully swollen feet. They had been on the road for the best part of a week, and sleep and whatever proper food was available was essential before the final push.

Once they had settled, Red led her gently by the elbow and they sat down together by one of the big coffee-boilers, while the cooks dished up a breakfast of fried oatmeal and eggs to the foot-weary men. As he ate, she was unable to halt the flood of words that poured forth from her lips. There was so much to tell—so much time to make up.

He was astonished to find her here, imagining, when informed that she was no longer in New Orleans, that she had gone home to England. 'But why, Aimée, why? You don't have to mix yourself up in this! It's not your war.'

She looked across at him through tear-blurred eyes. 'How can you say that, Red? It's your war, isn't it? And if it's yours, then it's mine too.'

He took her hands in his, looking down at her fingers with their painfully cracked nails, then turning them over to shake his head at the calloused palms. 'Oh, Aimée . . . *Ma belle Aimée* . . . What can I say?'

'You can say you love me.' Her voice was barely audible.

'I love you . . . I love you . . . and I adore you!' He lifted her work-worn hands to his lips. 'There can never be any doubt about that!'

He lowered his eyes and they alighted on the tiny gold necklet of interlocked hearts. 'You've still got it!' he exclaimed softly. 'You still wear it!'

'I've worn it every day since the day I found it. I've worn it since my wedding day.'

'Your wedding day!' His eyes clouded as he spat the words out. 'How could I? How could I have let you marry that son of a bitch!'

She shrugged helplessly. 'Remorse for the past is useless, Red. I learned that a long time ago. I'm Chas's wife only on paper. Not in my heart.'

'Only on paper! My dear, isn't that enough? It means you're tied to that bastard for life! Ordinary people don't get divorced—leastways not here in the South. And certainly not the MacDonalds! Weren't they Jacobite Catholics who fled the country after the 'Forty-five rebellion? I'm sure I heard tell of that.'

She nodded miserably. It was true. 'It—It seems so unreal . . . I don't even use his name! I don't even know where he is, now. He could be still "pleasuring" Tizzy —or killing even more slaves on the plantation, for all I know—pleading a weak heart or some such nonsense to evade conscription. Plenty do!' It was impossible to keep the bitterness from her voice.

Red's face hardened. 'He's not. He's up in Georgia, and a captain, the last I heard. Might even be a major, same as me, by now!'

Aimée fell silent. No matter what she now felt about her husband, she would not wish him in this hell. 'Does he know I'm still in this country?'

'Darned if I know; I haven't passed more than half a dozen words with him for over three years . . . But I haven't found you again to waste precious time talking of him! Can they spare you for a few minutes—just long enough to get out of the camp and take a walk down by the river? It might be the last chance we ever get.'

A shudder ran through her. The thought that he was on his way to what could be the last big showdown of the war, between the opposing forces of Lee and Grant, was too unbearable to contemplate. 'I'll have a word with Lizzie-Ellen. I'm sure she'll cover for me for a little while. She knows I'd do the same for her.'

He smiled and nodded, mopping up the last bit of grease from his plate with a piece of stale cornmeal bread. She picked up her skirts and ran back to the main building where her friend was still scrubbing the floor.

Lizzie-Ellen got to her feet, wiping the sweat from her brow with the back of a damp hand as she stared open-mouthed at her friend. 'Well, don't that just beat all! Lordy, Aimée, you never told me you had a beau in the war!'

Aimée flushed slightly at her friend's raised voice, and glanced around her nervously. 'Well, he's not a beau exactly,' she lied. 'More of an old friend. Anyway, he's only passing through. If you could double for me for a short while, I'd be truly grateful!'

'You take as long as you need! Ah know you'll do the same for me when Don gets back!'

'Of course I will!' She knew that Don would never be back. He lay somewhere in the green fields round Gettysburg, among the unaccounted-for thousands who would never know the dignity of an individual grave. She hugged her friend's spare frame to her, as she murmured her thanks.

It felt strange to be walking together through the chaos that was the hospital camp. To begin with, it was difficult to reconcile the tall, gaunt, uniformed soldier with the dashing, almost raffish, figure she once knew as Daniel Redmayne. He had aged. Even through the dust she could see the increasing number of silver hairs in the thick blue-black of his sidewhiskers. The laughter lines around his eyes had deepened, and a deep furrow had etched itself across the high, intelligent forehead. But the war had changed them all. Herself most of all.

When they wandered further from the camp, they could hear the deep boom of field-guns in the distance and the occasional burst of musketry, almost as inoffensive as the chirping of crickets on a summer's day. A small group of men were removing the spare wheel from a caisson to hammer it on the axle of a waiting howitzer. Everywhere there was movement. No one and nothing was still. Except the river. It snaked, blue-grey and beautiful into the distance, recognising no frontiers, no barriers.

As they stood on the bank and looked down on it, it reminded her of that day high on the bluff at La Terre d'Or . . . But all that was a lifetime ago.

'Come!' He reached out his hand and led her further down the bank to a small clearing edged on three sides by tall clumps of bent-grass. He took off his jacket and spread it on the ground for her to sit down, and she gasped in horror. There was a gaping unhealed wound halfway up his left arm. His shirt had been torn off at the elbow to form a makeshift bandage that was now stained a dark brown with dried blood.

'It's nothing!' He turned from her so that she could not see the offending wound. 'It's only a scratch. Most of the men have far worse!'

She shook her head. He had never talked of what they had just been through, and she felt ashamed of her own gush of personal information of half an hour ago. There was so much of his life now, and over the past few years, that she did not know—would probably never know.

'Where exactly are you headed?' She could not bear to think of the impending battle, but had to know. She must never lose track of him again.

An ironic smile, that brought a fleeting reminder of earlier happier days, flickered across his face. 'To meet up with two old friends of yours from New Orleans!'

She frowned. 'Who can that be?'

'Beauregard and Butler! If the old bully Ben is still

around, that is! It seems that Pierre and his men have got him bottled up good and proper down there!'

'I'd no idea he was back in the fighting; but it'll be a relief for the folk in New Orleans. Unless they've replaced him by someone worse, that is!'

Red laughed. 'I doubt it! The general who took over from him you could call the better of two evils!'

She frowned. 'Have you heard anything of your grandfather!'

When he did not reply, she looked at him, and there was real pain in his eyes. 'He's gone, Aimée—six months since. Old Edith wrote me. He blew his brains out. The war got to him in the end, I guess. He'd heard tell of some friends further north who'd had their homes and land ransacked by Sherman's bummers. He couldn't bear to live to see that happen to La Terre d'Or!'

She felt sick. She had heard of the trail of destruction that General Sherman's men were leaving behind them on their push through Georgia to Atlanta and the sea. Her hand found his. 'I'm so sorry, Red . . . So very sorry.'

'I'd have given them La Terre d'Or—ay, and Wildwood too!' he said bitterly. 'If only he'd realised that it's people that matter, not land and possessions! But he'd poured his heart and soul into that place . . . It would have killed him to see them take it away from him.'

'I heard that they're in Craven County, or will be soon,' she said softly.

She felt the muscles of his arm tense beneath her fingers. 'Too heavy a price may be paid for wealth, Aimée! My grandfather's death proved that. If Wildwood survives, then so be it . . . If not, we must just be grateful to God for having made it through to the end ourselves—if indeed we do.'

'And if we do, Red, what then?' Her eyes pleaded for answers that she knew he could not give, but longed with all her heart to hear.

'I can make no promises, *chérie*.' His eyes left hers to gaze out over the river. 'I have nothing to promise you—not even my life. It would have been better if we had never met—had never found each other again today. Loving me has brought you nothing but heartache, and it can bring nothing but unhappiness in the future. I've been selfish, Aimée, unforgivably selfish.'

'What are you saying, Red? Dear God, what are you saying?'

He turned to her in silence, his eyes studying her face, as though seeing it for the first time. Decisions were forming in his mind that she had no influence on. Decisions that brought a cold sweat of fear to her brow. He didn't know what he was saying! If he had any idea how much she really loved him, he could never talk like this!

He got up slowly and stood looking down at her for a long time before putting out his hand. 'It's time we were getting back. We'll be missed.'

'Does it matter, Red? Does it really matter? Does anything really matter but us?' She scarcely recognised her own voice as she stared at him wild-eyed. 'Are you telling me to forget you?'

He stooped to pick up his cape from the ground, and flung it over his shoulders. He was no longer her Red, her beloved, devil-may-care Red. It was a different man—a strange, gaunt man who wore the grey uniform of a Confederate major. A man with cold, dead eyes that now turned on her own.

'Yes, my dear, I'm telling you exactly that. Forget me, Aimée. Go back to London. Who knows, perhaps divorces are easier to get over there? Then you can forget this godforsaken country with its self-inflicted wounds. Find a nice safe Englishman to settle down with—and have children!'

CHAPTER THIRTEEN

RED TURNED TOWARDS her and held out a hand. 'Coming?'

She shook her head, unable to trust herself to speak. It wasn't happening. Please God, don't let it be happening! It couldn't—it mustn't—end like this!

He stood looking at her before smiling wearily as one might at a rebellious child. Then he shrugged and turned to walk slowly back towards the camp.

She sank to the earth, her legs unable to support her weight. Her eyes followed him until he became simply a small grey blur in the distance. But she couldn't cry. All her tears had been used up long ago. Her hands beat the ground in helpless frustration, then pulled at a clump of bent-grass until the thin dry reeds cut into her fingers. The bright red blood seemed appropriate, somehow. She could not recall walking back to the camp, but was aware of Lizzie-Ellen's supportive hand on her arm as she went to the shack that served as their living and sleeping quarters.

'What happened, Aimée? Tell me! You look awful!'

'N—Nothing. Nothing at all . . . I'm all right, really I am!'

'All right my eye! You look like you've seen a ghost —and you'd better tell me about it, or I'll nag you until you do!' Lizzie-Ellen poured a ladleful of water from a pail into a tin mug and handed it over. 'Drink this, it'll do you good!'

Aimée took it and sipped at the lukewarm contents. What could she say that would make any sense? She was already living a lie by using her maiden name and pretending she was unmarried.

'You love him, don't you? That Major—you love him?'

She nodded miserably.

'Has he told you he has another sweetheart some-where? Is that it?' Lizzie-Ellen was trying her best, determined to relieve the look of devastation on her friend's face.

'No, nothing like that. He—He just doesn't want us to see each other any more, that's all.' She laughed bitterly. 'That's all! That's all! My God, Lizzie, that's absolutely everything! He wants me to go back to England and forget all about him!'

'And you don't want to?'

Aimée shook her head emphatically, then pride got the better of her and she attempted a casual shrug. 'I don't know anything any more!'

They stared at one another—two once beautiful faces now drawn and haggard by months of toil. Then Lizzie-Ellen sighed. 'Well, I do! If we don't get our sleeves rolled up and get on out there, we'll have some explaining to do to the Superintendent!'

Aimée followed her out of the shack and on past the rows of grey-uniformed men—Red's men—who lay sprawled round the cook-house door. She deliberately kept her eyes fixed firmly on the middle distance in case they should fall on the Major in charge—Daniel O'Connell Redmayne.

For the remainder of the day she threw herself into ward work, changing dressings and administering what little quinine they could spare to the very worst cases. She was certain he would appear at any moment, take her in his arms and apologise for what had happened that morning. But it didn't happen, and when nightfall came and the regiment prepared to leave, a cold, empty feeling rose within her. What if she were never to see him again? What if he were to march down that road and never return? What if he were to be killed?

A Captain—a red-haired, freckle-faced young man who looked much too immature for the position—was standing less than ten feet away, packing the regulation supply of worm-tunnelled hard tack into his kitbag. She approached him nervously, unsure exactly what to say.

'Ma'm?' He glanced up enquiringly at her hovering figure. 'Can I help you at all?'

'Major Redmayne,' she blurted out. 'He's your commanding officer, isn't he?'

'Sure is, ma'm.' He looked at her curiously as he tightened the metal buckles of the bag and threw it over his shoulder.

She undid the tiny clasp of the gold chain round her neck. 'Would—Would you do something for me, please? Would you give him this? Not tonight, though. Wait until daybreak. Wait until you're well on your way down the road!'

She gazed down at the delicate interlocking hearts for the last time, then pressed them into his hands.

The Captain looked at the necklet, then shrugged and slipped it into the pocket of his tunic. 'I'll see he gets it, ma'm, you can rely on that. Will there be any message?'

She shook her head abruptly. 'No. No message'. Then she turned and hurried back to the ward. They would be forming ranks to march out any minute now, and she mustn't be here. She must never set eyes on that tall figure again.

She was changing the fouled straw beneath one of the countless dysentery sufferers when the faint shouts of command sounded through the plank walls. Then the sound of marching feet filled the night air. Despite her resolve, she ran to the door, gripping the rough wooden edge as her eyes followed the grey column as it snaked its way into the darkness. He was in there—somewhere —in that anonymous mass of humanity wending its way towards the war zone and almost certain death.

It took days to get back to some kind of normality in her mind. He was everywhere. In every dirty grey coat and every dust-encrusted face she saw him, until she thought she would go mad. The heartache was a deep, physical pain that refused to leave. Even in the exhaustion of sleep he was there, his gaunt face, with the sad, empty eyes staring at her. There was no escape.

When the chance came to move to Richmond with a band of much-needed medical reinforcements, she jumped at it. To get away from here was to escape from the memory of Red. In the Virginian capital there would be no river to haunt her with the recollection of that misty morning when he told her to forget him—to go back to England and find a nice Englishman and have his children.

She was sorry to leave Lizzie-Ellen, of course. Her friend had chosen to stay, feeling that if her husband were to be brought to any hospital camp, it would be here rather than the town itself. They said their good-byes in the early morning, with the dew still thick on the ground and the mist hovering in long grey wisps on the surface of the river. Aimée felt embarrassed that she could give no home address to resume contact after the war was over.

'You'll probably head on back to England, then?' Lizzie-Ellen's pale eyes were troubled as she clung to her friend's hand. It was terrible that they might never see each other again.

Aimée gave a tight little smile and nodded briefly. 'It doesn't seem as though there'll be much left for me here.'

'You'll come and visit us, though, before you go? You'll love Don, you really will!' She let go of Aimée's hand and pulled a scrap of paper from a reticule in the folds of her skirts. 'I've written our address down for you.'

'Mrs Elizabeth Helen Monihan . . .' Aimée looked up from the childish rounded hand, and smiled. 'I'll come and see you, Lizzie-Ellen, dear. I don't know when, but I'll be there!'

They looked at one another then hugged, and Aimée watched her friend disappear in through the closed doors of the isolation ward. Lizzie-Ellen was the nearest thing to a real friend she had made in America, but even

this friendship had had to be based on lies. Lizzie-Ellen
was of Irish Catholic stock and would never condone her
walking out of her marriage to Charles Macdonald. That
one fatal decision seemed to have blighted her chances
of any type of normal life, unless she was prepared to live
a lie. The thought appalled her.

'Fitzwilliam! Time you were on board!'

The Superintendent's strident voice shook her back to
the present, and she picked up her small valise and
moved wearily to the wagon. There were twelve of them
going to Richmond, six men and four women. One of the
men produced a mouth-organ once they were under
way, but the others had little enthusiasm for singing.
Most had been at this work for at least a year, and its
sheer drudgery had sapped what little surplus energy
they had ever possessed.

'They say it's worse in Richmond, you know!' It was
Greta Muller, an over-pious woman of about thirty, who
spoke, and all eyes turned to her dully. Greta was not
known for her optimism. 'Yes, it's a much bigger camp,
that's why. And there are camp-followers—lots of
them. Harlots, mainly!' She sat back primly and waited
for a reaction, but there was none.

'Well, just as long as they don't bother me!' the man
with the mouth-organ said with a wink in Aimée's
direction. 'Hell, Ah don't even have the strength to take
off these here boots at night, let alone anything else!'

There was a murmur of agreement, and the young
man sitting next to her sniggered, then they all settled
back in silence once more as the wagon bumped its way
to Hanover Junction. They were to board the mid-
morning ambulance train that was due in with more
casualties. Their help was essential in the unloading,
then, when that was finished, they would carry on down
the line in the same coaches to Richmond.

A slight drizzle of late spring rain was falling when
they finally rolled into the station. To their surprise, the
train had already arrived. Medical attendants, mainly
male but interspersed with a few females, were busy

carrying the injured men to the wagons. The walking wounded had to get out as best they could, and no matter how often she witnessed this scene—and it had run into many hundreds of times by now—Aimée's heart went out to the once able young bodies who hobbled along the platform, their missing limbs bound up in makeshift blood-caked bandages. It took almost two hours to get the last man loaded on the transport and then to settle themselves in a vacant carriage towards the front of the train. It smelt strongly of its previous inhabitants, an odour that would make the strongest of stomachs turn over, but they were used to it by now and it was barely commented upon as they made themselves as comfortable as possible on the wooden bench seats.

'How long d'ya reckon Richmond'll hold out, Jeb?' It was the youngest of the party—a boy of about eighteen —who spoke. He had been excused conscription into the Army because of epileptic fits, but no one could recall his ever having experienced one in the past three months of hospital duty.

The recipient of his question stroked his greying sidewhiskers and looked thoughtful. 'Ah don't rightly know, son. Ah heard tell ol' Grant and Meade, and a few other of them Union war-horses, held some kinda council o' war the other day. Looks like there could be some kind of offensive on its way. We'll just have to pray to the good Lord that he's agreeable to comin' down on ol' Bobby Lee's side. We sure could do with some good luck!'

'Well, if there is a good Lord—and the longer this war goes on, the more Ah'm beginning to doubt it—he sure ain't been anywhere near Georgia lately!'

The speaker was a gaunt-faced man of around fifty, with the soft liquid vowels of the true Georgian that Aimée recognised only too well.

'What d'ya mean, Harry?' It was the owner of the mouth-organ who spoke.

'Sherman and his bummers—that's what Ah mean!' Harry replied bitterly. 'From what Ah've heard, there ain't hardly a single house left standing where those varmints have passed through.'

Aimée's face grew even paler than its normal fair hue. 'You don't happen to know if they've got as far as Craven County yet?'

''Spect so, ma'm! Ah know they've been through Charlotteville. Plundered the house of a Minister of God there, so Ah heard tell, and trampled his cassock under their feet!'

She sank back in her seat. They would be gone, all gone, those beautiful houses—Wildwood, Four Winds, the Madisons' old house Magnolia Mount . . . all burnt to the ground, and the slaves fled to the freedom of the North. It was the end of an era. It wasn't just the young men who were dying out there, it was a whole way of life. And what of old Aunt Effie, and all the others? She had heard that many of the slaves who had been freed by the Unionists had turned on their former masters and mistresses and killed them. It was all so dreadful—so really dreadful.

A long sigh shuddered through her, and she leaned against the backrest of the seat and closed her eyes. Perhaps, one of these days, she would wake up and find it was all a terrible nightmare—that she was actually still back at the Gaiety Theatre in London. All that seemed a million years ago and a million miles away from where she was now, in this rickety old wagon on her way to a city under constant threat in this bloodiest of civil wars. The conversation dwindled to a stop as the other occupants of the carriage also took the opportunity to snatch a wink of sleep before their arrival at the much bigger camp. Each was immersed in his or her own thoughts. All had volunteered for medical service for very different reasons, but all were as heartily sick of the needless suffering as any soldier in the battlefield itself.

They were met at Richmond station by an official who informed them they would be stationed in some disused tobacco warehouses on the banks of the James River,

which had been given over for use as hospital units
during the worst of the fighting. Everyone in the city was
very conscious of the fact that it was no longer the capital
merely of Virginia, but also that of the whole of the
South. President Jefferson Davis himself had taken up
residence and was as aware as every one of his fellow
citizens that if Richmond fell, so would the Confederacy. It was all much bigger and more impersonal than
Aimée had imagined, and when they eventually arrived
at the hospital camp, a deep feeling of gloom enveloped
her. Why hadn't she stayed where she was? What on
earth had possessed her to move to this awful place?

Across the river, in the distance, they could make out
the great grey bulk of the Old Dominion Nail Works on
Belle Isle, which had been requisitioned for use as a
prison for Federal soldiers, and not much further away
was the notorious 'Castle Thunder', an old tobacco-
warehouse where even more Union men were incarcer-
ated to die of starvation and disease long before the war
was finally over.

Their own quarters seemed little different, with each
person allotted six square feet of space in a partitioned
warehouse. There had been a rudimentary attempt
at segregating the men from the women, but by the
sounds that emanated from the individual cubicles on
the first night, she became aware that fellowship was
being taken a good deal further than merely working
together.

The work itself was similar to that of the last camp,
although on a much greater scale. It appeared they were
in only one of many makeshift hospitals that had sprung
up in and around the city, and Aimée was told by the
Superintendent that a transfer to any of the others could
be easily arranged if she was not happy. Happy, here?
She had almost laughed in his face. How could anyone
be happy, here? 'The Slough of Despond' Harry had
named it on their arrival, and he wasn't far wrong. She
would stick it out, though, she decided. The suffering of
the men was the same, no matter where she was.

And she stayed—for month after weary month, as the
fighting dragged on. Although no one dared even whisper it for fear of being branded a traitor, it looked as
though the war was going the Unionists' way. Down in
Georgia, by the end of August, Sherman and his men
had succeeded in pushing their way as far as Atlanta.
But, for the native Georgians in the camp, the knowledge brought even more worry and depression. The
Federal route—a belt of country fifty miles wide and
over three hundred miles long—had been swept bare,
with most of the plantations, and their stately mansions,
destroyed. And when eventually in mid-December they
reached the sea, and later captured the important sea-
port of Savannah, deep gloom hung over the whole
camp.

Aimée could not bear to think about it. But, with
casualties still pouring in, there was little time for reflec-
tion. The Confederate soldiers were putting up a brave
last-ditch effort, but they were no longer the predomi-
nant army in the west. Indeed, there was not much of a
Confederacy left. The once proud state was now reduced to the almost independent area of Texas, the area
of south Virginia beneath Richmond, and the Carolinas.

Christmas Eve 1864 was like no other she had ever
known. They had not expected to be busier than usual,
but a fire at one of the other hospital camps in the city
had meant that those patients who had survived the
blaze had to be evacuated and shared among the remaining units. Aimée had had no experience of burns before,
and the sight of already seriously ill or wounded young
men being brought in with additional suffering was
almost intolerable. She had no wish to shirk her duties
and leave the worst jobs to others, but it was with an
enormous sense of relief that she was assigned to a
contingent of newcomers who simply required
competent nursing.

'They're mainly amputations, Fitzwilliam,' the Superintendent informed her briskly. 'Nothing too serious on

the whole, although there is one in the corner over there—who isn't expected to last the night. Lost too much blood at the outset, I'm afraid.'

She glanced apprehensively at the line of new arrivals, crammed tightly together through lack of space. In the distance, through the gathering dusk, she could hear carols being sung, and as she picked up her lantern to make her round of each bed, she found herself joining in—softly at first, then louder as others joined her.

Very soon the gentle strains of 'Silent Night' were filling the room. To her embarrassment she could feel the hot rush of tears, which rolled freely down her cheeks as she walked slowly from bed to bed. She was not alone, for there was hardly a dry eye among any of the young men. She stopped to have a quiet word with each one. Some wanted to hold her hand, others simply to smile their thanks with their eyes as she stooped to adjust a pillow or smooth a lock of damp hair back from a fevered brow. They were all so young.

She deliberately avoided the bed in the corner—the man pointed out to her as not expected to last the night. She had no wish to disturb the hollow-eyed young officer who lay gazing out of half-closed lids as she made her way back to her seat at the table.

'Nurse!'

She laid the lantern on the table, then turned abruptly as the hoarse voice assailed her ears. It was he—the dying young Captain!

'I'm coming!' She spoke softly so as not to disturb those trying to sleep, and returned to him.

He attempted to pull himself up on the mattress as she approached, but his missing left arm made the movement difficult.

'Here, let me help!' She bent down to clasp him round the chest, still in the stained grey coat of battle, and pull him further up on the pillow, when a strangled gasp caught in her throat.

Heaven! It couldn't be! The blood drained from her

face as she bent closer for a better look, then she shrank back aghast, burying her face in her hands. It was he—there was no doubt about it at all!

CHAPTER FOURTEEN

'AIMÉE . . . IS IT really you?' Chas MacDonald blinked incredulously at the white-faced young woman in front of him.

'Chas . . . Chas! I'd no idea it was you!'

He reached out a hand and she took it, clasping it to her as her eyes remained riveted on the pale, gaunt face; a face with death written in every pore. There was no bitterness in her heart any more, only a deep, over-whelming pity for the man she had once known, had once consented to marry.

He gazed up at her as if unable to believe what his eyes were telling him. As if this was yet one more of those awful nightmares that seemed to haunt his every mo-ment, waking or sleeping. 'It's been so long, Aimée, and now it's too late—much too late . . .' His voice was hoarse, and the words came out with difficulty. There were tears in his grey-blue eyes.

'Don't try to talk . . .' She couldn't bear to see him like this. This was not the man she had once known, had once believed herself to be in love with long ago, in another life.

'I must. I'm going, Aimée . . . This bloody war is all over for me.'

Tears flooded her eyes and she wiped them away with the back of her hand as she gazed at the shell of the man who had once been her husband. 'Don't say that . . . You're in safe hands now. You'll live, Chas. You'll see Four Winds again!'

He looked away as painful memories contorted his emaciated features. 'Four Winds,' he said faintly. 'Four Winds is dead, Aimée, like I shall be by morning. They have destroyed my beautiful land like they have destroyed my body.'

He started to sob; quiet painful sobs that came from the heart. 'Even Aunt Effie . . . They're gone, they're all gone.'

'They—They killed her too?' Surely not an old defenceless woman! Was there no end to this barbarity?

He shook his head wearily. 'Not with bullets—but they might as well. She had a heart attack after they raided the house. I heard from one of the Carmichael boys. I couldn't even get to her funeral.'

He had loved her. There were very few people in this world that he had loved, but in his own way he had loved the old woman.

'And the slaves? What of the slaves?'

He closed his eyes. 'Gone. All of them, even Ebenezer.'

'And Tizzy?' Her voice dropped to a whisper.

He could not speak, but shook his head, then said with difficulty, 'Gone, God help me, every last one of them. I—I don't blame her. She never forgave me for Jonah—never . . .'

'But if you haven't been to see for yourself . . . I mean, the Judge's son could be wrong?' She was trying to be of comfort, but he would have none of it.

'It's God's will . . . divine retribution . . . Call it what you wish.' His voice faded as he fought for breath, but he seemed determined to continue. 'I've seen a priest, Aimée. I'm not the man I was . . . not just in body . . . I understand more now. I know why you left. God help me, I know.'

He was trying to explain, to tell her he understood, but as each breath became more painful, the words refused to come. His hand clutched hers, squeezing her fingers until she had to force herself not to wince. She wanted to help him—to tell him that she understood too, that she forgave him. Didn't someone once say that to understand all was to forgive all?

'Don't, Chas, don't try to talk. There was so much we both didn't understand. There were so many mistakes . . . so very many mistakes—on both sides.'

She paused, trying to form the words to make him understand. She felt no bitterness towards him now, only sorrow. A deep overwhelming sorrow for what had gone before and for what had happened since.

'Fitzwilliam!'

The Superintendent's voice rang through the quiet ward, and she looked round in alarm as he stalked towards her. 'You're needed next door. They're a man short in fevers.'

Chas's grip grew tighter, and she glanced down at him again. He shook his head. 'No . . .' The word came out almost unheard as his breath rattled in his throat.

'They're waiting, Fitzwilliam! You can't waste time playing the angel of mercy at every bed!'

She looked down despairingly at Chas. His eyes were the only living part of his face. They pleaded with her to stay, but the Superintendent was getting impatient. 'I—I must go, Chas, but I'll be back soon. I promise.'

He shook his head as his fingers released their grip on her hand, and she bent over and placed the lightest of kisses on his damp brow. She could not look back. She could not bear to see the pain in those eyes.

'You know that man?' The Superintendent's gruff voice broke the silence as they headed for the door. 'He a friend of yours or something?'

She was silent for a moment. An image of Peter denying his Lord flashed through her mind, but she dismissed it instantly as blasphemous. 'Or something, Superintendent,' she said softly. 'We once knew each other a thousand years ago . . .'

It was almost two hours later when she had finished on the fever ward and slipped back into the warehouse where Chas lay. It was in darkness but for a single lantern. A few of the men recognised her and moaned softly in the gloom, but it was to the bed in the far corner that she headed. It was a long room, and the weight of the lantern made her wrist ache as she picked her way through the narrow passage between the rows of beds.

He was lying back on the pillow looking straight at her as she knelt down beside him.

'It's me, Chas, I'm back!' She kept her voice deliberately low so as not to disturb the others, but he made no response. He was looking past her, his eyes fixed unblinkingly on the darkness somewhere above her head.

'Chas!' Her voice was louder now, and she clutched the sleeve of his tunic. 'Chas! Answer me, Chas!'

But still he stared silently into the darkness.

'Oh, no!'

She put the lantern down on the floor with one hand as the other reached across and felt the pale brow beneath the thatch of fair hair. It was as cold as the grave. He was dead. Her husband was dead. The man she had once hoped to love, then learned to hate, was dead.

She gazed down at the pale face with its unseeing eyes. Then, very gently, she closed each eyelid. He was at rest. This awful war had done its worst and could do no more to the wreck of this once handsome man.

'Forgive me . . . Dear God, forgive me!' She raised the cold hand to her lips and kissed it. He was still wearing the gold signet ring on his little finger that she had given him before he sailed back without her to America.

'You knew the Captain, ma'm?'

She whirled round. The voice came from a young man in the next bed.

'He's dead, ain't he? Was he a friend of yours.'

She nodded briefly.

'He went just after you left with the Superintendent. Must have been hallucinating at the end . . . Called out for his wife. Was she a friend of yours, too? Did you know Mrs MacDonald?'

She turned back to look at the dead form of her husband. 'I knew Mrs MacDonald,' she said softly.

'She'll be real upset, if she's still alive.'

She stood up, lifting the lantern from the floor, to look down into the upturned face of the young soldier. He had two stripes on his sleeve, but looked scarcely more than eighteen. 'Don't worry, Corporal,' she said quietly. 'Mrs MacDonald died a long time ago . . . A very long time ago.'

She walked slowly back up the ward, for once ignoring the pleas for attention as she headed for the open door. She needed air—fresh air, for the smell of death was all around.

The moon hung like a silver orb in the star-spangled sky, and somewhere in the city beyond a bell rang out to signify the midnight hour. It was Christmas Day now—the first seconds of the Lord's birthday, 1864.

Her eyes turned skywards. 'Dear Lord, if you're out there somewhere—if there's anyone there at all—look after him. Look after all those who have died, or are about to die, in this awful war.'

She could not sleep that night, or the next. She attended his funeral in the soldiers' section of Hollywood, Richmond's principal cemetery on the western outskirts of the city. They were burying fifty more that day. But it was impossible to identify the man she had once known with any part of the brief ceremony. The Charles MacDonald she had known was not in that cheap pine coffin; that cold, shattered body had nothing to do with the young man who had been master of Four Winds. If there was any afterlife, then his spirit was miles from this bleak, unhappy place. It was back amid the trees and flowers of Craven County. He had been conceived, born and bred in that beautiful land, and it was to there he would return. The Yankees might have destroyed those parts made by man, but they could never destroy the rest. Georgia would survive, and every one of her sons would return, in spirit or in body, when this bloody war was over, she was certain of that.

The night before New Year's Eve brought a surprise visit from the Superintendent just before she did her last ward round at midnight. His thin face looked even more gaunt in the ghostly glow of the lantern, but his words brought a comforting glow to the end of another tiring day.

'Fitzwilliam, it's time you had some time off!'

'Really? But we're so busy, sir, I never even thought to ask!' She looked at him in astonishment as she snapped shut the lid of the medicine-chest and replaced it in the drawer for sake keeping.

'Exactly! And that selfless attitude is why you're to be one of the lucky ones. There's to be a New Year's Eve ball tomorrow night in the City Hall, organised by the Richmond War Wives' Committee, and I've been given six invitations to be distributed as I think fit among my workers.'

'And you want me to go?' She stared at him in amazement. She had almost forgotten what a ball was!

'Yep! That's about it. You can finish at six tomorrow night to give you a couple of hours to prepare. There's a coach coming to pick y'all up at eight-thirty. But I'd appreciate it if you didn't go spreading your good fortune around—it'll only cause a heap of bad feelin' among them not so fortunate!'

She nodded mutely, as he pushed a gilt-edged invitation card into her hand. A ball in the middle of all this carnage—what was the world coming to!

The washing facilities at the camp were primitive, to say the least, but she did manage to half-fill a tin tub with two buckets of lukewarm water when she finished work the following night. Ringlets were out of the question —there simply wasn't the time for her hair to dry twisted round the long rags, but, while it was still damp, she succeeded in arranging it in a presentable chignon at the nape of her neck.

A gown of heavy black taffeta, trimmed with white Nottingham lace, was unearthed from the depths of her chest, and with the aid of one of the other female nurses, she successfully squeezed into the tightly-laced stays so necessary for the eighteen-inch waist of the basque. A dark grey long-fringed shawl completed the outfit, but because of a lack of an adequate mirror, she was denied the opportunity to admire the result of almost two hours' concentrated effort.

'Purty . . . Mighty purty, young lady! It sure gladdens an old man's heart to see such a sight among all this misery!' Harry gave a low whistle of appreciation when she emerged from her quarters to head for the waiting coach. The compliment gave her a surprisingly warm glow. It seemed—and indeed was—years since a man had complimented her on her looks.

She did not know by name any of the others who had been chosen to go. They were simply other youngish women she nodded to on the occasions that their paths crossed in the course of their duty. In a way she was glad, for it enabled her to keep her counsel and quietly think her own thoughts as the coach trundled along the darkening streets towards Capitol Square.

The dancing was already in full swing, and streamers of gaily coloured flags criss-crossed the high ceiling of the entrance porch, fluttering gaily in the draught. A liveried footman at the door took their invitations, and announced each by name before they proceeded through into the main body of the building.

Everywhere seemed awash with colour, as girls in rainbow-hued gowns whirled past, their full, hooped skirts revealing not quite respectable glimpses of white-silk-stockinged ankles or the occasional sight of lace-trimmed pantalets. For a long time Aimée could only stand and stare. She had quite forgotten what it was like to feel so pretty, so feminine. The air seemed filled with their laughter as they tossed their ringleted heads above bare white shoulders draped with long-fringed shawls of the finest silk. Beautifully painted fans trimmed with snow-white swansdown hung from narrow satin ribbons attached to their wrists. And everywhere, absolutely everywhere, there were flowers—in their hair, tucked into the broad velvet sashes of their gowns, and arranged in colourful displays on the white cloths of the tables that ran along one wall.

The young men were almost all in the grey tunics and blue trousers of the Confederacy. Those still not able to join the dancing stood around the walls; many were on crutches, or sporting black silk arm slings or the occasional swathed white head bandage that contrasted vividly with the weathered complexions resulting from months of field warfare.

At the far end of the hall hung a huge Confederate flag that quivered constantly in the draught from the open doors and the continuous breeze engendered by the swirling skirts of the dancers. On the wall under it hung a large oil-painting of the Confederate President, Jefferson Davis. The tall spare figure in the black frock-coat seemed to dominate the whole of the festivities; the keen eyes in the high-cheekboned face looked directly into her own as she gazed up at it. Someone said he was now in Richmond and might even attend the ball, and the possibility had added a buzz of underlying excitement to the proceedings. The sight of so many brilliantly coloured crinolines swirling in gay abandon before her eyes had a curiously stunning effect. She had seen nothing but dark, dull hues and unsmiling faces for so long that at first such gaiety seemed almost immoral. Within half an hour, however, her card was filled and she, too, was being whirled round the floor by more than her fair share of handsome young men. Most were in uniform, and like the majority there, were able to attend only because they had been invalided home to recover from a particularly bad injury or illness.

Dance followed dance, and halfway through the evening it had become very obvious that her energy was not what it had been a few years ago. When Strip the Willow was announced, she thought seriously of pleading exhaustion, but the elegant young man with the single gold star of a major on his collar would not be deterred, and very soon she was swept up once more in the colourful whirl.

'Mrs MacDonald! . . . Mrs MacDonald! Aimée!' From somewhere in the swirling mass of humanity someone was calling her name. A female voice that grew more insistent as the dance progressed. Then, at last, she was face to face with its owner. At first it was difficult to place the red-haired young woman in the sky-blue organdie gown. 'Don't you recognise me?' The wide-set pale eyes glanced across in amusement as they swung past each other for the second time.

But it was the eyes—those fair-lashed eyes that had once reminded her of a startled rabbit but were now sparkling with excitement—that succeeded in stirring the chords of memory, or that she called out, 'Becky Madison!' in delight as her partner swung her down the long row of clapping dancers once more.

This time, at the end of the dance, she was adamant that the red-haired lieutenant who appeared at her elbow should accept her apologies and excuse her from not taking the floor. Nothing and no one was going to deprive her of the chance of talking to her old friend.

'But you look so—so grown up!' Her green eyes gazed in delighted approval at the exquisitely attired young woman with the bouncing titian ringlets.

'I am grown-up!' Becky exclaimed. 'And I'm no longer Becky Madison, don't you know! I'm a married woman now!'

'No!'

'Yes! There—see!' She held out her left hand proudly, and Aimée gazed down at the gleaming gold ring beneath the white net mitten. 'I'm Mrs Rebecca Sanders, if you please! He's a captain, with General Hood, down near Nashville right now.' Her face grew serious. 'I heard tell that the Unionists have been involving them in quite a bit of fighting recently, but I guess everything must be fine with Jack or I'd have heard, wouldn't I?'

Aimée nodded reassuringly. 'Of course you would, my dear! I wouldn't give it another thought. I'm sure it would upset your husband to think you were worrying yourself needlessly, tonight of all nights!'

Becky squeezed her friend's arm gratefully. 'You always were good for me, Aimée! To tell the truth, I feel a mite guilty about being here without him, but being on the Committee for War Relief—well, there really wasn't much choice. Anyhow, I do so love a ball, don't you?' She fluttered her feather-trimmed fan gaily before her flushed face as she glanced back at the dancers re-forming for the Dashing White Sergeant. 'But, tell me, what are you doing here? What on earth are you doing in Richmond? I thought you went back to England when you left Four Winds.' She gave a faintly embarrassed smile, 'Or, at least, so the rumour went . . . But then there were so many rumours at that time.'

Aimée sighed and gave a weary smile. 'It would take far too long to explain. Let's just say that, at the moment, I'm here working for the medical corps.'

'You mean you're a nurse!' Becky exclaimed in astonishment. 'How long have you been doing that?'

'It must be getting on for two and a half years. To tell the truth, I stopped counting a long time ago.'

'Well, in that case, it's time you had a well-earned rest! How do you feel about coming to stay with me? Jack's not at all happy about me staying on in Richmond on my own, with my folks so far away and all. I'm sure it would put his mind at rest if he were to hear I had an old friend keeping me company for a bit, while he's gone. Do say you'll come! Do?'

Aimée looked at her in astonishment and began to shake her head. 'Oh, I don't know, Becky. It's very kind of you, but there really is so much work to be done at the hospital . . .'

'And you're the only one there to do it? Fiddlesticks! I'm sure they can spare you for a short while. And I know it'll do you the world of good. Why, you must have lost at least twenty pounds since I last saw you!'

Her friend's admonishing tone made her laugh as she glanced down at her figure. She had been noticing how the hollows of her shoulder-blades had become much deeper of late. Perhaps Becky was right, perhaps they

could spare her for a short while—a few days maybe . . .
That wouldn't be too much to ask.

'You're swithering, I can see that! Say you'll come!
Oh, do say you'll come!'

Aimée smiled into her pleading eyes. 'You've talked
me into it, you wicked girl! Yes, I'll come. But not for
long, mind—a few days, that's all.'

The squeal of delight that greeted her decision
made heads turn all round them, but Becky Sanders
didn't care as she hugged Aimée in delight. 'This has to
be the best start to a New Year that any girl could ask
for!'

As the dance progressed, Aimée realised how
wonderful it would be to escape for a few days. Just to
sleep in a real feather-bed again would be sheer heaven.
Suddenly the whole world seemed brighter. She was
actually able to laugh with her eyes as well as her mouth
as young men vied with each other for her attention.
Except for the numbers of them with arm slings or on
crutches, one could almost forget the war.

Even the food! She had never seen the like since she
left New Orleans. Whole honey-roast hams nudged
platters full of chicken legs and other delicacies; while,
in the centre of the table, the biggest cake she had ever
seen stood etched with the date 1865. It was to be cut
when the last stroke of midnight had sounded.

The evening seemed to fly past on enchanted wings,
and she could hardly believe it when a portly man whom
she took to be the Governor mounted the podium and
called for silence as the bells of the city rang out the old
year and rang in the new. When the time came to join
hands and sing 'Auld Land Syne', she found herself in
between a captain and a much older man with bushy
sidewhiskers and a red, perspiring moon of a face that
positively beamed at her throughout the whole of the old
song. When it ended, however, it was the young Captain
to whom she turned first, to shake hands and to wish a
Happy New Year. There was something vaguely familiar about the bright red hair and freckled countenance,

and from his puzzled look it was obvious he felt the same.

'I know . . . You're the lady from the hospital! You're that nurse who gave me the necklace to give to Major Redmayne! You're old Red's friend!'

She stared open-mouthed as the memory came flooding back. 'Yes! Yes, that was me.' It was pointless to deny it. 'How is he? How is Red?' The words came out with difficulty, but it would have looked terrible not to have asked.

The young man paled beneath his freckles and shifted uncomfortably from one foot to the other. 'You—You didn't hear, then? They never informed you?'

'Informed me of what?' Aimée's voice rose an octave as she gazed at him in mounting apprehension. 'He is all right, isn't he? Red's still all right?'

The young Captain swallowed hard, his Adam's apple clearly visible above the collar of his tunic. 'Red's dead, ma'm. He's dead.'

CHAPTER FIFTEEN

'DEAD? HE CAN'T be dead! What do you mean?'

Her white, aghast face upset the young Captain, who reached out a steadying hand. 'I'm sorry, ma'm, I really am! I wish it wasn't true. God, how I wish it wasn't true! Red was my friend as well as my commanding officer.'

Still Aimée shook her head, unable to take it in. 'No—he can't be . . . He just can't be! They misinformed you, that's all. You misheard! Mistakes like that happen in wartime—in the confusion of battle.'

The Captain shook his head sadly. 'It's no mistake, ma'm. I was with him when he died. The shell that got him got me too. That's how I came by this!'

He lifted the empty right-hand sleeve of his tunic. She had not noticed it before.

Her mouth went dry. 'You—You lost your arm with the same shell that killed Red?'

He nodded, a strange, haunted look in his hazel eyes as he lived the moment once more. 'I—I'm sorry, ma'm. I really am. I gave him the necklace, though. I did that for you.'

'Thank you, Captain . . . Thank you.' She turned from him and walked blindly back to the side of the hall where Becky was waiting.

Her young friend looked with consternation as she approached. 'Is something wrong, Aimée? What is it? Tell me.'

Aimée shook her head and glanced back towards the floor, where the young Captain was still looking at her with despair in his eyes. 'Nothing, it's nothing—really. I've had rather a shock, that's all. An old friend—a very old friend—has been killed in battle. I've only just found out.'

Becky clucked sympathetically. 'I do declare, that's a

terrible thing! Why, there's hardly a day passes when you don't hear about someone you know who won't be coming back. But don't you worry about it any more. You'll be able to put this terrible old war behind you, for a while at least, when you come home with me. Now when will that be? Is tonight too soon?'

Aimée stared at her dully, hardly taking in what she was saying. All she could see was Red's shattered form lying on a bloodied field somewhere.

'I said, is tonight too soon?' Becky repeated the question impatiently.

'No. I mean, yes . . . I really don't know. I must speak to the Superintendent first.' All the excitement she had felt earlier at the thought of a few days' holiday had vanished. In fact, she really didn't want to be here at all with all these smiling, laughing people. Somehow the New Year revelry had become an obscenity. People were lying dead out there—young men were dying —giving up their lives so that everyone in this hall could dance the night away as if they hadn't a single care in the world. Every smiling face became an insult to his memory. She wanted to be alone, to collect her thoughts, to learn to cope with what she had just learned.

But Becky had other ideas. She was impatient to get things moving, and excited at the prospect of having her old friend to stay. 'Well, you must see about permission right away. In fact, I'll call my carriage and ride out there with you. That Superintendent can't refuse the pleas of two young ladies, can he? Good heavens, it's not as if you're actually in the Army; you are a volunteer, after all!'

Becky grasped her elbow, and before she knew what was happening, she was being propelled towards the door and out into the street. As insistent hands helped her into the carriage, she felt she was no longer in control of her body or her thoughts. She had started out this evening thinking, for the first time in months, that she might actually enjoy herself, and now—and now . . .

*   *   *

'Fitzwilliam, you put me in a difficult position!' The Superintendent's thin face wrinkled into a frown as he looked at the young woman in front of him. 'Good nurses ain't easy to come by, you know!'

Aimée looked down at the ground. She felt like a traitor running out on him like this—running out on all those young men who needed her. 'I know . . . Believe me, I know. I wouldn't ask, only it's sort of a favour for a friend. She's lonely living by herself with her husband at the front. It wouldn't be for ever. I'm sure I'll be back before too long.'

The Superintendent scratched the grey stubble of his chin. 'Well, you lady nurses ain't in the Army, y'all know that. I sure can't do anything to keep you against your will!'

Taking it to be acquiescence, she grabbed his hand. 'Thank you . . . Thank you so much!'

The elderly man shrugged helplessly. 'Well, you've bin one of the best I've ever had, m'dear. I have to say that. I guess all that's left for me to do is to wish you a very Happy New Year!'

'A Happy New Year!' She repeated the words slowly, as her mind went back to that terrible vision on the bloody battlefield. Never had those four words seemed more ironic.

The Sanders' house was a spacious three-storey building on Leigh Street, one of the best addresses in the city. Becky and her husband possessed no slaves, but had plenty of servants, and they were greeted at the door by Mary-Ann, a small Irish girl with a head of wild curly hair beneath her neat white cap.

'Mary-Ann, this is Mrs MacDonald. She'll be staying with us until I inform you otherwise. I trust you'll do all you can to make her stay a happy one!' Becky addressed her briskly as she undid her cape and handed it to the girl.

She dropped a curtsy in her mistress's direction, then Aimée's. It had been a long day, and she was just glad to have her employer home again so that she could put out all the lamps and retire to her own room in the basement.

Becky suggested a cup of coffee to round off the evening, but Aimée declined with an apologetic smile. 'I'd really love to, but I was on duty on the wards at six this morning. I don't think I could keep my eyes open for another minute!'

Her friend looked suitably abashed. 'Mercy, I'd no idea; you really should have been tucked up in bed long ago! And don't you worry about the morning. I'll tell the servants you won't be requiring breakfast until you ring for it. If I'm gone when you get up, don't worry. I usually go out during the day for a few hours of Committee work. They'll be needing all the hands they can get hold of tomorrow to count those lovely dollars that the ball must have brought in. Wasn't it simply swell? I bet you're so glad you went! Why, you wouldn't be standing here now if you'd remained in the hospital.'

Aimée stared into the smiling eyes. If she had remained in the hospital, she wouldn't be going through this agony now—this terrible, agonising pain of knowing that he was dead. Her beloved Red was dead. Was it better to know, or to continue living in ignorance and being spared this awful heartache? It was an impossible question to answer. Almost anything would be better than this—the terrible finality of death.

Her room was pretty and colourful, with pink floral curtains and a pink silk spread on the wide bed, but she took in none of it as she undressed in the lamplight and then threw herself on to the thick feather pillows. This time last night she had been almost happy. Oh, she had been exhausted, as she always was after a long day, but she had the comfort of knowing that she had made her peace with Chas before he died, and the continuing satisfaction of doing her best by the other young men who passed through her hands in the hospital. But now, just twenty-four hours later, her whole world had come to an end. How could things ever be the same? How could she go on living, knowing Red was dead?

She had tried to put him out of her mind after he had marched off into the night, down that dusty road, with his battle-weary men. She had even tried to tell herself that she had never loved him. But that had been easy when there was always the possibility that he would come back to her. And, deep in her heart, she had always believed he would return. He would walk back into her life one sunny day when the war was over, his blue eyes searching out hers to tell her that nothing had changed. But that would never happen now. All those dreams that had kept her alive over the past few years were dead—buried—along with the man who now lay in some cold, unknown field of battle. Tears flooded her eyes as she stared into the darkness. She should pray: pray for his soul so that it might find rest; pray for the peace of mind that would allow her to continue her life without him. But how could she? How could she ask anything of a God who would allow this to happen?

She rolled on to her stomach and beat her clenched fists into the soft pillows. There was no God! There was nothing but this war—this bloody war that went on and on and on . . .

Morning came slowly—a cold, grey day that promised little and delivered less. The rain pattered monotonously on the windowsills as she sat in the comfortable drawing-room and tried to occupy her mind by immersing herself in some of Becky's ladies' journals. But, somehow, the tinted pages with their pictures of the latest Paris fashions only seemed to increase her misery. Who could bear to think such trifles were of any importance at a time like this? She got up and paced the polished wood of the floor. It had been a mistake to come here. She felt alone and useless—guilty, even —staying here in this beautiful house with servants at her beck and call when the others were still working their fingers to the bone at the hospital.

When, at three-thirty, Becky eventually came home and announced she had arranged a soirée for that evening in Aimée's honour, it was all she could do to keep from bursting into tears.

'But, Aimée dear, why the long face? You'll simply adore everyone!' She clapped her slim hands in delight as she added confidentially, 'I've even invited a young man who is positively one of the most sought-after beaux in the whole of the city. And, what's even better, he's a doctor! Dr Arnold J. Holzenbein, to be exact! You'll have ever so much to talk about. He's been very much involved with the Sanitary Commission—he even threatened to resign when there was an objection to female nurses!'

Aimée stared at her dully. How could anyone imagine she was in the least bit interested in meeting eligible young men? But, then, she couldn't really blame Becky. She had never told anyone—no, not a single living soul—what Daniel Redmayne had meant to her.

'I'm sure that's very thoughtful of you, my dear. I'll look forward to discussing medical matters with the good doctor.'

In fact, Arnold James Holzenbein turned out to be a very charming young man indeed, and despite her forebodings Aimée found herself enjoying the long chat they had on the leather sofa by the fire. The young doctor was more than happy to hear her experiences of life in the wards, and for her own part, she found it almost a cleansing process to be able to talk about it to someone who understood the problems.

Becky came across from time to time to offer sweetmeats and coffee when she felt the supply in their cups and plates to be diminishing, and whenever that happened, Aimée got the distinct feeling that the good-looking Dr Holzenbein was more than a little taken by his young hostess. His grey eyes lit up as they alighted on Becky's slim young figure whether from across the room or near at hand. And, by the end of the evening, Aimée was convinced that the good doctor might well still be one of the diminishing ranks of eligible bachelors, but his heart was well and truly engaged. When the guests departed at a little after ten-thirty, she could not resist mentioning her suspicions when her friend brought up the subject, and to her intense embarrassment, Becky's fair skin flared a fiery red.

'Why, Aimée, whatever do you mean? I do declare that is the stupidest thing I ever did hear!' Her fingers plucked nervously at the long fringes of her shawl as her eyes darted across the room to where Aimée sat nibbling the last of the chocolate truffles. 'Whatever makes you say such a silly thing?'

Aimée's eyes took on a far-away look as she gazed down at the flickering logs in the grate. 'Oh, I don't know—just a feeling, I guess . . . Perhaps when you've been in love once yourself—really in love—it makes you more sensitive to the existence of that same feeling in others. Has he been a friend of yours for long?'

Becky passed a hand over her flushed brow, then patted the thick cascade of ringlets behind her head. 'Well, I don't really know that I can regard him as a friend! He's my doctor, my dear Aimée, and it's hardly the same thing! Anyway, he's a very old friend of Jack—they went to school together—so there's no question of his believing I'm a merry widow or any such nonsense!'

The two young women looked at one another, then Becky giggled. 'You do put the wickedest thoughts in a gal's head! Why, I swear I'll go pink all over next time I come within a mile of the poor man! In love, indeed! And just what is this exotic emotion that you seem to have such intimate experience of? I 'spect I'm in love with Jack—I must have been, mustn't I, to have married him? I mean, you just don't go round marrying people you're not in love with, do you?'

Their eyes met, and this time it was the turn of Aimée's cheeks to colour. 'If you're really sensible you don't, Becky. But how many of us can make that claim?' It was the nearest she had ever come to a public admission that her marriage to Charles MacDonald had been a mistake.

She was to look back on this conversation with a good degree of embarrassment a week later when Becky was the recipient of the news that every wife of a serving soldier dreaded. Jack had been killed in the fierce hand-to-hand fighting that had taken place outside Nashville the previous month. His body had been found in a ditch, hidden beneath the carcass of a horse, so that identification had taken much longer than usual. There could be no question now of the newly-widowed Becky allowing her friend to return to the hospital in the foreseeable future. She needed her far too much in Leigh Street, so Aimée resigned herself to at least another month of comfortable tedium in the Sanders' household.

The days dragged by, each one as comfortable but as utterly boring as the next. The young Dr Holzenbein found it necessary to call almost daily to assist the young widow of his friend in her recovery, and Aimée could tell, with each passing day, that Becky would not be in widow's weeds for very much longer.

It was ironic, she thought. There must be thousands of young widows just like poor Jack Sanders', who went through the obligatory public mourning period with hardly a moment of true mental anguish, their greatest preoccupation being where to purchase the most fashionable black gowns and bonnets now that this annoying blockade had made decent material so difficult to come by. It was often difficult to keep the bitterness from becoming all-consuming as she thought of the others like herself who were suffering in private—really suffering—but whose pain was invisible, and must always remain invisible. Their love was born in secret, lived in secret and must die in secret, while life went on around them.

She sighed and rose from the button-backed chair a

the drawing-room window to glance at the small brass
perpetual calendar on the chiffonier. The twentieth of
March 1865—the war was almost four years old. It
hardly seemed possible. It seemed only yesterday that
she had heard the news of the firing of the first shots at
Fort Sumter that had signified the opening of hostilities.
She smiled bitterly as she recalled the newspaper reports
of the crowds that had rushed to watch the sky flare into
life beyond the harbour as the first shot of the war
brought the population cheering in the streets until their
voices were hoarse. How many would still be cheering
today, she wondered. How many still believed that
all the bloodshed had accomplished anything at
all?

Walking back to the window, she gazed up at
the gathering stormclouds in the afternoon sky. The
weather had been oppressive for days, close and sultry;
the kind of weather that gave you a headache and left
you on edge wishing the storm would break. If she was
still a romantic, she told herself, she would regard it as
symbolic of how the war was going for the South.
Everything seemed to be going wrong. The re-election
of Abe Lincoln as President of the United States, the
failure by the South to obtain recognition by foreign
powers, Sherman's successful march through Georgia to
the sea and Grant's continual hammering at the thin grey
lines round Petersburg. Each happening was one more
nail struck in the coffin of the Confederacy, although no
one dared yet make such a treacherous statement out
loud.

Even the South's whole raison d'être had been jetti-
soned in January, when President Davis sent an envoy to
Europe to offer the abolition of slavery in exchange for
recognition of the Confederacy by foreign governments
—a recognition which was not granted. When the details
of the mission were announced, Becky's parents had
been staying in Leigh Street, on a visit of sympathy to
their newly-widowed daughter, and Aimée could still
recall the former Master of Magnolia Mount's face as he

had exploded over his morning paper at breakfast.
Civilisation as they knew it was at an end, he had
declared, and never ceased to declare, for the remainder
of their visit. He had very sensibly sold up and moved
out of Craven County, buying a chain of stores in
Charleston instead, just before war broke out, but he
still held the entrenched beliefs of the rest of the planter
class from which he had sprung.

Now Aimée remembered the agitated conversation
that morning. She had been pouring the last of the maple
syrup on her hot waffle when Dr Holzenbein breezed
into the breakfast-room. He had been making a habit of
taking his second cup of coffee of the morning with
Becky, but instead of the usual cheerful smile there was
a distinctly preoccupied look about his handsome
countenance as he threw his hat and gloves on a chair
and took his usual seat at the end of the table.

'Why, Arnold, what ever's the matter? I do declare
you look like you've lost a dollar and found a dime!
Don't you know we rely on you to bring some joy into
our boring little lives at the start of the day?' Becky's
pretty lips pursed reprovingly as she passed the coffee-
pot across the table to him.

The doctor looked suitably chastised and attempted a
consoling smile. 'I'm sorry, my dear. I guess the day
didn't get off to too good a start this morning. I met one
of my patients—a Captain Jardine—who's just been
invalided home from the front for a week or so. Seems
things are pretty bad round there. He reckons General
Lee is in one mighty dilemma. He's going to be forced to
move his troops out of their trenches before General
Grant and the Yankees completely surround them, but
if that happens and Petersburg is abandoned, then
Richmond will fall almost immediately.'

Becky went quite pale—memories of Sherman's
march through Georgia to the sea were still a vivid scar
on her mind. She glanced across at Aimée, then back at
the young man sitting opposite her. 'I really don't hold
with that kind of talk, Arnold. It's important we keep

our spirits up in these dark days. If you see your Captain Jardine again, I'd tell that particular young man to keep his lip buttoned. It does no good at all to frighten us folks like that—and what it must do for morale on the field, heaven only knows!'

The subject was dropped abruptly for the rest of the doctor's stay, but when he left to resume his daily round, Becky turned immediately to Aimée with a look of alarm on her face. 'Mercy, what news to start the day with! I guess I was a mite hard on the poor boy, but we could really do without that kind of scaremongering, don't you agree?'

Aimée raised her eyebrows but said nothing. They were going to have to face the facts of the situation sooner or later.

'Well, say something! Don't just sit there looking at me like that! You don't really believe there's any truth in it, do you?'

Aimée sighed, then grimaced slightly as she drained the last of the bitter dregs from the bottom of her coffee-cup. 'Quite frankly, my dear, I do. I think there's a distinct possibility that's what will happen, and that there could be Yankee soldiers in Richmond within a week.'

Becky sat back in her chair with a defeated sigh. It was simply too much to take in. She had deliberately avoided reading the local newspapers over the last few weeks because they never seemed to have anything positive to say about the war—but this was just too much. 'Well, if there really is something in it, and the worst comes to the worst, then I shall simply go right back home to Charleston. I know my folks wouldn't want me to be on my own here without them at a time like that! But you must come too, of course. The family would love it if you came back with me.'

Aimée smiled gratefully, but shook her head. Wherever she was going, she was not going to Charleston. She had reached a crossroads in her life, and now was not the time to be sidetracked. Anyway, she was pretty certain

that the handsome young doctor would never be agreeable to his beloved Becky disappearing back to South
Carolina, so the situation would probably never arise.
'We'll see, my dear. Let's just hold on and see what
happens . . . It's not going to happen today—or even
tomorrow, God willing!'

It had been enough to remove the worried look from
her friend's face temporarily as she rose from the table to
prepare for another day of committee work. But, for
Aimée, left alone in the silent house, it meant one more
thing to worry about as she sat quietly in the drawing-
room and attempted to amuse herself with a little
reading or sewing.

All that was hours ago, and a glance at the clock told
her it was about time for Becky to return. It would be
nice to have her home again and have someone to chat
to. Becky could always be relied upon to have enough
amusing anecdotes to keep them cheerful over their
evening meal, and could be very entertaining when there
were just the two of them. Perhaps that was her now!
Footsteps were hurrying along the passage outside the
door.

It was thrown open, and Mary-Ann stood there.
'Begging pardon, ma'm, there's a gentleman asking for
you. He says it's urgent!'

Aimée's brows furrowed. 'For me? Are you sure?
Don't you mean it's your mistress he's asking to see?'

'Oh, no, ma'm! Mrs Aimee MacDonald, he said.
Sure, an' there's nothin' wrong with my hearing!'

'Did he give a name, by any chance?'

Mary-Ann's brow wrinkled beneath the curly fringe.
'That he did, ma'm. It's a Major Redmayne to see you!'

CHAPTER SIXTEEN

'No!' AIMÉE GASPED the word out loud as she stared at the startled face of the maid. 'No! He's dead! How could you lie to me like this?'

Mary-Ann's freckled face flushed. 'Beggin' your pardon, ma'm, but I'm not lying! The gentleman says his name is Major Redmayne—so if you've any quarrel, you'd better take it up with him.'

She was quite serious. It wasn't some horrible, unforgivable jest. There was actually someone downstairs calling himself by Red's name. Perhaps he had a cousin —a brother even—that she'd never heard of . . . someone who had heard what he had meant to her, and had come to offer his condolences. Yes, that was it—a relative had come to inform her of what she already knew. Despite her determination not to allow her imagination to run riot, her heart pounded mercilessly in her breast as she glanced across at the maid. 'Yes, all right, thank you, Mary Ann. Tell the gentleman I'll come down at once.'

The maid dropped a quick curtsy and hurried from the room, leaving Aimée white-faced in the middle of the carpet. Her whole body was now bathed in perspiration. She felt hot and cold at the same time as a shiver of gooseflesh ran over her skin. Her legs, beneath the wide hoops of her skirts, were trembling. She was not prepared for this—not prepared at all. Her hands flew to her cheeks. She could almost feel the blood draining from them. She must look absolutely dreadful!

Hardly aware of what she was doing, she turned and walked shakily to the mirror on the wall by the fireplace. The face that stared back at her was devoid of all colour and looked much older than its twenty-four years. The war had taken its toll. Her green eyes had lost their sparkle, and the dark hollows beneath them paid silent testimony to the long nights without adequate sleep in the hospital. She had lost even more weight than before, for her appetite had vanished completely after hearing of Red's death. The high cheekbones, once a coveted beauty feature, now emphasised the gauntness beneath the pale skin. Whoever was waiting for her downstairs, she hoped he had not known her before, in those carefree days before the war, for the change in her appearance was almost embarrassing. She was putting it off—she knew she was. But he would have to be faced. This stranger with Red's name would have to be received with as much aplomb as her trembling being could muster.

Her nervous fingers smoothed the dark grey cotton twill of her dress over the hoops of the crinoline and tucked a stray lock of hair back into her net-covered chignon. What was it she used to do in the nerve-racking seconds before going out on stage to face an impatient audience? She closed her eyes and took six long breaths, letting the air out of her lungs slowly, as she silently counted to twelve. It did little to calm the butterflies that cavorted wildly in her stomach, but it gained her a few precious seconds to collect her chaotic thoughts. It must be a relative . . . If this war had taught her anything, it had taught her that miracles simply didn't happen. Red was dead. It was a relative, or some other stranger with his name, waiting for her down there. And, whoever it was, she was as ready for him now as she would ever be!

As she descended the staircase, her hands gripping the polished banister and though her life depended on it, she saw a tall figure in the grey jacket and cape and faded blue trousers of the Confederate Army standing by the hall window gazing out over the gardens. She paused, her heart beating wildly, as she narrowed her eyes and attempted to identify him. Then he turned, and there could be no doubt.

'Dear God! No!' Her legs went from her as his deep blue eyes gazed into hers.

'Aimée!' He tried to rush forward as she crumpled into a heap on the broad steps of the stairs, but the heavy strapping on his left leg made walking awkward.

'I—I'm all right . . . Don't worry . . .' Her voice was faint as she grasped a piece of furniture and started to pull herself upright. Then, suddenly, she was in his arms, his right hand smoothing the hair back from her brow as she clung to the shabby battle-scarred uniform. 'They told me you were dead! They told me you were dead!'

She gazed up into the face she thought she would never see again. A deep scar ran down his left cheek and neck, disappearing beneath the collar of his tunic, and, for the first time, she noticed that his left arm and hand were also heavily bandaged. Although an attempt had been made to clean up the uniform, it was heavily stained a deep, dark brown. Without a word she took him by the hand and led him into the morning-room. A fire of birch logs was burning in the grate, and they sat down together on a small settle in front of it. Never for a second did her gaze waver from his face. She felt that if she were to look away, he might disappear again. It would be no more than a dream—one of the countless hundreds she had experienced since learning of his death.

'Who told you, *chérie*? Who told you I was dead?' His eyes were troubled, as with his one good hand he stroked hers.

'The young Captain—the young man I gave the necklet to . . .' Her voice was barely audible.

'Ah—yes, of course, Will. Will Crockett.' Understanding dawned in his eyes, and he nodded slowly. 'He was alongside me when the shell came over. Neither of us knew anything about it. In fact, for a long time —God, how long a time—they thought I was dead! When the skirmish and all the shelling finished and they came looking for the dead and injured, they took Will away to hospital . . .'

His voice faltered, his blue eyes clouding as his thoughts returned to that dark rain-sodden field. 'He was moaning. That's how they can tell in the darkness —if they moan when you prod 'em, they're still alive and might be worth saving!' He gave a mirthless laugh. 'I guess I was still too far gone to make any sound, so they left me for dead. It wasn't till almost two days later that I was found and taken back to camp. By then, of course, before they were moved on to one of the hospital trains for Richmond, Will and the others had been told I was a goner. I guess that's where you met up with him!'

She nodded ruefully, as the sentimental strains of Auld Lang Syne echoed in her head. 'At the New Year's Eve ball . . . It's where I met Becky again, too. You cannot imagine, Red, how I've felt these past three months!' She shook her head at the memory. The scars would remain with her for ever.

Sympathy softened the war-ravaged contours of his face. 'I can imagine, Aimée. I guess I felt pretty much the same when I went back to that hospital to find you and discovered you'd moved on. You took some finding, I can tell you! Your old Superintendent at the Richmond camp told me you'd gone off with one of the ladies from the War Wives' Committee after their ball, and it was only after going round almost every single member that I discovered your whereabouts. Do you know, I went to nine different houses today before I met someone who suggested that a Mrs Rebecca Sanders might have a friend living with her who had once worked as a nurse!' He gave a wry smile. 'Mind you, I'd resigned myself to knocking on every darned door in Richmond if it should prove necessary!'

A deep breath shuddered through her. He looked so tired—so very tired. He had not told her the half of it. Heaven only knew what he had been through before he had arrived on Becky's front step a few minutes ago. 'You'll stay here, of course. Becky will insist on it—I know she will. She'll be back any minute now.'

He shook his head, stemming her flow. 'No, *chérie*, I

have a place to stay, with the family of my ordnance sergeant. I promised him, before he died, that I'd visit his folks and tell them he didn't suffer—leastways not too much . . . They're good folks, Aimée, and they've prepared a bed for me for tonight. I'll not disappoint them. And, anyway, I'm moving on tomorrow . . .' His voice faded and he looked at her with a disconcerting intensity in his gaze. It was as though he had been thinking about something for a very long time, but putting his thoughts into words did not come easily.

'Moving on?' She stared at him in disbelief, as her heart sank. He couldn't be leaving, not so soon . . . Life couldn't be as cruel as that. 'But where—where to?' She could not bear to look at him as her lips formed the words.

There was a pause, while he stared into the dancing flames of the fire. His voice, when finally he spoke, was soft, almost wistful, but there was a finality about it that left no doubt of his intention. 'Wildwood, Aimée. I'm going back to Wildwood.'

'Wildwood!' Her eyes misted over at the very mention of the name. But Wildwood was in Georgia—miles away. He would have to pass through the battle zone. But Wildwood and all those other beautiful places would be gone. The Yankees had seen to that. 'They say there's nothing left, Red! Sherman's soldiers have destroyed it all. It's true. I know it's true—Chas told me.'

'Chas told you! You've spoken to Chas MacDonald recently?' His voice was harsh, and his eyes hardened as he looked across at her. 'Where and when did you meet up with him, for Chrissake?'

Her hands were nervously clasping and unclasping on her brow once more. Why did he have to glare at her like that? 'At Christmas, in the hospital camp. He's dead. Chas is dead . . .'

There was a long silence as both fought to control their very different emotions. She started to say something —to try to explain—but the words wouldn't come, and she shook her head helplessly as tears formed in her eyes. Then Red reached across and took her hand.

'I can't suddenly pretend I liked the guy, Aimée—you know better than that. But I wouldn't wish him dead. There's been too much blood spilt in this land—far too much. If his death means anything, it means that you are now free . . .' His voice dropped to barely above a whisper. 'You realise that?'

When she gazed up at him, there was an intensity in his deep blue eyes that knotted her stomach. What was she supposed to say? What did he want her to say? Long, long ago, in another time, another place—in Wildwood, perhaps . . . 'What are you saying to me, Red? What do you want of me?' Her voice faded as she fought to keep her composure.

When he eventually spoke, his voice was huskily low. 'I want you to come with me, Aimée. I want you to join me in Wildwood. When I came here today, it was to ask you to join me there—to live with me there—as the woman I love. But now, with Chas dead, that's no longer enough. I want you to come back to Wildwood with me . . . But as my wife.'

'Your wife!' Her heart was bursting as she stared across at him. 'Go back to Wildwood as your wife!'

He nodded, his dark brows furrowing slightly. 'I—I guess it's a lot to ask now that you're mistress of Four Winds. It's yours now, Aimée—you realise that? With Chas dead, Four Winds is yours.'

She stared at him. His wife . . . Four Winds . . . The words swam in her brain. Never, never had she imagined this could happen! She attempted to compose herself, but the words continued to whirl in some crazy dance in her head and she passed a hand over her brow as though the action could clarify her chaotic thoughts. 'I—I never gave it a thought,' she said softly. 'It never for one second crossed my mind that Four Winds would ever be mine. Property and land mean nothing to me, Red . . . There is only one thing—one person—that matters —and has ever mattered.'

Her voice dropped to barely a whisper as she looked up and found his eyes. 'I'll come back with you to Georgia—to Wildwood and Four Winds. I'll be your wife, my beloved Red—and that small gold ring will mean more than all the land in Craven County!'

Her gaze remained locked in his until his face became blurred by her tears. His right hand touched her cheek as he whispered her name. Then, suddenly, his lips found hers. All those years of loneliness and heartache rolled back, the war and all its misery disappeared in the warmth of his embrace to leave its mark on their physical bodies alone. Nothing—and no one—could part them ever again . . . Their spirits, now fused as one, were already flying through time and space to the rich red rolling hills and forests on the other side of the Blue Ridge Mountains.

Becký could only stand open-mouthed in amazement when she returned ten minutes later to find Daniel Redmayne standing in the middle of her morning-room. And to find that he was, in fact, the mysterious friend of Aimée's who had come back from the dead—with whom she was leaving for Georgia the very next day!

'Well, I just don't know what to say—I really don't!' She shook the raindrops from the dark blue satin of her bonnet and handed it mechanically to the waiting Mary-Ann as she stared into the flushed face of her friend and then at the grey-clad Major by her side. 'Daniel Redmayne—Red—you ol' son of a gun! Whoever would've guessed it? I do declare you've both left me speechless . . . I just don't know what to say!'

'Try "Good luck", Becky, dear—I'm sure that will suffice!' Aimée glanced up with a nervous smile at Red standing beside her, and he nodded his agreement as he shook the astonished young woman warmly by the hand, then, throwing propriety to the wind, kissed her on both cheeks and administered a bear-hug that left her grasping for breath but grinning delightedly.

'How are you, Becky, honey? I guess my surprise is as

great as yours to meet here like this—and I'm sure sorry
to be taking Aimée from you at a time like this, but you
could say my need is greater than yours!'

He winked down at the blushing face of his new
fiancée, and for the first time in years Aimée caught a
glimpse of the old Red she had once known. It would
come back, she was sure of it. That old devil-may-care
spirit would return. But neither of them would ever be
quite the same again. Too much had happened for that
to be possible. The war had changed them both, in mind
and body, but they could bring to their life together a
new maturity: a maturity born out of shared suffering, a
maturity that could only stand them in good stead for the
years ahead.

Wildwood . . . Four Winds . . . The very names brought
a mercurial tingle running down her spine as she packed
her trunk that evening. Red was collecting her in the
wagon early the following morning and they would make
their way back to Craven County, avoiding the fighting
that was still going on near Petersburg as best they
could.

Becky sat on the edge of her bed, swinging her
satin-slippered feet, and watched the gowns being taken
down from the hangers in the wardrobes and packed into
the large trunk in the middle of the floor. Aimée had
preferred to do it herself, rather than turn the task over
to one of the maids. She simply had to do something to
occupy herself tonight, or she would go mad with excitement at the prospect of what lay ahead. When the last
one was pressed into position and Becky had been
persuaded to sit on the lid of the trunk in order to get the
metal fastenings to close, they looked at one another and
burst into excited laughter.

'Oh, Aimée, I really don't know why I should be
laughing at a time like this! I shall miss you terribly, I
know! You've been my very best friend. I don't know
how I would have survived this awful time without
you! The very thought that you're about to leave me

tomorrow . . . Well, I just can't bear to think about it, so there's an end to it! What will you do down there among all that destruction? Why, I go quite weak at the very thought!'

Aimée nodded sympathetically as she lifted a bonnet from the shelf on top of the wardrobe and stroked the swirl of peacock-feathers on its brim. 'We'll work, that's what we'll do! Red once told me his father and mother had created Wildwood from out of the wilderness of forest—and we must do the same. We'll rebuild that lovely old house brick by brick if we have to—even if it takes a lifetime to do it!'

Becky looked thoughtful. 'You'll do it, too! I have no doubt about that. Although I can't bear to think about Craven County any more. I think I'd die if those Yankees had done anything terrible to Magnolia Mount—I just thank God we got out before that awful man Sherman got there . . . But what's going to become of me up here? What's going to become of Richmond, and the rest of the South? Why, I could cry, just thinking about it! Pa says it's the end of civilisation as we know it. Is that true, Aimée, is that really true?'

She looked down at Becky, her eyes thoughtful, as she sat down on the bed with a sigh. 'I guess your Pa's partly right, my dear. If the South lose, it will be the end of one type of civilisation; but another—a better one—will rise to take its place. Did you read the report of Abe Lincoln's inauguration speech earlier this month?'

Becky shook her head. 'Pa once said he wouldn't sully his eyes by reading anything that two-bit lawyer said! I guess I've always followed suit.'

Aimée reached across to the drawer of the bedside cabinet and drew out a little leather-bound common-place book. 'I wrote down part of his speech,' she said quietly. 'To me, it says just about everything I myself would hope for when peace finally comes.' With an embarrassed glance, she held the book in front of her, beneath the opaline shade of the lamp, and began to read:

> With malice towards none; with charity for all;
> with firmness in the right, as God gives us to see
> the right, let us strive on to finish the work we are
> in; to bind up the nation's wounds, to care for him
> who shall have borne the battle, and for his
> widow, and his orphan—to do all which may
> achieve and cherish a just, and a lasting peace
> upon ourselves, and with all nations . . .

Her voice trailed off, and when she looked up, there
were tears on the face of the young woman seated on the
trunk at her feet.

'You'll give me a copy of it before you go, Aimée
—you'll write those words down for me!' Her blue eyes
glistened in the lamplight, underlining her plea as she
looked up into those of her friend on the bed. 'I'll be
needing to remind myself of them in the days ahead. We
all shall . . .'

The last thing Aimée did before leaving her room for the
very last time the following morning was to write out
those words once more on a page of the small book. She
then tore it out carefully and clasped it in her hand as she
descended the staircase to wait for Red.

Becky was waiting on the front porch, gazing up into
the overcast sky. For late spring the weather was terrible, but it seemed to match her mood exactly—even as
a child she had always hated farewells. But she had
resolved to try at least to be cheerful when her friend
finally appeared. At the sound of approaching footsteps
she turned, her face lighting up as the door opened.
'Why, Aimée, you look real beautiful!'

Aimée flushed with pleasure and glanced down at
her dark blue bombazine travelling-dress. She had deliberately avoided silks in favour of something that
would withstand the hazards of the long journey. Red
reckoned it could take up to two weeks to make their
way back to Craven County—often sleeping rough in
the wagon itself if Unionist forces were in command of

the small towns and villages they would be passing through.

She had hardly been on the porch more than two minutes when he rolled up at a little after eight o'clock. Becky gave a wail of dismay. 'Lordy, he's here! You're leaving me, Aimée! You're really going!'

Aimée glanced down the road to see Red aloft on the wagon—a scarcely recognisable figure in a tan-fringed buckskin jacket and trousers. He gave a wave at the sight of her—an action which necessitated changing the reins into his bandaged hand. 'How are you, honey? I'm not late, am I?'

'No, you're not late!' The mere sight of him made her stomach turn somersaults beneath the tight basque of her gown. She turned to Becky, while two of the servants carried her luggage down the steps and into the wagon. 'I—I wrote out that part of the speech you asked for,' she said softly, pressing the folded sheet of paper into her friend's hand. 'I hope it brings you comfort in the days ahead. You will write to me, won't you?'

Becky nodded, too full of emotion to speak, as they hugged one another for the last time.

'You'll come to visit us? You'll come back to Craven County, even if only for a visit. You will, Becky! This war will soon be over and life will return to normal again—just you wait and see.'

She raced down the path and out through the white-painted front gate, then turned to wave once more as Red bend down to help her on board the wagon beside him, but her friend's blue muslin gown was already disappearing inside the front door. Only Mary-Ann and a few of the other servants stood silently watching the departure.

Aimée felt like a bride already as she clambered up on to the wooden-planked seat and lifted her hand in farewell. 'Becky never could stand goodbyes.' She smiled ruefully. 'Perhaps it's just as well. I couldn't have borne seeing her cry.'

Red gave her a beaming smile as she settled her skirts.

'There'll be no crying anywhere near us today, *ma belle* Aimée! We're on our way, my gal! We're heading home—together!'

With a rattle of the reins and a shout of 'Roll on there!', the wheels of the wagon creaked into action and they were off at last. Within half an hour they would have left this beautiful but doomed city behind and be on their way along the open road—towards Wildwood —towards home.

She gazed up to the heavens. The bank of grey cloud that had been obscuring the sun all morning suddenly parted and a shaft of golden sunlight broke through, making her shield her eyes. It seemed as though even God was on their side.

He had noticed it, too, as he turned to smile down at her. 'It won't always be sunshine, Aimée. We've a long, hard journey ahead of us. Sure you've no regrets?'

She shook her head. 'No, Red—the hard part is behind us now.' Her eyes alighted on the glint of gold against the bronze of his throat beneath the open-necked checked shirt. He was wearing the necklet—the two tiny interlocking hearts. 'No, my love, I have no regrets.'

And, as she rested her head on the fringed buckskin of his shoulder, she knew she never would.

EPILOGUE

ON THE OLD stage road between Richmond and Lynchburg, in the little Virginian village of Appomattox, two men met in the local Court House on the ninth day of April in the year of Our Lord 1865.

General Ulysses S. Grant, commanding officer of the Unionist Army, stood to attention, his five feet eight inches belied by the slight stoop of his shoulders. At forty-three, his brown hair and full beard were untouched by grey, despite the strain of the past four years. His appearance was slightly dishevelled: the dark blue single-breasted tunic unbuttoned, and the black mud-spattered riding boots, with his trousers tucked inside, were without spurs. He had removed his beige thread gloves and felt stiff-brimmed hat before entering the room, and the latter now rested on the small table at his side. No sword or sash adorned the battle-worn uniform; a pair of shoulder-straps were the only insignia to indicate his exalted rank. The victor had no wish for any outward display of pomp.

The man standing opposite him was taller—a good six feet one inch—his bearing erect although he was now in his sixtieth year. General Robert E. Lee, commanding officer of the Confederate Army, looked every inch a leader of men. His thick locks and full beard were silver; the hair thinning slightly at the front. In direct contrast to the man opposite, he wore a new uniform of Confederate grey, buttoned to the neck, and a handsome sword and sash. His riding-boots were complemented by a pair of shining silver spurs. His felt hat and long grey buckskin gauntlets lay alongside those of General Grant on the table.

On that same table lay the documents signed by the two men only seconds before. The war was over. Robert

E. Lee had offered the surrender of the South, and it had been accepted. There was little more to be said. The two soldiers shook hands, then Lee turned and walked out on the small porch of the building.

The Union officers sprang to attention and saluted the man who had until a few minutes ago been their enemy in chief. The General returned the courtesy, then slapped his gauntlets against his hands three times, and in a voice thick with emotion, called for his horse. His animal was summoned and he mounted, his deep sigh audible to all those around. Then General Grant himself appeared on the steps of the porch. The victor removed his hat and waited in silence, and the other Union officers followed suit.

Without a word Robert E. Lee raised his own hat in silent salute, then turned his horse and rode bareheaded back to his own men. The tears that streamed down his cheeks said all there was to say.

At that very moment, over the distant horizon in the foothills of the Blue Ridge Mountains, a man and woman stood on a plateau overlooking the soft, rolling red earth that epitomised the land of North Georgia.

'We're home, Aimée. We're home at last!'

Tears filled the eyes of the young woman as she looked up into those of her husband of four days, then down at the ruined mansion that had once been Four Winds.

Leaving their horses and wagon tethered to the spreading branches of an old hickory tree, they walked hand in hand down the long slope towards the place where they had first met. The once gleaming white walls stood stark and naked of all but the last peeling shreds of paint that revealed the bare wood beneath, now cracked and weathered to a dull ash-grey. Silently they walked through the long grass and weeds of the once immaculate lawns to what before the war had been the elegant front porch, where he had handed her back to her husband-to-be all those years ago.

A gaping hole showed where the front door had been.

It had been ripped from its hinges and lay at a grotesque angle halfway down the front steps. Almost nothing of the veranda remained, and weeds grew tall and green through the broken boards. The tall Doric columns that had supported the balcony on the floor above were, miraculously, still intact, but the balustrades were red with rust. Items of furniture lay forlornly where they had been thrown on the floor of the upper balcony. Someone had made an attempt at boarding up the windows on the ground floor, but on the floors above, the jagged broken panes were covered with grime and gaped forlornly out over the unkempt gardens.

Red reached out his hand and Aimée took it, and together they entered the house. She could not bear to look as they walked past the destruction of what had once been one of the most elegant entrance halls in the whole County, then continued on up the great curving staircase.

They emerged on the balcony of the floor above to look out over the rolling acres of the plantation. High on a hilltop above the dense green of the forest between, they could just make out the contours of Wildwood. Unlike Four Winds, it was made not out of clapboard but of strong red brick from Georgia's own river-beds.

'There she is! There she is, at last!' Red's eyes lit up as he gazed across at the proud walls even the damned Yankees had not been able to destroy. 'We're going home, Aimée . . . We're going home. We're almost there, my love . . .'